QUELLING THE DEMONS' REVOLT

TRANSLATIONS FROM THE ASIAN CLASSICS

QUELLING THE DEMONS' REVOLT

A NOVEL FROM MING CHINA

ATTRIBUTED TO LUO GUANZHONG

Translated by Patrick Hanan

Introduction by Ellen B. Widmer and David Der-wei Wang

COLUMBIA UNIVERSITY PRESS
New York

Columbia University Press wishes to express its appreciation for assistance given by the Pushkin Fund in the publication of this book.

Columbia University Press
Publishers Since 1893
New York Chichester, West Sussex
cup.columbia.edu

Library of Congress Cataloging-in-Publication Data
Names: Luo, Guanzhong, approximately 1330-approximately 1400, author. | Hanan, Patrick, translator. | Widmer, Ellen, writer of introduction. | Wang, Dewei, writer of introduction.
Title: Quelling the demons' revolt : a novel of Ming China / attributed to Luo Guanzhong ; translated by Patrick Hanan ; introduction by Ellen B. Widmer and David Der-wei Wang.
Other titles: Ping yao zhuan. English
Description: New York : Columbia University Press, 2017. | Series: Translations from the Asian classics | Includes bibliographical references.
Identifiers: LCCN 2016049404 (print) | LCCN 2017008949 (ebook) | ISBN 9780231183062 (cloth : acid-free paper) | ISBN 9780231183079 (pbk. : acid-free paper) | ISBN 9780231544733 (electronic)
Classification: LCC PL2690 .P513 2017 (print) | LCC PL2690 (ebook) | DDC 895.1/346—dc23
LC record available at https://lccn.loc.gov/2016049404

Columbia University Press books are printed on permanent and durable acid-free paper.

Printed in the United States of America

Cover design: Noah Arlow

CONTENTS

INTRODUCTION

ELLEN B. WIDMER AND DAVID DER-WEI WANG

As Patrick Hanan wrote in an article of 1971, "*Quelling the Demons' Revolt* is the most neglected of the early Chinese novels."[1] He attributes this neglect to the relative inaccessibility of the twenty-chapter version, as opposed to the forty-chapter version edited by Feng Menglong. The repetitions and non sequiturs that Feng sought to correct are actually part of what makes the original precious, for it is an unvarnished example of the Chinese novel as the form was getting under way. Embedded in the text is material drawn from short stories, but the closest cousin of all is the great Ming novel *Water Margin* (*Shuihu zhuan*). Whereas *Water Margin* was groomed by intellectuals, *Quelling the Demons' Revolt* (*Pingyao zhuan*) appears to be closer to the original story cycle as delivered by oral storytellers.

The end point of *Quelling the Demons' Revolt* is a revolt by Wang Ze. This revolt took place in 1047, but the novel is much more interesting at the beginning, where it is at its least historically accurate. The exploits of heroine Eterna are described with humor and compassion, qualities that must have been common to the best oral storytelling of the mid-Ming. To readers who think of the early Chinese novel as misogynist, the depiction of Eterna will come as a surprise. Although she eventually turns out to be a "demon," she is not exactly that at the beginning. One has sympathy for the childlessness of her parents until her birth, the poverty of her family that she helps to alleviate, and the system of arranged marriages that paired her with a grossly inadequate husband. Issues of poverty and alienation drive the characters of *Water Margin*, too, and in fact there are several types of episode that the two novels share. The issue of the lively woman paired with an inadequate husband lies at the heart of another great novel of a little later, *The Plum in the Golden Vase* (*Jin Ping Mei*). Since we do not know who wrote *Quelling the Demons' Revolt* and when it was written (the same is true of *Water Margin* and *Plum*), we cannot be sure which novels influenced which or whether, instead of influence at the level of the completed novel, there was only shared inheritance from oral storytelling. Whatever the case, the patterns of mutual interconnection seem quite clear.

Quelling the Demons' Revolt also deserves attention because of its unique relationship with *shenmo xiaoshuo* (fiction about gods and demons), a popular genre of late-imperial Chinese fiction. While the best-known works of this genre, such as *Xiyouji* (*Journey to the West*), feature fantastic adventures and supernatural marvels, *Quelling the Demons' Revolt* points to a different style. It is characterized by a degeneration of fantastic motivations to the human and subhuman levels, whether it be in plotting, setting, or characterization, and by a distinct penchant for black humor oriented to human foibles. The author appears less interested in generating an autonomous world of the supernatural than evoking the macabre and funny parallels between the other world and this one. Human vanities and fixations, as well as social injustice and corruption, are examined through the prism of grotesquery to induce sardonic laughter.

As such, *Quelling the Demons' Revolt* anticipates a series of comic novellas about the ghostly and the grotesque from the seventeenth to the nineteenth century, such as *Zhangui zhuan* (*A Tale of*

Devil Killing, 1688), *Pinggui zhuan* (*A Tale of Quelling Devils*, 1785?), and *Hedian* (*What Sort of Book Is This?*, ca. 1820). These works drift somewhere between social satire and supernatural fantasy. The way they conjure up a nonhuman world with all-too-human motifs paves the way for the rise of late-Qing exposé fiction, which likens social evils to monsters, specters, fox sprits, and demons.

The finale of *Quelling the Demons' Revolt* suggests the return of a moral order. But such an ending has an ambiguous overtone. Since the demonic characters are condemned souls at the outset, they are supposedly not subject to, or worthy of, the constraint of human laws. The moralist vein of the novella is thus undercut by its thesis, which recognizes the vulnerability of any human pursuit of order in a world haunted by demonic forces but also beset by corruption. In other words, the final return of law and order is subverted by the novella's pretext holding that the world of demons and ghosts lacks the agency needed for moral rejuvenation, even though some of what the demons and ghosts react to is true injustice. Next to the façade of imperial rule, the threats of revolt and otherworldly subversion always loom.

Patrick Hanan did not enter the field of Chinese studies as a translator. It was only after many years of teaching the history of the vernacular Chinese novel at Stanford and at Harvard that he embarked on his first translation, of Li Yu's *Carnal Prayer Mat* (*Rou putuan*) in 1990. That translation has been appreciated for many reasons, especially its humor, which is said to capture the spirit of the original. In *Quelling the Demons' Revolt* we have another example of a humorous original matched by a spirited translation. Readers will appreciate the work for the insights it provides into the early novel, but the humor may be what they most enjoy.

Bringing this translation into print has been a cooperative enterprise. Before Patrick Hanan died, in April 2014, the manuscript had been passed to his son Guy, who died three months later, not long before the death of Anneliese Hanan, Patrick's wife and Guy's mother. The devoted efforts of Guy's wife, Iris, led to its eventual retrieval from a computer, then our colleague Professor Mingwei Song brought the retrieved version into intelligible form. About a year later, granddaughters Elizabeth and Joanna Hanan signed the contract for the book version. Jennifer Crewe at Columbia University Press has expertly guided the transition from manuscript to book, with Jonathan Fiedler as her able assistant. We are grateful to the whole Hanan family and to Columbia University Press for the roles they have played in realizing Patrick Hanan's hope that this, his final translation, would reach printed form. We are happy to see Hanan's legacy carried on through the posthumous publication of a great late-imperial novella. Our collective effort salutes an outstanding scholar, translator, and teacher, as well as the novel *Pingyao zhuan*.

QUELLING THE DEMONS' REVOLT

1

MASTER HU ACCEPTS A PLEDGE AND OBTAINS A FAIRY'S PORTRAIT;

MISTRESS ZHANG BURNS A PICTURE AND BEARS A DAUGHTER.

POEM:

If the ruler's up early, his court is, too—
In the hour before dawn they convene;
But for many of the capital's richest men
The morning star is a sight unseen.

Let us tell how in the time of Emperor Renzong of the great Song dynasty, the Eastern Capital, the city of Bianzhou in Kaifeng prefecture, glowed like a brilliant tapestry. Thirty-six imperial highways did it boast, as well as twenty-eight city gates, thirty-six lanes of brothels, and seventy-two music halls, and any idle space in the city was given over to flower gardens or football fields. Let us put aside the powerful officials in the capital and speak instead of the many merchants of varying degrees of wealth. There was Master Wang of the dye works, Master Li the pearl merchant, Master Zhang the merchant adventurer, Master Jiao of the colored silks—the list goes on and on. Among them was one man so rich that "his stack of money rose higher than the stars, and his rice was so abundant that it rotted in his granaries." He had three pawnshops in front of his house, the one on the left taking in silks and satins; the one on the right gold, silver, pearls, and kingfisher feathers; and the one in the center musical instruments, calligraphy, paintings, and antiques. Each pawnshop was staffed by a manager and three assistants. This merchant was named Hu Hao, style Dahong, and he had a wife, Mistress Zhang, but no children. "Of eyes he had a pair, but of children not a one."

One day he and his wife were taking their ease in their hall when a sudden thought occurred to him and he began to weep. Noticing his tears, his wife rose to her feet. "Master," she said, "you have all that you need in life—you lack for nothing—and you enjoy many luxuries as well. You may not compare with the richest in the land, but you're far better off than the poorest. Why are you so upset?"

"This has nothing to do with either necessities or luxuries. I do own some property, it's true, but we have no children. When the time comes, who can we depend on to see to our last rites? That's what makes me sad."

"But we're not old, and who's to say we can't still have a baby? Perhaps we're destined to have one later in life. I've heard that in the Precious Amulet Temple the Veritable Helpful and Saintly Master of the Polestar is wonderfully effective.[1] Why don't we choose an auspicious day to go over there, burn some paper money, and pray for a child? Even if it's a girl, we'll at least have someone to tend our graves." She gave orders to the maidservants: "Set out the wine. The master and I are going to cheer ourselves up." They drank several cups together before clearing away the wine things and going to bed.

An auspicious date came along several days later. Master Hu told a servant to buy some incense and paper money and arrange for a sedan chair. Then, with their servants in attendance, he and his wife set off for the temple, where they alighted and walked inside. In the main hall they burned incense and then, needless to say, did the same in the other halls and porticoes. At the Zhenwu Hall,[2] Master Hu prayed most devoutly, giving the date of his birth and praying to the god for a child to continue the family line. He bowed down "like a tower toppling, a pillar falling," clicking his teeth[3] as he kowtowed. His wife bowed too, bobbing up and downlike a supplicant holding a candle in a candlestick. They prayed and burned paper money again before departing for home, which is where we shall leave them.

For about a year after that, on the first and fifteenth of every month, they returned to the temple to burn incense and pray for a son. One day in the fifth month, when the weather was turning hot, the door curtain in the central pawnshop rose and in walked a Daoist priest. How was he dressed?

He wore an iron-frame Daoist cap of fishtail shape
And a black-bordered, fiery red gown;
In his left hand he held a bramble basket,
In his right a turtle-shell fan;
Puttees he wore around his legs
And hempen shoes with grommets.

Now, a Daoist immortal has four remarkable qualities:

He travels like the wind;
He stands still as a pine;
He lies bent like a bow;
His voice sounds like a bell.

Raising the door curtain, the priest entered the pawnshop. He glanced at one of the assistants, who noticed his venerable appearance and quickly rose and welcomed him in, then bowed and sat down with him and ordered tea. When they had drunk it, he said, "Well, sir, and what instructions do you have for us?"

"This is the pawnshop that deals in musical instruments, calligraphy, and paintings, is it not?"

"Yes, sir, that's correct."

"In that case I have a small painting that I'd like to pawn. I'll come back later to redeem it."

"Kindly show it to me, sir, so that I can estimate its value." The assistant assumed that the priest would have a servant with him to carry the painting, but the man reached into his basket and brought out a painting that was less than a foot wide and handed it to him. The assistant took it and said nothing, but he wondered to himself, could this priest be making fun of me? At most this painting can't be worth very much. But of course the assistant had to take the picture pole and hang the painting up, only to find that it was less than five feet long. He looked at it close-up, and he looked at it from a distance; it was a painting of a beautiful woman, but although well executed, it was too small to be of much value.

The assistant turned back to face the priest. "And how much money did you hope to raise on it, sir?"

"It's no ordinary work, you know. I'd want fifty taels for it."

"*But sir!* I'm afraid we can't give you that much. A small painting like this is worth only from thirty to fifty strings of cash. How could we give you fifty *taels*?"

The priest kept insisting, however, and the assistant continued to refuse. In the midst of the argument, footsteps sounded outside the door, the curtain rose, and the master came in from his private quarters. "Have you burned the noon incense today?" he asked the assistant.

"Yes, sir, I have."

The priest looked at the master and said, "Master, I bow my head in greeting."

"Please take a seat, sir, and have some tea," said the master, returning the greeting. He assumed that the priest had come to solicit alms.

"The reverend gentleman has a small painting that he would like to pawn for fifty taels," explained the assistant. "I couldn't see my way to accepting it, but he keeps on insisting."

The master took a look at it. "It's a good painting, my dear sir, but it's not worth very much. How can we offer you fifty taels on it?"

"But Master! You don't know *everything* about this picture. It may be small, but it has a certain marvelous quality."

"And what might that be?"

"This is hardly the place to talk. Let's go somewhere else, and I'll explain to you."

The master took the priest by the hand and led him into the study, where they were alone. "Well, and what is this marvelous quality it possesses?"

"Don't let anyone see you as you do this, but in the dead of night take that painting and hang it up in some very private place. Burn some fine incense, light two candles, cough once, knock three times on the table, and then in a reverent tone of voice invite the divine maiden to step forth from the picture and take tea with you. There'll be a sudden gust of wind, and she'll step down."

If that's the case, this must be a divine painting, thought Master Hu. As he left the study with the priest, he told the assistant, "Give the reverend gentleman the full amount that he asked for."

"Then don't blame me if he never comes back to redeem it!" said the assistant.

"That's not your concern. Just enter it in the account book." He invited the priest to tea, at the same time slipping the painting into his sleeve. He then took his guest into his private quarters and, after a vegetarian meal, saw him out to the shop again. The assistant paid him the fifty taels, and the priest took his leave.

The master could hardly wait until evening. He told a servant to sweep out the study and set up a censer, candlesticks, a teapoy, a kettle of water, and the like. When evening arrived at last, he had dinner with his wife, and then came up with a plausible excuse. "You go off to bed now, my dear," he said. "I have some accounts I need to check. I'll be along in a little while, once I'm done." Then, before he knew it, the drums sounded from the watchtowers and the bells from the temples, and quickly it grew dark.

> Over the *ten* parts of the earth there falls a sudden pitch-black pall;
> In the *nine* margins of the sky stars move amid the clouds;
> From all *eight* directions merchants head for inns to lay down their loads;
> The *seven* stars of the Dipper appear above and beside Heaven's Gate;[4]
> In the *green*[5] willows' shade small boats tie up on weed-covered shores;
> By the *five* planets' light animals are driven into their pens;
> In all *four* quarters brightness illumines the world for a hundred miles;
> The *three* marketplaces[6] fill with cool night air;
> *Two* by two husbands and wives retire to their chambers;
> And *one* circle of vivid whiteness shines all over the land.

Master Hu walked to the study, pushed open the door, which was fitted with a window, and went in, telling the servants to wait outside. Then, turning around, he shut the door and lit the lamp. The kettle on the wall stove was boiling vigorously. He lit a stick of incense and the two candles, then used the picture pole to hang the painting on the wall. It was indeed of an enchanting beauty, one so realistic that she looked as if she could be plucked right out of that painting. The master gave a cough and knocked three times on the table. A slight gust of wind sprang up. What was it like, that wind?

It could push the courtyard plants together—
Or part the duckweed in the river;
Kindhearted when it moves the curtains,
Heartless when it extinguishes the candle.
From the temples it brings forth a peal of bells;
From the towers it sends out a roll of drums.
All you hear is its roar among the trees,
For it shows no trace of visible form.[7]

Once the wind had passed by, the beauty in the picture, in plain sight, jumped down onto the table and from there onto the floor. She stood five feet three inches tall and was as pretty as a flower, with pure-white skin and jet-black hair. But what was so beautiful about her?

One inch more, and she'd be too tall;
One inch less, and she'd be too short;
One touch of rouge, and she'd be too red;
One dab of powder, and she'd be too white.
Without powder or rouge, a natural look
Such that no artist could ever convey.
A face to make fish dive and birds drop,
And put moon and flowers to shame.

She glanced at the master and gave a deep curtsy, and he was quick to bow in return. He poured a cup of tea from the kettle on the stove and handed it to her, then poured a cup for himself, and they sat there drinking together. When they had finished, he returned the cups and saucers to the teapoy. He had still not said a word when there came a sudden gust of wind, and she returned to the picture. The master was thrilled. He quickly put away the painting and called the servants in to tidy up, then returned to his bedroom, where we shall leave him.

Following this incident he spent every evening in his study checking his accounts.

For her part, Mistress Zhang began to wonder. For half a month now, she thought, the master has been spending every evening checking his accounts, and I simply don't believe he has *so* many accounts that need to be checked. Unable to restrain herself any longer, she told a maid to bring a lantern and lead the way to the study. As she listened outside the room, she fancied that she could hear a woman's or a girl's voice inside. Tiptoeing up to the door, she moistened her little finger with spit and pressed it gently against the paper windowpane to make a peephole. As she peered through it, she saw a woman sitting down chatting with her husband. Twin columns of fury surged from the soles of Mistress Zhang's feet to the crown of her head, while the irrepressible rage in her heart flared up into the sky. Stretching out a hand, she pushed open the door and charged in.

Startled, the master scrambled to his feet. "My dear, what are you doing?"

"What am *I* doing?" she raged, beside herself with anger. "You old beggar, you! You old fool! A fine thing you've been up to! Utterly shameless! Every evening for over half a month now, you said you were going to check your accounts, and all the time you were in here doing these disgraceful things!" In the midst of her tirade the divine woman returned to the painting in a sudden puff of wind. Fuming with anger, Mistress Zhang called out to the maid, "Come in here and find her for me!" "Don't you worry!" she added to the master.[8]

The master said nothing, but to himself he thought, even if you turn the study upside down, you'll never find her.

Failing to find the woman and seething with anger, his wife suddenly raised her head and, looking around, noticed the painting of a beautiful woman on the wall. She tore it down and set fire to it by holding it against the lamp, then flung it onto the floor. Because of the state she was in, the master did not dare to try and wrest it away from her. By now the painting was ablaze, and the ashes swirled around on the floor and then swirled up beside his wife's feet. She took a step or two backward, fearful that her clothes would catch fire, and the ashes spurted into her mouth, at which she gave a loud scream and collapsed on the floor. Panic-stricken, the master called on the maids to help her up, sit her on a chair, and pour hot water from the kettle down her throat. They helped her up and sat her on a chair. "A fine thing you've been up to, you old fool!" she said. Then she turned to the maids. "Help me to the bedroom. I need to rest." She slept until about midnight, when she began to feel unwell. From that point on, she became listless and distracted, her breasts swelled up, and her belly rose—she was pregnant! Master Hu was thrilled. There was just one thing that troubled him: now that his wife had burned the picture, how was he going to return it to the priest when he came back to redeem it?

Time sped by like an arrow, and after a year his wife was about to give birth. The master went before the spirit tablets in the ancestral shrine, burned some incense, and was in the act of making a pledge to the gods when he heard a sudden commotion outside the door. A servant came in and reported, "That priest who pawned a painting with us is back again!" Although this news almost gave the master heart failure, he had no choice but to go out and greet his visitor.

"Well, sir, it's been a year since we last met," he began. "I hardly dare mention it, but we are blessed with your visit on the very day my wife is due to give birth."

The priest burst out laughing. "I have some medicine here, in case there are any complications." He picked up a gourd from his basket and tipped out a red pill that he gave to the master, explaining that if his wife took it together with a drink of pure water, she would immediately give birth. The master accepted the medicine and asked him to stay on for a vegetarian meal. Afterward the priest left, without saying anything about redeeming the picture.

Let us leave the priest and tell instead how the master gave the pill to his wife, and how soon after, to his great delight, she gave birth to a baby girl. The midwife took charge of the baby, which, we need hardly say, passed through the successive stages of Third Day, First Month, Long Life, First Year, and Name Bestowal. Because the ashes had twisted and turned as they rose up and led to the pregnancy, they named the girl Eterna.

Time sped by like an arrow, and soon Eterna was six. The master asked a tutor to come in and teach her to read and write. She proved to have a quick intelligence, and once something had been taught to her, she was able to remember it. She grew and grew, and soon she was nine. On the evening of the fifteenth of the eighth month, Master Hu gave the managers and assistants of his pawnshops time off to celebrate the Midautumn Festival at home. He told his servants to secure all the gates and take great care with the candles and lamps. That evening there was a brilliant full moon:

The cassia flower[9] rises from mountains and sea;
Clouds bestrew the highway of heaven.
A vivid radiance shines like silver for a thousand miles;
The Jade Hare's[10] brilliance turns endless hills to water.
Sheer whiteness in a single circle
Divides the cosmos with vivid clarity;
Reunion throughout the four seas[11]
Makes heaven and earth manifest.
The moon's shadows quiver in the wilds,
Startling the crow that nests alone.
Its light, streaming in through the secluded window,
Shines on the spinster in her lonely bed.

The icy wheel rolls on, crushing the myriad worlds;[12]
The Jade Spirit[13] devours a thousand miles of autumn.
This night the orb is full;
There's brightness over all.

Master Hu, his wife, and Eterna, attended by the nurse and their servants, enjoyed the festival in the Eight-Sided Pavilion in the back garden and celebrated the moonlight with wine. But because of what happened on that night, certain consequences followed: Master Hu was left in desperate poverty, and he and his family almost starved to death.

Blessings have always come singly;
Troubles, we are told, come in pairs.

But what troubles were they? Turn to the next chapter to find out.

2

ETERNA BUYS STEAMED CAKES IN THE MIDST OF A SNOWSTORM;

PRIESTESS PIA TRANSMITS THE MAGIC OF THE DARK GODDESS.

POEM:

The kitchen's bare of the commonest food;
The child cries: there's nothing on his plate.
The mother whispers to her little boy:
"Daddy has a poem for the head of state."[1]

That evening Master Hu, Mistress Zhang, and Eterna were all in the Eight-Sided Pavilion in the back garden celebrating the Midautumn Festival with wine when the gatekeeper came rushing frantically up. "Master, something terrible has happened!" he said.

"What was it? Where did it happen?" asked Master Hu.

"The center shop is on fire!"

Shocked, Master Hu and his family stepped down from the pavilion and went to see. It was indeed a huge fire. How huge?

First like a firefly,
Then like lamplight,
Finally as overwhelming as a thousand candles,
As powerful as a myriad sacrificial fires.

Had it happened on top of Mount Li,
Baosi[2] would have gloried in it;
Had it occurred at Three Rivers,
It would have rivaled Young Zhou's[3] brilliant ploy.
Its smoke and flames weaved and whirled, darkening heaven
and earth;
Its flashing red glow linked up with the fiery clouds above.
It threatened to lay waste the land for thousands of miles,
It seemed apt with its blaze to burn down millions of homes.

As the fire attacked the house, the master reassured his wife and Eterna, "Don't worry! Even if the house is totally destroyed, we won't have to spend the rest of our lives in poverty." But just at that moment the fire shot upward, flaring and crackling as it went. The wind also picked up strength, and despite the efforts of many locals to put it out, the fire went on burning all night. Master Hu and his family were forced to spend the night in the pavilion. At dawn they got up, and Master Hu told his servants to rake over the burned foundations of the house. As they did so, they stood openmouthed at the sight that met their eyes. Master Hu's property had been obliterated by this fire of mysterious origin; the front buildings, the rear buildings, the exits and entrances, the pawnshops, the side buildings—all of them had burned to the ground. The master's only remaining hope lay in his stock of valuables and appliances that, even though they would have been melted by the heat, were stored below ground. He told his men to rake through the ashes and look for them, but his whole stock had been removed by heaven. Hitherto he and his family had had the good fortune to enjoy these things, but now fortune had deserted the family, and when their men raked over the scene of the fire, they found nothing at all.

And so the family stayed on in the pavilion. They had no food, but relatives and friends brought them some. Inevitably they were forced to borrow rice and fuel, but it was something one could do only once or twice. As the days turned into months and the months into a year, they found themselves growing short of both food and clothing. They asked someone to sell the vacant lot, but there were no takers, and soon they became so poor that they were dressing in rags. When they sought help from friends, the friends sent out word that they were not at home. They were snubbed by people whom they used to know well. As the saying goes, if you are poor and live in the city, no one will call on you, but if you are rich, even though you live in the mountains, relatives will come from afar. And there's another old saying: It takes but a single fire to make a rich man poor. If Master Hu and his family continued to live in the pavilion, where there were no walls to protect them, how were they going to shelter from the elements? They had no choice but to move into an almshouse. (Almshouses were like our modern homes for orphans and the elderly.)

It was the middle of winter, a time of dense red clouds filling the sky, of biting northerly winds, of heavy snow filtering to earth. How heavy was that snowfall?

Bitter winter weather;
Auspicious clouds crisscross the sky.
Along the river the myriad mountains grow dark and dim.
The peach tree vies in beauty with the plum:
The frost competes in brilliance with the snow.
Above the river flocks of egrets wheel and dive;
In the sky hosts of gulls whirl hither and thither.
From the vast heavens snowflakes fill the ends of the earth.
In the wilds the snow, like goose down, dances its frantic dance
And before the eaves, like white powder, gathers in great banks.
Unless you are among the poorest of the people,
How would you know how harsh this winter snowfall was?

Indeed
Snow betokens a good year, it is said,
But how can it stand as a lucky sign?
For the sake of the poor in the capital,
Let's have the lucky sign, just not too much!

The people who enjoy snow are the young gentlemen in their mansions, while those who detest it are the poor in their mean streets. In the Eastern Capital the newly impoverished Master Hu, with his wife and daughter, Eterna, had once possessed vast wealth, but now, because a fire had ruined them and wiped out their entire fortune, they had moved into an almshouse. It was winter, and snow was falling. Master Hu and his family were huddled around the stove, and although it was midday, they had still had nothing to eat. Master Hu's wife jabbed a finger at her husband, and he raised his head and looked at her. "Is something the matter?" he asked.

"What do you mean, is something the matter?" she demanded. "Here we are in the midst of a snowstorm, and there's no food in the house. It's all right for you and me to go hungry; we've lived well. But she's only fourteen," she said, pointing at Eterna. "What has *she* ever seen of the good life? You're letting my child starve!"

"I don't know what I can do about it. What do you expect me to do?"

"*You're the head of the household!* It's just started snowing, and if it freezes up in a little while and there's some emergency, we won't be able to get in or out of here. Surely we're not going to just wait here until we die? Take this chance to go out and call on a few people that you know. If you can bring back three or four hundred cash, we'll be able to get by for the next few days."

"Who do you suggest I call on, then?"

"If you won't go, you surely don't expect *me* to go, do you?"

Master Hu could stand the pressure from his wife no longer. "I suppose I'll just have to buckle down," he said, getting to his feet.

He opened the door and went out, but for every two steps he took he was beaten back three steps. "What bitter cold!" he muttered to himself. The chill wind struck his face like a flight of arrows; the cold cut into him like a knife. Blown back a few steps by the northwest wind, he was about to reenter the house when he found that his wife had locked the door behind him. There was nothing else for it; he had to brave the snow and go on. And so he set out from the almshouse on his quest for help, and there we shall leave him.

Mother and daughter were left sitting lonely and dejected together. "Daddy has gone out to ask for help," said Eterna. "I wonder how he'll get on." She continued, "Mama, the snow is coming down *so* heavily and the wind is *so* cold. Who could Daddy possibly go and see?"

"Child, we have no money in the house. Suppose I hadn't made your father go out, would you want me to go instead? Look beside the head of the bed and you'll find a few cash. Take them and go and get us some steamed cakes for breakfast. When your father comes back, we'll decide what else we ought to do."

Eterna looked beside the bed and found eight cash. "Go out to the main road and get us some steamed cakes," said her mother. "You can go ahead and eat a few yourself, you're so hungry."

With the lapels of her coat drawn up around her head, Eterna trudged through the snow and out of the almshouse. At the place on the main road that sold steamed cakes, she curtsied to the vendor and said, "I'd like seven cash worth of steamed cakes, please."

He took the money, noting how ragged the girl's clothes were. She kept one cash over, tying it to her belt. The vendor wrapped the cakes in a lotus leaf and handed them to her.

It was early afternoon as she headed home. Hugging the walls under the eaves, she happened to meet an old woman coming toward her who was also hugging the walls. The woman walked with a bamboo cane and carried a basket over her arm. She was bent and hunchbacked, with eyebrows like streaks of snow and hair tied up in a bun. Her eyes were like murky autumn water, and her hair was as pale as the clouds over Mount Chu. She looked like a spring flower after spring has left; her life was like a chrysanthemum nipped by the autumn frost. In fact, she was a beggar woman. She curtsied to Eterna, and the girl reciprocated.

"What have you bought?" the woman asked.

"My mother told me to buy some steamed cakes," replied Eterna.

"My dear, let me tell you something. I had no supper last night, and I've had no breakfast this morning. Would you be willing to offer me one of your cakes?"

Eterna said nothing in reply, but she thought to herself, my mother had no supper last night or any breakfast this morning, either. But this woman is so *old*, I can't bear to see her in such a state! Opening the lotus leaf, she gave one cake to the old woman, who took it and looked at it, and then said, "This is very nice, but it will never be enough to fill me up. Why don't you give them all to me?"

"But ma'am! I don't dare give them all to you. Our family has had nothing to eat for two days, and my mother told my father to go out to ask people for help. She had only eight cash left, and she sent me out to buy some steamed cakes. The big cakes are for her, the little ones for me. Because you begged me for one, I felt I had to let you have it."

"When your mother asks you why you bought one cake too few, what are you going to tell her?"

"I shall just say I was hungry and ate one on the way home."

"What a kind girl you are! I was only teasing you just now. I'm really not hungry. Here, I don't want to eat this. Let me give it back to you."

"But I gave it to you. How can you give it back?"

"I was just testing you. It's rare to come upon such a kind-hearted girl and dutiful daughter. Do you know how to read and write?"

"A little."

"Well, in that case, my child, there's a predestined bond between us!" She reached into her basket and took out a purple silk bag. "Here, take this bag," she said to Eterna.

"What's in it, ma'am?" asked Eterna, as she took the bag.

"It contains what's known as a wish-fulfillment manual, and there'll be times when you'll need it. In case of an emergency, you just open it up and read what it says. See that you put it away securely, now. If there are any words in the manual that you don't understand, just call on Priestess Pia without letting anyone hear you, and you'll automatically know what they mean. But whatever you do, don't let anyone else into the secret."

Eterna stuffed the bag into her breast pocket and thanked the old woman, who went on her way.

Eterna took the cakes home. "Why are you so late, dear?" asked her mother.

"It was slippery with all that snow on the road, and I found it hard to walk."

They ate the cakes, and before long the master returned. "You've been away a long time," said his wife. "Who did you see?"

"Let me tell you. Along the street I met someone I know, and he invited me to share a meal with him. He also gave me three hundred cash."

His wife was delighted. "Go out and buy us some rice and charcoal," she said. "Let's make do with that for the next two or three days. Then we'll have to think again." Needless to say, she cooked them a meal.

That night they went to bed, but Eterna was unable to sleep. She kept thinking to herself, when that old woman gave me the manual today, she said that in the case of an emergency I should take it out and read it. Well, we don't have any food to eat, and that's an emergency if ever there was one. I'll just open it up and take a look. She got up ever so slowly and quietly dressed herself, but even so she awoke her mother. "Where are you going?" her mother asked.

"I have a stomachache, and I want to go to the privy." She got down from the bed, put on her shoes, and went into the kitchen, which the moonlight that was reflected off the snow had turned as bright as day. She took the purple silk bag from her breast pocket, shook out a manual, and read it.

Reading this manual and learning its magic had consequences unheard of in history and rare in the present day. Indeed,

> Bushels of rice appeared at the touch of a hand;
> Millions in wealth arrived in a matter of days.

But was she really able to create cash and rice? Turn to the next chapter to find out.

3

ETERNA TRIES OUT THE MAGIC FOR CREATING CASH AND RICE;

MASTER HU GETS ANGRY AND BURNS THE WISH-FULFILLMENT MANUAL.

POEM:

An amazing one is the Dark Goddess,[1]
Though I fear we've lost her authentic art.
The master, in a moment's fit of rage,
Heedlessly destroys a constant heart.

Eterna noticed that the booklet was titled "Magic of the Dark Goddess of the Nine Heavens." Opening it at page 1, she read as follows:

> How to Create Cash: (An illustration depicted a piece of string passed through a copper coin.) You should tie a knot in the string and place it on the floor, then cover it with a washbasin. With a cup full of water in your hand, recite the charm seven times, then take a mouthful of the water and spit it on the floor, at the same time shouting, "Presto!" When you lift up the washbasin, the objects underneath will have turned into a string of cash.

She found a piece of string and took from her belt the copper coin left over from her purchase earlier that day. She threaded the coin on the string, tying a knot in it and placing both items on the floor. She then fetched a washbasin and placed it on top of them. From the water pitcher she dipped out a cupful of water. Taking the cup in her hand, she recited the charm seven times, then took a mouthful of the water and spat it on the floor while shouting, "Presto!" She put down the cup and lifted up the washbasin to see—and found beneath it a pile of cash coiled up like a green snake! In her astonishment, she didn't know what to do with the money. If I give it to my parents, she thought, they're bound to ask me where I got it. Then she had an idea. Opening the back door, she tossed it out onto the snow-covered ground inside their fence, where it could be explained away as an anonymous act of charity. Finally, she locked the back door and returned to the bedroom, where she hid the manual.

"Do you still have a stomachache, dear?" asked her mother.

"No, it's better now," said Eterna, as she climbed back into bed.

At dawn the family rose and heated the water for washing. When Eterna's mother opened the back door to throw out the slops, she was astonished to find a string of cash lying on the snowy ground. Snatching it up, she showed it to her husband. "I wonder who could have thrown this money into our yard," she said.

"My dear, it's better to be poor but honest than rich and dishonest," said the master. "Our daughter is growing up, and I'm afraid some disreputable young fellow may be trying to stir up her feelings and using this money to trifle with her."

"Oh, how little you know!" retorted his wife. "The Eastern Capital is full of rich men who do good deeds to help the poor. One of them must have seen the heavy snowfall and realized there would be many people in the almshouse with nothing to eat. Then he must have come during the night and thrown this into our yard as an act of charity. Our daughter has never been out of the house! Don't be absurd!"

"I daresay you're right. When I went out yesterday, I asked people for a mere two or three hundred cash, and I still didn't get anything. Now that we have this string, let's spend five hundred on rice, three hundred on firewood, and two hundred on salt, soy sauce, vegetables, and side dishes. Let's not worry about the snow!"

That evening they went to bed, but around the second watch Eterna began thinking to herself, when I made that string of cash yesterday, it went off well. Let me see if I can set things up again tonight. Ever so slowly she eased herself out of bed and put on her clothes. "What are you doing?" her mother asked.

"I have another stomachache, and I need to go to the privy."

"Oh, dear! You missed a good many meals before, but these last two days we've had both rice and firewood, and you must have overdone it and eaten too much. Tomorrow I'll get your father to go and buy you some medicine."

Eterna got down from the bed and went to the kitchen, where she set out the items as she had done the day before. She followed the magic formula in threading a piece of string through a coin, covering them both with a washbasin, reciting the charm, spitting out a mouthful of water, and then raising the basin to find a string of cash underneath, exactly as before. She opened the back door, placed the string on the snow-covered ground, then shut the door and went back to bed.

At dawn her mother arose and heated the water for washing. Then when she opened the back door to throw out the slops, she found another string of cash. Thrilled, she brought it back inside. "That's odd!" exclaimed Master Hu. "There's something very strange about where this money comes from."

"Nonsense! *I'm* not in the least afraid. It was all because the local god couldn't bear to see us in such misery and came to our aid, and now he's come and left us another string of cash." The master had no choice but to take the money and go out and buy firewood, rice, and vegetables and store them in the house.

A few days later the snow melted and the skies cleared. Mistress Zhang said to the master, "Now that we have a few days' supply of food in the house, why don't you take this chance to go out for a walk? If you meet someone you know, try and get a few hundred cash out of him." The master had no choice but to go. Meanwhile his wife, free of the concerns that had been plaguing her, went off to visit a neighbor and enjoy a chat over a cup of tea.

Eterna saw her mother leaving and realized that she was alone in the house. She shut the front door, took out the manual, and turned to page 2, which was headed "How to Make Rice." Thank heaven, she said to herself. Once I can make rice, we'll never have to worry about running short of food again. She found an empty bucket and placed it on the floor, dropped a dozen grains of rice inside, covered the bucket with one of her garments, recited the charm, spat out a mouthful of water, and shouted, "Presto!" at which point the rice started surging out from the bucket. In her alarm, she failed to recite the release formula, and the rice quickly rose higher and higher. The hoops on the bucket had long since corroded, and with a sudden crack they now burst and allowed the rice to spill all over the floor. Eterna let out a cry of dismay.

Next door her mother heard the cry and rushed over with the neighbors to see what was the matter. The arrival of outsiders broke the spell, and the surge stopped, leaving the floor covered in rice.

Her mother and the neighbors were aghast. "How did all this rice get here?" they asked.

Eterna resorted to the desperation move known as Total Fabrication. "Let me tell you what happened, Mother," she said. "A great big man came along carrying a sack of rice over his shoulder. He pushed open the back door, poured out the rice, and then left. I got such a scare that I let out a cry."

"What sort of man was he, and why would he do such a thing?" asked her mother.

"Oh, Mrs. Hu, you simply don't understand these things!" said her neighbor, Goodwife Zhang. "It's that same wealthy merchant as before. He saw that it's been snowing for days and he knew that there are thousands of people in the almshouses with nothing to eat, and he did this noble deed. Throwing money and rice into people's houses without letting the people know—those are 'good deeds done in secret.' He's afraid that, if he did it openly, people would come along and pester him. It's all perfectly obvious." The neighbors then left, and mother and daughter set about cleaning up the kitchen floor.

They had still not finished when Master Hu happened to return. At the sight of the two women sweeping the rice off the floor, he flared up: "I've never seen anything like the way you two carry on! You no sooner get a couple of meals of rice inside you than you start wasting the stuff!"

"I'd *never* waste any rice!" retorted his wife. "Take a look around you. All our jars, pots, vases, and buckets are full of it. And there's a lot more over here that we don't have containers for."

The master looked. "Where did it come from, then?" he asked in astonishment.

"After you left," said his wife, "I was drinking tea next door when I heard Eterna cry out. I rushed back home and found the whole floor covered in rice."

"How extraordinary! Where did it come from?"

"According to Eterna, a great big man brought in a sack of rice through the back door, poured it inside the house, and then left."

Master Hu was no fool. He opened the back door and looked outside. No tracks were visible in the snow inside or outside the hedge. Shutting the back door, he came in and found himself a rod. "Eterna!" he barked.

Eterna didn't dare come forward, but the master dragged her over. "How can you beat that child for no reason?" said his wife.

"Hold your tongue!" said the master. "This is a serious matter. The other day two strings of cash mysteriously arrived here, and today rice appears out of nowhere. Get this little hussy to tell me the truth, and I'll let her off. But if she says one word that's not true, I'll beat her to death! I'm asking her how those two strings of cash came to be on the ground outside and how that rice got into the house."

At first Eterna held out, but eventually the beating became too much for her to bear, and she had to tell the truth. "Let me tell you both what happened. That day when it started snowing, Daddy went out, and Mama told me to go and buy some steamed cakes. On the way back I met an old woman who said she was hungry and begged me for a cake. I couldn't bear to see her in such a state and gave her a little one. She said, 'I don't want to eat your cake, I was just testing you.' She gave the cake back to me, saying, 'It's rare to come upon such a kindhearted girl and dutiful daughter.' Then she gave me a purple silk bag with a manual inside and said to me, 'If you need money or rice, just read the charms in this book and you'll be able to make it yourself.' I know it was wrong of me, but when I came back, I started looking at the manual just for fun. Then when I recited the charm from the manual, it really did create some money."

At these words, Master Hu began moaning to high heaven. "The authorities have recently put up notices calling for the arrest of demons, and now you've gone and implicated *me* in it! I'm going to kill you, you little hussy, in order to clear myself of any crime." He raised the rod and began hitting her.

"Help!" cried Eterna. The old woman who lived next door heard Eterna being beaten and rushed over to intercede, but found the door locked. She called out, "Master, spare that child! You don't normally get into such a state! Why are you hitting her? Ma'am, why don't you stop him?"

"But the little hussy . . ." The master didn't dare say more, but he did let slip the remark, "What's in that manual is sheer bunkum!"

When the old woman heard the word "manual," she called out, "Your daughter's very young and doesn't understand anything at all. It must be some good-for-nothing local youths who are trying to provoke her. If the manual isn't worth reading, just burn it. Why beat the child?"

"You're right," said the master. To Eterna he said, "Bring me that manual!" She took it out from her breast pocket and handed it to him.

"Do you remember what it says?" he asked her as he took it.

"No, Daddy, I don't," she said. "If I had it in front of me, I could read it to you."

The master told his wife to light a lamp and burn the manual. To Eterna he said, "Out of regard for our neighbor, I shall forgive you this time, but if you do anything like this in the future, I shall beat you to death!"

"Oh, Daddy, I wouldn't dare," said Eterna.

The neighbor went back to her house. "Once again we've been blessed," the master told his wife. "We're the only ones who know about this. If someone outside the family had gotten to know of it, we'd be in terrible danger!"

From this point on their rice jars were full of rice, and there was plenty of money beside their bed. However, as the ancients said, if you sit idly at home, you'll soon use up all you possess. Day followed day, and before half a month had passed the rice jars were empty and there was no more money beside the bed. Once more they found themselves skipping the odd meal. There was nowhere they could go to ask for help, and they were in constant despair. Once more there was nothing left to eat.

Her mother recalled how Eterna had created both cash and rice, and she complained bitterly to her husband: "You beat her, and you burned her manual! You're the one who deserves to starve to death, but you're dragging my daughter and me down with you. How could you *do* such a thing? "You're 'starving to death beside the rice jar' while forcing your wife and daughter to suffer from hunger!"

"At this stage there's nothing I *can* do. Why do you keep blaming me?"

"Just when we had some food to eat, you had to go and stir up all this trouble. Since you took it upon yourself to beat her, you ought to be making yourself useful by getting us some money and rice. Yet here we are, barely alive, and that manual has been burned to ashes!"

"I wasn't thinking when I did that. I definitely shouldn't have burned it. I realize that now."

"It's too late now to keep your mouth shut. Ever since you gave her that beating, she never comes out to join us but stays in her room."

"Well, there's nothing else for it. I'll pocket my pride and go in and plead with her. I expect she still remembers and can come to our aid by making some more cash and rice. Let me go and ask her."

He went into the bedroom and said to his daughter with a smile, "My dear, your daddy would like to ask you something. Do you remember how to make cash and rice from that manual?"

"No, Daddy, I don't."

"Useless creature! Out of my way!" shouted his wife to Master Hu as she stepped forward. "My dear," she said to her daughter, "do try to remember, for my sake. You'd be saving your mother's life."

"And I won't beat you this time, either," added her father.

"Because Daddy beat me that last time I've forgotten all of it, but I do have a faint memory of something . . . I don't know if it would be any use. Daddy, sit yourself on the table, and I'll show you."

The master did as she said and sat on the table. The girl recited something, shouted, "Presto!" and the table rose up into the air, scaring her mother speechless. "Help!" cried the master, as his head bumped against the rafters. He couldn't get down, no matter how hard he tried. If it were not for the ceiling, he would have soared up into the sky.

How terrified he was! "What sort of magic is this?" he cried to his daughter. "Let me down!"

"Daddy, I've forgotten how to make cash and rice," said Eterna. "This is the only magic I remember, and it won't save us from going hungry or help us out in a crisis."

"*Let me down!*"

Eterna recited some words and shouted, "Presto!" and the table sank down to earth.

"That was terribly dangerous," said the master. "I nearly fell."

"Daddy, get me two pieces of string and I'll make a couple of strings of cash for us."

The master came back with three pieces of string and said to Eterna, "You go ahead, my dear. One guest shouldn't trouble two hosts. If you can do three or four *hundred* more strings of cash, you'll make me a very happy man. If it should ever come to the ear of the authorities, we'll deal with it then." His wife and daughter could not contain their amusement.

Eterna tied a coin to each piece of string, and one piece of string became ten, ten became a hundred, and a hundred became a thousand. From that day forward, there was always rice in the rice jar, and the master had money to spend on wine and food as well as gradually to buy clothes.

One day, as he was returning from buying a few items, Eterna said to him, "Daddy, there's something I'd like to show you." She felt in her sleeve and produced an ingot of silver.

The master held it in his hand. It weighed twenty-four or twenty-five ounces. "Where did this come from?" he asked.

"This morning I saw an old man selling paper money who was passing by our door, and he had some papier-mâché imitation gold and silver ingots on his cart," she said. "I snatched one of them away from him, and it turned into the real thing."

"In that case, it's hardly worthwhile making a hundred strings of cash. If you can make gold and silver ingots, we'll be rich again!" He went off to the paper money shop and came back with three strings of gold and silver imitation ingots. "If you make just one or two ingots, that won't be much use," he said to Eterna. "You might just as well make twenty or thirty. Then we'll be able to enjoy ourselves for the rest of our lives."

Eterna placed the gold and silver imitation ingots on the floor, then took off her skirt and covered them up. She recited the words, spat out a mouthful of water, and shouted, "Presto!" When she lifted up the skirt, she found two piles on the floor, one of gold, the other of silver. The master, needless to say, was ecstatic. His joy was due entirely to his daughter's prowess in making so much money.

He talked their situation over with his wife and daughter. "Now that we have all this gold and silver, we're rich, and we surely won't want to go on living in the almshouse. I'd like to buy a house in a prosperous part of town and open up a shop selling colored silks. What do you think?"

"All winter we've been scraping about for food and trying to get help from others," said his wife. "If we suddenly open up a colored-silk shop, I'm afraid people will get suspicious."

"That's no problem. I'll just tell the fellow merchants I know that I've recently acquired an official as my patron and borrowed some capital from him. I'll ask a broker to buy half the property for us, then get the rest on credit. They won't suspect a thing."

"You're right."

That day the master dressed up neatly and went out to try and meet a few of his acquaintances. "I've recently received patronage from an official and borrowed some capital from him, and I'd like to open a small shop. Would any of you gentlemen be interested in helping out? I'll raise only half the money on credit, putting up the other half myself. I hope you'll agree to help."

"That's no problem at all," they said. "Just leave it to us."

Having secured their agreement, the master went to the business district and rented a house and bought furniture for it. He chose an auspicious day for the opening and sold his goods for eight hundred cash when they were worth a full string. Everyone loves a bargain, and when people saw that he was selling his goods cheaply and that they were superior to those of his competitors, they flocked to his shop. The entire stock sold out, and the master could hardly contain his delight. Gradually the family's wealth increased, and they engaged an assistant for the shop and two menservants and two serving women for the house. Within two years the master and his family were living in style, and he became once more the Master Hu of old.

But when the other shopkeepers saw the customers coming to his shop, they grew suspicious. How very strange, they said, "He fetches all his stock from *inside* his house." The assistants also became suspicious: "Why aren't his goods displayed on the shelves? Why do they always go in to fetch them?" The master realized that people were suspicious because the goods came from inside. We haven't bought a thing, he thought, all the goods have been made by my daughter. What am I going to do, now that people are so full of suspicion and envy? The evening of the following day he tidied up the shop and went into the inner quarters and gave orders for supper to be served. The serving women brought it in, and as the master and his family were drinking their wine, he said to the women, "You may take a break. We have family business to discuss." The women left the room.

"My dear," the master said to Eterna, "we owe our entire fortune to you. We have countless quantities of gold, silver, and silk. We have menservants for the outer part of the house, serving women for the inner quarters, and an assistant for the shop. But when people come to buy, they get suspicious of the fact that we sell stock but never buy any. From now on you mustn't go into the shop and listen to customers' requests. After all, what are a hundred strings of cash worth when, if the slightest hint of this ever got out and people realized what was going on, we'd be in terrible danger and lose our entire fortune? From now on you mustn't make any more goods."

"Daddy, I shall stay inside. I won't go out and listen to orders in the shop."

"Splendid," said the master as he ordered the food brought in again. Following supper Eterna returned to her room.

After the master gave Eterna these instructions, if a customer requested something that the shop had in stock, they would sell it to him; if not, they would send him elsewhere for it. Previously his daughter had created the things they did not have in stock, but now she no longer came into the shop to listen to requests. Master Hu was vastly relieved, but after a month or more this thought suddenly occurred to him: these days I've been so preoccupied with the business that I haven't paid any attention to my daughter at home. If she can suppress the ideas she cherishes, fine, but if she does something wild and the serving women get to hear of it, we'll be in terrible danger!

This thought of checking on his daughter led to certain consequences: the court mobilized an army and sent it forth, while Eterna threw half the world into chaos and plunged several cities into tumult.

Peasants bore regimental insignia on their backs;
A fisherman flew a commander's flag on his boat

What strange thing was it that she did? Turn to the next chapter to find out.

4

ETERNA CUTS UP STRAW TO MAKE HORSES; ETERNA SCATTERS BEANS TO MAKE SOLDIERS.

POEM:

The evil arts are rarely to be found;
The Five Thunder God Rites[1] are known to few.
But if you transform evil into good,
The gods will assuredly favor you.

Master Hu looked for Eterna in the hall, but she was not there. Nor was she in the bedroom or in the backyard. But as he passed by the woodshed, he noticed that the door was ajar and wondered if she could be in there. He strode over and stepped inside, to find her sitting on a small stool in the middle of an open space, a cup of water in front of her and a vermilion gourd in her hands. I couldn't find her anywhere, thought the master; what is she doing in here? He didn't dare disturb her, but stood where he was and watched what she was doing. Removing the stopper from the gourd, she tipped a couple of hundred red beans and inch-long snippets of rice straw onto the ground. Then she recited something, took a mouthful of water, and spat it out, crying, "Presto!" as she did so. The beans and snippets of straw at once turned into mounted horsemen three feet tall, with red helmets, red armor, red battle dress, red tassels, red flags, red insignia, and red horses. They wheeled about on the ground and then took up battle formations. As long ago as the tenth of last month, thought the master, I drummed it into Eterna not to dare make anything ever again, and yet here she is playing games with her magic. Let me watch and see how she brings this to a conclusion. She removed the stopper from a white gourd and tipped out a couple of hundred white beans and inch-long snippets of rice straw, recited something, took a mouthful of water, and spat it out, crying, "Presto!" again. The beans and snippets turned into mounted horsemen with white helmets, white armor, white battle dress, white tassels, white flags, white insignia, and white horses. They arrayed themselves like a wall of steel before they, too, took up battle formations.

Eterna plucked a gold comb from her hair and cried, "Change!" The comb in her hand turned into a priceless sword, which she pointed at the two armies while crying, "Engage!" The two forces closed on each other, filling the air with shouts of "Kill! Kill!" Master Hu was so shocked he was rendered speechless. It's a good thing I was the one to see all this, he thought. Had it been anyone else, it would have been a very serious matter. Sooner or later the little hussy is going to get me into trouble. To protect myself, I'll have to put my paternal feelings aside and take drastic action right now. Furious over the sight he had just witnessed, he left the woodshed and went to the kitchen in search of a knife.

With the sword grasped in her hand, Eterna was ordering the troops to maneuver this way and that and engage in battle. A wild melee ensued from which no clear victor emerged. Then after a long time the formations broke up, and the red and white forces regrouped. "Withdraw!" cried Eterna, at which the red and white soldiers and horses reverted to their original form as red and white beans and snippets of straw. She then returned them to the red and white gourds.

Master Hu raised the knife and slashed at Eterna, severing her head and leaving her lifeless body sprawled on the floor. Then, nearly driven out of his mind by the sight before his eyes, he threw the knife away and dragged his daughter's body to an out-of-the-way spot and covered it up. He then locked the woodshed door and went with a heavy heart to the shop, where he sat himself down and began to excoriate himself: What a crime I have committed! My daughter brought us in a large fortune, but just now in a brief moment I saw her doing something wrong and I took her life. But I can hardly be blamed for it. If I'd allowed her to go on like that, I'd certainly have had to face charges. Far better to take her life now, so that my wife and I can live in peace. But if my wife learns what I've done, she's bound to be furious. After missing the girl all day, she's sure to ask what possible reason I could have had for killing her.

Too restless to settle down, he was in and out of that shop a hundred times. When in the evening the shop closed and the assistants left, he told the serving women, "Set out the wine things. The mistress and I are going to have a drink." In talking to his wife, he made no mention of their daughter, but when each of them had drunk five or six cups of wine, he heaved a sigh, and two streams of tears trickled down his cheeks.

"Why are you crying like that for no reason?" asked his wife.

"There's something troubling me, and it's all my fault. At a time in our lives when you and I have begun to enjoy ourselves, I caught our daughter doing something very wrong, and on the spur of the moment I couldn't bear it and took her life. I'm afraid you'll blame me for it, but you mustn't be angry."

"Why are you telling me all this? What peculiar thing has she done this time?"

The master gave a full account of how Eterna had changed objects into soldiers and horses. When his wife heard the story, she struck her breast and stamped her feet and began to sob.

"You've forgotten how three years ago we were hungry and freezing in that almshouse; but for her we wouldn't be alive today. Despite all that, you were so heartless as to take her life!"

"Just at that moment I lost my temper, but *please*, for the sake our marriage . . ."

"You killed my daughter—how can I help being furious?" she exclaimed, but then she began to have doubts. I saw her just now in her bedroom, she thought, and she seemed perfectly all right. How can he say he killed her? "When was it that you killed her?" she asked.

"During the day."

"If you killed her during the day, I have someone here that I'd like you to meet."

She was gone a little while before she came back again pulling someone by the arm. The master took a closer look. It's my daughter, he realized. But I killed her with a single blow! How could she still be alive? He was so shocked that he blurted out, "One day the unnatural little hussy is going to get us into trouble. We'll have to find some scheme to safeguard ourselves."

He managed somehow to get through that night, then rose early the next morning and went straight to the woodshed. On opening the door and looking inside, he was stunned by the sight that met his eyes: there was the knife, lying off to one side, but the corpse that he had beheaded was nothing more than a bamboo broom. "Oh! Oh!" moaned the master. "We can't keep her here anymore. I have to get her out of the house."

He went and discussed the matter with his wife. "As the saying goes, when boys and girls grow up, they must be wed, and Eterna is now grown up. We can't keep her at home indefinitely, but we still haven't arranged a marriage for her."

"Quite right," said his wife.

The master sent a servant around town to invite two matchmakers. The servant took only a little while to summon Goodwives

Zhang and Li, who came into the hall and curtsied to the master and his wife. She asked them to sit down and ordered tea, and after they had drunk it, she ordered wine to be served. Goodwife Zhang then rose to her feet and said, "May I ask what instructions you have for us in inviting us here?"

"Do sit down," said the master. "Have either of you ever seen my daughter?"

"Yes, I saw her when I was here before," said Goodwife Zhang. "And a pretty young lady she is, too!"

"We have just the one daughter, who's now seventeen," said the master. "We want to arrange a marriage for her, and we've specially invited you two over to discuss the matter."

"Thank you, sir, thank you, madam, for calling on me," said Goodwife Zhang. "Since the young lady is to be married, I'm wondering whether you would want the son-in-law to move into your house or have your daughter marry into his family."

"Only to marry into his family."

"In that case," said Goodwife Li, "a marriage can be arranged."

The master produced six taels of silver. "This is for your trouble. If a marriage is successfully arranged, you will, of course, be handsomely rewarded." The matchmakers thanked the master and left, then proceeded to divide up the money between themselves.

On the way back Goodwife Zhang asked, "Where are we going to find a suitable match?"

"I know a good one. I'll take you with me."

"Who is it?"

"Master Zhang the cooper has a son who's twenty-one, and he wants a marriage with a good daughter-in-law. Let's go over and get a few drinks out of him."

They went over, and when Master Zhang saw them arriving, he asked, "And what brings you two to my door?"

"We have a fine match that we've come specially to propose."

"Lots of matchmakers come here with proposals, but none of them has been successful so far. I wonder whose daughter you have in mind."

"It's the daughter of Master Hu, the owner of the colored-silk shop. She's seventeen years old and very pretty."

"I saw her once at Jinming Pond, and she really is pretty. But I have just the one son and I wouldn't be willing to have him marry into her family."

"But Master Hu wants to marry his daughter out of the family."

Master Zhang was delighted to hear this news. He set out the wine for the matchmakers, who drank several cups. He also handed them three taels, saying, "If the match is successful, I'll give you a handsome reward on top of this."

The matchmakers took the money, thanked the master, and left. On the way back, they discussed the suit. "Today must be our lucky day, everything has gone so smoothly," they said.

Returning to the Hu residence, they met the master, who invited them to sit down. "What hard workers you are!" he said. "You only just went out to find a match, and you're back already!"

"Sir, the match we've arranged is with the son of Master Zhang the cooper. He has just the one boy, who's twenty-one. The Zhangs' social position is on a par with yours, and the son is extremely clever, good at writing and accounts—a young man of outstanding talent."

The master waited until she finished and then said, "Drop it."

"But sir!" protested the two matchmakers, "how can you possibly drop such a good match?"

"I just don't care for it. But if you have any other matches to propose, do bring them along." The matchmakers had no choice but to take their leave.

"Although the match didn't come off, we did make a few taels," said Goodwife Zhang, as they were about to part. "Let's go back home and give this matter some further thought."

Next day after breakfast Goodwife Zhang went to see Goodwife Li. "Have you come up with any good matches?" she asked.

"I've been thinking all night, and I don't have any good ones to suggest. When we proposed that match yesterday, Master Hu still refused despite the fact that the other family was a perfect match, socially speaking."

"I know a good one. Master Tang the alchemist[2] has a son who's nineteen. I've proposed several matches to Master Tang, but none of them appealed to him. If we put forward Master Hu's daughter, we're bound to succeed."

"Good! I'll go with you."

At Master Tang's residence they found the master sitting in front of his door. When he saw them coming toward him, he asked them in and invited them to sit down. "Sir," said Goodwife Zhang, "we have a good match, and we've made a special visit here to propose it for your young master."

"Who is it?"

"It's the daughter of Master Hu, the owner of the colored-silk shop. She's seventeen."

Master Tang laughed. "I know about Master Hu's daughter. She's good-looking and highly intelligent. Several times I've sent people over there to propose a match, but each time Master Hu has shaken his head and turned me down. Why are you proposing it now?"

"Yesterday Master Hu called us in," said Goodwife Zhang. "He gave us three taels each and offered us several cups of wine and asked us to find a match of equal status. That's why we're calling on you."

Master Tang was delighted, and he at once had wine brought out and offered to them. When they had drunk it, he handed them four taels and said, "If this match is successful, you'll receive a handsome reward on top of this. Now, see that you do your best." The matchmakers thanked him and took their leave.

On the way back, they said to each other, "We've earned our retainer. This match is bound to succeed."

When they arrived at Master Hu's, he said, "And what match are you proposing this time?"

"Sir, it's the son of Master Tang the alchemist, who's nineteen. We've been sent to you to propose a match."

"I know Master Tang's son."

"I really wouldn't dream of exaggerating, but the young man is extremely intelligent and good at both writing and accounts—altogether a most suitable young gentleman."

"Drop it," said Master Hu. "If you find another match, do come and tell me about it." The matchmakers had no choice but to leave.

To spare you the repetition, whenever it seemed that the matchmakers had a good match to propose, the master told them to drop it as soon as he heard that the young man was intelligent. After a few days of this treatment, they thought to themselves, what an extraordinary man that Master Hu is! When first we went to see him, he gave us wine and money and treated us well, but when we offered him seven or eight good matches, he refused them all. I wonder what's behind it.

"We have nowhere to go today," said Goodwife Li. "Let's go over to his house and do him out of a few cups of wine and, with any luck, a couple of taels as well. Let's have a little fun."

"What match are you going to propose?"

"Don't you worry about that! You just come along with me, and I'll treat you to some wine."

The two women arrived at Master Hu's and were invited in to sit down and have some tea. Then the master asked them, "Well, what match do you have for me today?"

"Sir, today we're proposing the son of Master Jiao, who owns a colored-silk shop just like yours."

"How old is he and what's he like?"

Because Goodwife Li opened her mouth to propose this match, certain consequences followed: Eterna Hu could not marry and instead became a runaway.

Green dragon, white tiger walk side by side—
Good and bad fortune cannot be foretold.

But did this match succeed? Turn to the next chapter to find out.

5

MASTER HU'S DAUGHTER IS MARRIED TO DAFFY; ETERNA FLIES IN SECRET TO ZHENGZHOU.

POEM:

Talk too much, you're bad; too little, you're dumb.
If you're bad, you're reviled; if good, you're cheated.
If you're rich, you're envied; if poor, you're scorned.
But which to heaven's plan is better suited?

"Master Jiao's son is in his thirties," Goodwife Li told Master Hu. "His hair is drawn up in two tufts, he drools at the mouth, he has to have a nurse dress and feed him, and he's unfamiliar with the facts of life."

"I'd like you two to do your best to arrange a marriage with him," said Master Hu. The matchmakers said nothing, but they wondered to themselves, after turning down countless good matches with brilliant sons-in-law, is he now going to marry that perfectly good daughter of his to this idiot?

They drank several cups of wine and received two taels each, then thanked the master and left the house. On the opposite side of the street was a teahouse, and the two women stopped by for a cup of tea. "You didn't need to make me laugh like that," said Goodwife Zhang. "I was on tenterhooks the whole time lest

Master Hu get angry and take it out on me, too. Whatever were you thinking of?"

"Well, we'd offered him those wonderful matches, and he'd turned them all down, so I thought I'd have a little fun at his expense. If he'd got angry, I'd have just said it was all a joke. It never occurred to me that he'd accept."

"It must have appealed to him, though. Otherwise, he'd hardly have offered us any money or wine."

They bustled along, chuckling as they went, through Academy Gate as far as Master Jiao's. He invited them in to sit down and have some tea.

"You're both matchmakers," he said. "What business do you have with me?"

"We've come especially to drink some of your wine, sir," said Goodwife Li, "and also to propose a match for your young master."

"But my son's a simpleton. He's not familiar with the facts of life. Who would be willing to marry his daughter to him?"

"Master Hu, the owner of another colored-silk shop, has a daughter who's as pretty as a flower and just seventeen. Her father has refused many proposals, but just now, when we mentioned your son, he agreed and sent us over to propose the match."

Master Jiao was overjoyed. "If you can complete this match, you'll be handsomely rewarded." Each of them drank several cups of wine and received three taels of silver.

From Master Jiao's house they went straight back to Master Hu's. "When Master Jiao heard of the match with your daughter, he was absolutely delighted and told us to come back and ask you to choose an auspicious day for the exchange of money and gifts. It's up to you to decide the arrangements." Master Hu was overjoyed and sent the matchmakers back to report as much.

"I didn't like to say anything in front of those matchmakers," his wife said to Master Hu, "but I simply don't understand your reasoning. Why on earth didn't you accept a match with a good son-in-law instead of telling them to propose marriage to an idiot?"

"If we'd kept our daughter at home," said the master, "she would eventually have undoubtedly got us both into trouble. Even if we'd married her into another family and she'd had a smart, capable husband, she wouldn't have been able to suppress her ideas but would have let something slip out, and then we'd have been in trouble, too. Now that we're marrying her to a dim, feebleminded husband, even if she does let something out, he'll never understand."

"But to marry such a fine girl to an idiot—aren't you ruining her whole life?"

"To get her out of the house—why, that's a blessing from heaven! Why are you so concerned about it?"

To cut a long story short, in due course the two families sent matchmakers to deliver the money and gifts as well as the goose[1] and the letter. Before long an auspicious date had been chosen and the wedding arranged.

Master Jiao and his wife called in the nurse and gave her instructions. "When the young master is married, his bedroom affairs will be your responsibility. If the couple get on well together, we'll reward you handsomely."

"Thank you, sir, thank you, ma'am," said the nurse. "I know what to do."

"In that case, you'd better take your time teaching him," said the mistress.

She and the nurse went into Daffy's bedroom, and the nurse said, "Daffy, tomorrow you're going to take a wife." (Daffy was the bridegroom's childhood name.)[2]

"Tomorrow you're going to take a wife," replied Daffy.

"What fun!"

"What fun!" he replied.

The nurse said nothing, but she thought to herself, how stupid that master is! What's the point of finding a wife for an idiot like this? It'll be the ruination of someone's daughter! And what a fool that Master Hu is, too! I've heard that his daughter's a perfect beauty, and that she's smart and intelligent as well as good at needlework, and yet he's marrying her to this idiot! I can't imagine what either man was thinking!

The following evening Mistress Zhang accompanied the bride to the Jiao household, where, needless to say, she bowed to the gods, performed the rituals, and enjoyed the banquet. But when the nurse helped Daffy out of his room and Mistress Zhang set eyes on him, she was aghast:

Layers of grime on his face,
Drool from the corners of his mouth.
His cap, all shiny,
Sat askew on his twin tufts.
His gown, quite new,
Was stretched tight across his body.
Bushy eyebrows, sunken cheeks,
Jug ears, and slanting eyes.
Boots coming up to his thighs made his gait unsteady—
It took several men to pull him along.
Snot hung down to his open lips, fouling his mouth—
He wiped it away on his sleeves.
He stared at people but said not a word,
As if he were some repulsive beast led forth;
His curled whiskers merged with his hair, thirty years' growth,
As if he were some monster conjured up.
With his clumsy body, he found it hard to stand,
Like some weird tree trembling in the wind on a far-off peak.
His ugly face confronted the spirits' images,
Like a demon fox worshipping the moon in a remote vale.
He saw only the colored lanterns,
Not realizing they were there for his own wedding.
Although he had met his destined partner,

He did not understand that this was his wedding night.
Seeing off the guests, he displayed alarm,
Causing those present to burst out laughing.
Inside the bridal chamber, under the colored candles,
It was like the Weaving Maid meeting Nata.[3]
Within the bed-curtains, as the red lanterns flickered,
It was like Guanyin encountering Pigsy.[4]
Even Momu[5] would have detested him;
Even Wuyan[6] would have scorned to be his wife.

When Mistress Zhang saw what her son-in-law looked like, the tears trickled down her cheeks, and she silently bemoaned her daughter's fate: That old fool! To throw away my own flesh and blood on such a creature! How will her marriage end? But Mistress Zhang was like the proverbial dumb person who bites into something bitter and can only suffer in silence. She had no choice but to spend the night celebrating with her many new relatives. And the next morning she had to abandon her daughter, say good-bye to her relatives, and return home to take her anger out on her husband.

When Eterna saw her mother leaving, her cheeks streamed with tears and she felt an inexpressible misery. One after the other she saw the relatives off and, after eating supper, thanked her mother-in-law and bade her good night, then accompanied the nurse into the bedroom. When the nurse saw Daffy sitting on the bed, she said to him, "You'll be sleeping with the young lady."

"You'll be sleeping with the young lady," he replied.

"Sleep with the young lady!" ordered the nurse.

"Sleep with the young lady!" he replied.

He just repeats whatever I say, thought the nurse, and he'll go on doing it forever. I'd better get the young lady ready for bed. First she undressed Daffy and helped him into bed, covered him up with bedclothes, and then said to Eterna, "Please, miss, undress and get into bed."

Eterna's eyes filled with tears when she heard this request. Oh, Father and Mother! she cried to herself. How did I ever let you down that you should marry me to this idiot? You've forgotten the days when we suffered in the almshouse, and now that you're rich, you don't realize who you owe it all to. *No, no, that's not it!* Now I understand Daddy's reasoning! He was afraid that if he married me to an intelligent man, I would teach him something, and realizing that, he married me to this idiot! Wiping away her tears, she said good night to the nurse and undressed and lay down beside Daffy, while the nurse returned to her own room. Once in bed, Eterna wrapped the bedclothes tightly around herself and slept on one side, not sharing any of the bedding with Daffy.

Time slipped by, and half a year passed. It was now the sixth month, and the weather was fiercely hot. One evening Eterna went to the hall and said good night to her parents-in-law, then took Daffy out to the courtyard for the cool air. "Daffy, how hot it is!" she said.

"How hot it is!" he replied.

"We're going to enjoy the cool air together. Now, don't be afraid."

"We're going to enjoy the cool air together. Now, don't be afraid," he replied.

It drove her to despair that Daffy's talk was so nonsensical. They were sitting on a bench at the time, and as she recited a formula, the bench turned into a tiger with slanting eyes and white brows. With Daffy and herself straddling the tiger's back, she recited another formula, and the tiger soared up into the sky, carrying them both with it. It went as far as the tower of the gate known as Anshang, when she shouted, "Halt!" and the tiger came to a stop on the tower over the gate.

Eterna said to Daffy, "How nice and cool it is!"

"How nice and cool it is!" he replied.

They stayed there enjoying the cool air until the fourth watch, when Eterna said, "Let's go back."

"Let's go back," he replied.

She recited a formula and the tiger soared up into the sky and went directly to their own courtyard and landed. "Daffy, let's go to bed!" said Eterna.

"Let's go to bed!" he replied.

Every night from then on Eterna and Daffy rode on the tiger's back to the tower of Anshang Gate, returning at the fourth watch.

One day Eterna said, "Daffy, let's go and enjoy the cool air."

"Let's go and enjoy the cool air," he replied.

She recited a formula, and the bench turned into the tiger that soared up into the sky and went straight to the tower of Anshang Gate so that they could enjoy the cool air. That night, however, there was no breeze. Eterna said, "How hot it is tonight!" and kept fanning herself with a circular white paper fan. The moon was partly obscured as two soldiers on night duty came out on patrol. One was named Zhang Qian, the other Li Wan. When they returned to the gate, Zhang looked up at the moon and exclaimed in astonishment, "Li Wan, do you see what I see? Two people sitting on top of that roof?"

"But how could any people, if they *are* people, ever get up there?"

Zhang Qian looked hard at the rooftop. "They really are two people!"

"If you ask me," said Li Wan, "they're just two crows." Eterna was steadily fanning herself on the rooftop, and Li Wan added, "If they aren't crows, why are they flapping their wings up there?"

"One looks to me like a man and the other like a woman," said Zhang Qian. "Anyway, whether they're people or crows, they're going to get a taste of one of my arrows!" From his kit he picked out his bow and an arrow, fitted the arrow to the bow, bent the bow to its full extent, took aim, and let fly. The arrow sped unerringly to its mark, hitting Daffy squarely in the upper leg. Letting out a yell, he tumbled down from the tower, twisting this way and that before striking the ground like a ripe melon. Zhang Qian and Li Wan promptly seized him and bound him, but when they looked up again, the other person was nowhere to be seen.

The next morning the soldiers brought Daffy under guard to the Kaifeng prefectural yamen. The prefect happened to be at his tribunal, and Zhang Qian and Li Wan took Daffy in and had him kneel down. "We were on night patrol," they reported, "and last night at the third watch we had gone as far as Anshang Gate when suddenly we looked up and saw two people sitting on the ridge of the tower roof and fanning themselves with a white paper fan. The moon was not very bright at the time, but they appeared to be a man and a woman. We calculated that, since there was no way they could have climbed up such a tall tower without a ladder, and since there was no ladder in evidence, they must be the kind of thieves who leap onto roofs and vault over walls, and so I took my bow and shot this one down. However, when we looked up again, the one who appeared to be a woman had vanished. We've now brought this man before Your Honor and await your orders."

"What sort of man are you?" the prefect demanded of Daffy.

"What sort of man are you?" replied Daffy.

"Tell me the truth, and you'll be spared from torture."

"Tell me the truth, and you'll be spared from torture," replied Daffy.

His replies angered the prefect, who rounded on him. "Despicable creature! Don't you dare pretend to be mad in front of me!"

Daffy stared back at him. "Despicable creature! Don't you dare pretend to be mad in front of me!" he replied, sending the people who packed the chamber into fits of laughter.

The prefect was left with no choice but to have the members of the audience come forward and try to identify the prisoner and establish where he was from. They stepped forward, but all of them said, "We've never seen this man before." The Anshang Gate tower is as high as the sky, thought the prefect. How could those two ever get up there? And even if they could get up there, how is it that the one who looked like a woman was able to sneak off without anyone seeing her come down? She must surely be some sort of demon or ghoul who bewitched this fellow into going up there and then, when he was unexpectedly shot down, promptly left the scene. Judging from the nonsense of his replies, this one must still be out of his mind. But how am I going to solve this case without knowing his name and where he comes from? After pondering the matter for some time, he barked out an order: "Clap this man in a head cangue and take him out to the crossroads on the highway." To Zhang Qian and Li Wan he added, "I want you two to stand guard, and if anyone comes along to see this man and ask him questions, you are to bring that person to me immediately."

Before long the jailers brought out a head cangue and placed it on Daffy, and then Zhang Qian and Li Wan led him to the crossroads. The sight caused a sensation among the people in the neighborhood, and they crowded around, jostling each other to get a good look.

Early next morning, when the nurse and the maids in Master Jiao's household brought the hot water for washing into Daffy's and Eterna's bedroom, they found to their astonishment that neither of them was there. In great agitation they rushed off to tell the master and his wife, who were dumbfounded. "All the doors are still locked. Where *could* they have gone?" the master and his wife asked themselves.

Master Jiao went out and then in again, still at a complete loss. Then suddenly he heard conversations among the small groups gathered on the street outside: "Last night two people were sitting on the ridge of the Anshang Gate tower. One of them was shot down by a soldier on patrol, while the other escaped." Someone else remarked, "Haven't you seen him? He's locked up in a cangue at the crossroads."

When he heard this, Master Jiao felt as if someone were propelling him out the door. He went straight to the crossroads, forced his way through the crowd, and when he got close enough, found that the man in the cangue was his own son. He burst out sobbing. "How ever did you get on top of that tower?" he asked. "And where's your wife?" Zhang Qian and Li Wan saw that he had come to see the man in the cangue and without giving him a chance to explain dragged him off to the yamen.

"What is your name?" demanded the prefect. "What is your relationship to the man in the cangue? Why did he go and sit on top of a tower in the Forbidden City, and what nefarious scheme did he have in mind? And why was he with that woman who escaped? Tell me the truth, and I'll set you free."

Kneeling before the prefect, Master Jiao testified as follows: "My name is Jiao Yu, and I am a resident of this prefecture. The man in the cangue is my son, who has lived a useless life for over thirty years. He doesn't understand the simplest thing. He even needs to have someone constantly at his side to dress and feed him, and if anyone asks him a question, he repeats it. For that reason we gave him the childhood name of Daffy. I've had the nurse who attended on him as a child continue to look after him, and we never let him take a step outside the second gate. Six months ago a matchmaker happened to come by with a marriage proposal, which put me in a quandary. If I accepted, I was afraid that I'd be ruining the life of someone else's daughter. On the other hand, if I didn't accept, since he's my only son, there'd be no one after me to carry on the family sacrifices. I'm indebted to a man named Hu Hao of this prefecture, who was undeterred by my son's stupidity and married his daughter to him. Moreover, Eterna, the daughter, is both beautiful and clever. Last night after supper we went to our respective bedrooms to sleep, but this morning, to our astonishment, neither she nor my son was anywhere to be seen, although the doors were still locked. I haven't the slightest notion how they got out of the house and up onto that tower, nor do I have any idea how she was able to get away without anyone seeing her come down."

"Nonsense!" shouted the prefect. "They're your son and your daughter-in-law, so *of course* you opened the door and allowed them to get out! You've undoubtedly got your daughter-in-law hidden away somewhere in your house. Bring her here to see me at once!"

"I'm a law-abiding citizen—I would never dare tell any lies. You may torture me to death, but you would be committing a terrible injustice!" The prefect thought that the man's protestations sounded sincere, and moreover, his description of Daffy's speech rang true, so he sent another two men to bring Eterna's father in for questioning in the hope of finding out the girl's whereabouts. Armed with a warrant, the runners raced off to Master Hu's house.

Master Hu had heard gossip on the street about these events, and he realized at once that his daughter must have been responsible for the harm done to Daffy. He was commiserating privately with his wife when the runners rushed up, shouting, "Is the master in?"

Although Master Hu was scared half to death, he still had to go out and receive them. "What can I do for you?" he asked.

"We have strict orders from His Honor the prefect to summon you to court. Be so good as to come along with us."

"But I've not done anything wrong! I can't imagine why you've been put to all the trouble of summoning me."

"His Honor is waiting for you as we speak. You will find out the reason for the summons as soon as you get there." They would not even allow the master to turn around, but pushed him out the door and then took him straight to the yamen.

The prefect was in a testy mood from having to wait. As soon as he saw Master Hu brought in, he launched into an account of how Daffy had been shot down from the tower and Master Jiao had been unable to give any clear answers about Daffy and Eterna, and he demanded that Eterna be brought out for questioning. To all of which Master Hu pleaded ignorance.

"I understand that your daughter is extremely bright and intelligent," said the prefect. "Her husband being so stupid, she must have taken a lover and had an illicit affair with him. You were afraid that I would force her to tell me the truth, so you insisted on hiding her away in your house in order to conceal the facts."

From the other side of the court, Master Jiao, who was on his knees, broke in. "If you have her in your house, bring her out at once and save my son's life!"

"It's always the man who involves the woman in this sort of activity," retorted Master Hu. "Clearly, for some unknown reason you sent her away and then deliberately bribed the soldiers on patrol to say that the two of them were sitting on that rooftop and that one was shot down while the other escaped. Your Honor, that tower reaches up to the *sky*! They didn't have a ladder, and they could hardly have grown *wings* in order to get up there! If she was with him, how is it that the tiles didn't make a sound when she ran away so fast? Women's feet being so small, how is it that the soldiers couldn't catch up with her, but let her escape before their very eyes and then come back to my house to hide?"

Hearing this eminently reasonable explanation, the prefect shouted an order: "Put Daffy's father and also Zhang Qian and Li Wan in the press!" Pointing at Master Jiao, he said, "No doubt you plotted the death of that girl and colluded with Zhang Qian and Li Wan to concoct this plan, using your crazy son as a convenient cover. Unless you're beaten, you'll never confess!" He ordered a severe beating for all three of them. The runners who lined both sides of the courtroom sprang into action and beat the men until their skin was broken and blood oozed from the welts.

Master Jiao could stand the pain no longer. "May Your Honor in your wisdom decide the issue," he pleaded. "I did not plot the death of Eterna Hu. Please allow me to have a portrait made of her face. I am also willing to put up a three-thousand-tael reward. I would ask you to issue a general order for her arrest and circulate it throughout the prefecture together with her likeness and the announcement of the reward. If no news comes to light, I'll willingly take the punishment."

Noting that the three men would not confess even if practically beaten to death, the prefect had already begun to relent. Moreover, Master Hu had been noticeably lukewarm in demanding the return of his daughter. "Good idea," said the prefect. He released the three men and had Daffy brought into the yamen and his cangue removed. All of them were allowed to arrange bail and go home to await a further summons. He ordered the Jiaos to have a portrait made of Eterna, then put out a general order for her arrest and had it posted everywhere. And there we shall leave him.

Meanwhile, when Eterna saw Daffy hit by an arrow and falling to the ground, she recited a formula and soared up into the sky. Noticing a deserted spot in the countryside, she brought herself gently down to earth. Then, leaving the stool behind, she set off alone along the road, sunk in gloom. Where should I go, she asked herself. I can't go back to my in-laws, any more than I can go to my parents. She recalled that on her wedding night she had dreamed of Priestess Pia saying to her, "This is not a place for you to settle down in. If ever you find yourself in trouble, come to Zhengzhou and seek me out." I have nowhere to stay right now, she thought, and if the authorities learn where I am, what shall I do? I'd better go to Zhengzhou and seek refuge with Priestess Pia, then see what develops.

It was late, and she had been walking for a long time when she came to a roadside shelter from the sun and found an old woman in there making tea. Eterna entered and sat down to rest her feet, and the old woman poured her a cup. When she had drunk it, Eterna asked, "What is this place called, and what lies up ahead?"

"Up ahead you'll come to Eight Corners Village of Plank Bridge. Beyond that you'll find the main road to Zhengzhou. But miss, where are you going so casually all on your own?"

"My parents are in Zhengzhou, and I want to join them," said Eterna.

"It's late, and all you can do is spend the night at an inn in Eight Corners before you go on. I hope there's a place where you can stay, because it's simply not advisable to travel on your own at night."

Eterna created a dozen cash to pay for the tea and thanked the woman. After walking another half a mile or more, she came upon a young man:

Less than six feet tall,
Twenty-one or -two years old.
A thin mustache over his mouth and a goatee beneath.
A fairly slim waist and broad shoulders.
A peaked cap in heart-of-papaya style,
A white silk gown like silver filigree.
A red and green belt of the spider type,
A pair of brown leather shoes with grommets.
A pack on his back,
An umbrella over his shoulder.

He was walking along when he noticed Eterna. She had no bonnet on her head, and her hair was bound up in a simple tuft and fastened with two gold hairpins, but although she was dressed in everyday clothes, she looked quite attractive. He approached her and bowed with his hands folded in front of him. "Where might you be going, miss?"

"I'm going to Zhengzhou to seek refuge with my relatives."

The young man was of a raffish nature. "I'm taking the Zhengzhou road, too," he said. "It's hard for anyone to travel alone, and besides, you're a woman—how can you possibly go there on your own? Let me walk with you." At the same time he tried to frighten her with scary stories. When they came to a wood, he said, "Miss, this wood is the worst place of all. Tigers appear here all the time. If we go together, we'll be all right, but if you were on your own, a tiger would spring out and carry you off."

"In that case, brother, I'll need to depend on you to see me through the wood."

Along the way, whenever they came to a tavern, he would buy a few cakes and share them with her. They walked for a while, then rested, then walked some more. The evening was drawing on. "Brother, it's getting late," she said. "Is there an inn up ahead?"

"Miss, there's something I need to tell you. A month ago, two spies were caught around here, and the authorities have issued an order forbidding the local inns from giving shelter to anyone traveling alone. You and I will not be able to get rooms for ourselves."

"But in that case, where will we sleep tonight?"

"If you'll do as I suggest, we will be able to get a room."

"Then I shall do as you suggest."

"Miss, we're not married, but if we just pretend to be married, we'll be able to get a room."

She said nothing, but thought to herself, what a despicable creature! But he doesn't know me, and I'm going to make him do such and such.[7] "Please take me with you tonight," she said.

"That will be just fine!" he replied.

In Eight Corners he passed by several perfectly good inns in favor of one at the far end of the village. Going in, he shouted,

"Innkeeper! Do you have a room? My wife and I need a room for the night."

"I'm sorry, but we have no rooms vacant," said the assistant.

"What a pity! Whether I'm coming out or going back, I always stay at your inn. How is it you don't have any vacancies tonight?"

"All our rooms are full. We have only one left. It has two beds in it, one of which has just been taken by a shoemaker, a fellow with a beard. I'm afraid that you and your wife wouldn't find that too convenient."

"What is there to be afraid of? He'll be on one side of the room, and we'll be on the other."

"In that case you can go in." The young man led the way, with Eterna following. The assistant pushed open the door and showed them into the room. How revolting this fellow is, thought Eterna. Making me pretend to be his wife in order to get a room! But I'll show him who he's dealing with!

Certain consequences followed from this situation: Eterna Hu destroyed tens of thousands of lives, and the court mobilized a hundred thousand infantry and cavalry. Several cities were thrown into chaos, and Hebei province was plunged into turmoil.

How ridiculous he was, this stupid dolt
Who took another man's wife as his own!

Just what did Eterna do that night? Turn to the next chapter to find out.

6

ETERNA CHANGES HER APPEARANCE IN THE INN; CARTER BU PURSUES HER, AND SHE FALLS DOWN A WELL.

POEM:

How laughable, this frivolous young rake
Who met a young girl and claimed they were wed!
But beauty and wealth, wine in great mansions—
Which of us would not by these be misled?

Surely he must have heard the old saw, "Never love another man's wife or ride another man's horse." How could this young fellow harbor lascivious intentions toward an attractive woman whom he had just happened to meet on the road?

"Bring me some hot water to wash my feet," he said to the assistant.

"Coming!" said the assistant. To the shoemaker he said, "This man and his wife are here from the Eastern Capital. All the other rooms are full except this one, which has a spare bed. We'll have to let them spend the night in here."

"I'm using just the one bed," said the shoemaker. "If people want to sleep in the other bed, by all means let them." Eterna came in and curtsied to the shoemaker, who bowed in return.

"We're causing you a lot of trouble," said the young man to the shoemaker.

"Please suit yourselves," he replied. They don't sound as if they come from the Eastern Capital, he thought, and from the way they traveled up here on their own it would seem that they aren't married, either. Nor do they agree on everything—they have their differences. Still, it's none of my business. Let them do whatever they want to do. "Please suit yourselves," he repeated.

Eterna and the young man sat on the other bed. The assistant brought in the water, and the young man washed his feet, then asked for a jar of oil for the lamp. The bearded shoemaker, who was not working that night, said good night, turned over to face the wall, and fell asleep.

"My dear, we were in such a rush that we neglected to have any supper," the young man said to Eterna. "I'll go out and get us something to eat and drink." He turned and left the room.

What a loathsome creature, thought Eterna. And I don't even know him, either. All the way here he tried to scare me with his stories. He forced me to act as his wife so as to get a room, and now he's gone off to buy us some wine. Well, he doesn't know me, and I'm going to play a trick on him. First she recited something or other, then blew in the direction of the bearded man's bed and touched her own face. At once she turned into a bearded man with a florid complexion, the image of the shoemaker, while he turned into the image of her. Then the make-believe shoemaker lay down and pretended to be asleep.

The young man paid for some wine and steamed cakes and brought them back to the inn, thinking to himself, this is my lucky day, meeting up with such a pretty woman. Everybody in the inn believes I'm her husband, and I'm going to enjoy myself sleeping with her all night. He pushed open the door of the room, put the wine and cakes on the table, and trimmed the lamp, but when he looked at the bed, it was the shoemaker that he saw there, not the girl. Why did that fellow change beds, he wondered. Then he looked at the other bed—it had a woman in it. She must have been worn out from all the walking we did today and gone off to sleep as soon as her head touched the pillow, he thought. "My dear," he called out, shaking her with both hands, "I've bought the wine. Do sit up. Do sit up." But instead it was the shoemaker who leaped to his feet, seized hold of him, and began pounding him with both fists.

"What do you think you're doing, hitting your husband?" yelled the young man.

"I'm *not* your wife!" roared the shoemaker.

The young man took a closer look—it was the shoemaker who was hitting him! He hastily apologized: "My mistake! Please forgive me! Please forgive me!"

Having heard the commotion, the assistant came in. "What are you doing?" he asked.

"This swine came right up to my bed and shook me and called me his 'dear.'"

"You're not blind," said the assistant to the young man, "and your eyes aren't inflamed, either. That's your bed over there." Now that the assistant had restored peace, the shoemaker went back to his bed and lay down again.

The young man had received several blows. Just my luck, he thought. He looked exactly like a woman, but he proved to be the shoemaker. Then he looked at the woman sleeping in the other bed and called out, "Miss! Get up and have some wine." But when he looked more closely at her, he saw that she had bright red hair, green eyes, and a blue face with long fangs. "A ghost!" he cried, slumping to the floor.

The assistant was in the front of the inn having his supper when he heard the cry of "Ghost!" He rushed into the room to find the young man flat on the floor and helped him to his feet. The shoemaker had received such a scare that he got up, too. All the people staying in the inn came to the aid of the young man. Some of them spat mouthfuls of water at him; others bit his middle finger. After the ill-treatment he had been subjected to all night, he finally came to his senses, awoke, and said, "How horrible! A ghost! A ghost!" The assistant seized hold of him and spat twice in his face: "This is a clean house—we don't have any ghosts here. Who told you to come and ruin our business?" He brought the lamp over and demanded, "Now, where's that ghost of yours?"

"That woman in the bed there is a ghost!"

"He's playing games with us," said the assistant. He turned to the young man. "That's your *wife*, man! How can you say she's a ghost?"

"She's *not* my wife. I met her on the road, and we came here as husband and wife in order to get a room. I'd just been out to buy some wine, and when I came back, I saw that it was the bearded man in the bed, not the girl, so I called out to the shoemaker by mistake and got beaten up. Then when I looked at her again, she had bright red hair, green eyes, and a blue face with long fangs—she's a ghost, I tell you!"

They were all astounded, but when they looked at her by the light of the lamp, what they saw was a beautiful young woman, as pretty as a flower. "Your eyes must have deceived you," they said to the young man. "How can you call a pretty woman like that a ghost?"

"Gentlemen," said Eterna, "this loathsome creature has no morals whatsoever. I wanted to go to Zhengzhou to seek refuge with my parents, but this man met me on the road and walked along with me. All the way he kept telling me scary things in order to frighten me. He also told me that two spies had been caught and that the inns weren't allowed to take in anyone traveling alone, and so he forced me to pretend to be his wife in order to get a room for the night. This whole evening he's been talking nothing but nonsense—I don't know *what* he has in mind."

The others rounded on the young man. "What a swine!" said the assistant. "Disgraceful! Get him out of our inn! If he won't go, let's get together and beat him to a pulp!" They drove him out of the inn and locked the gate behind him.

It was pitch-dark outside, and the young man did not dare go any further. He was also afraid of being arrested by the night patrol, so he had to spend the night in an isolated spot in front of a nearby doorway. At dawn he thought he had better set out. Leaving the inn behind, he had gone a couple of miles and was about to make his way through a wood when Eterna Hu came walking out. "Brother," she said, "I'm ever so grateful to you for taking me to that inn last night, but why did you say I was a ghost?"

Gazing now at her flowerlike beauty, he was in two minds. Perhaps my eyes really did deceive me yesterday, he thought. "My dear, I would like to travel with you, but twice last night you gave me a terrible scare," he said. "I just don't believe you're a good woman. Get away from me!"

"Last night you wanted us to pretend to be a married couple, but now you're afraid of me. Well, let me introduce you to a friend of mine." She pointed and cried out, "Come!" A slant-eyed, white-browed tiger came bounding out of the wood and leaped at the young man, who gave a scream and collapsed on the ground. Eyes shut tight, he thought to himself, this time I'm a dead man! For a long time nothing happened, and when he cautiously opened his eyes again and looked about him, both the tiger and the girl had vanished. I always liked to play around, he thought, but I should never have tried to seduce that woman yesterday. I got a beating from the bearded man and a scare from her—in fact, she frightened me half out of my mind. Today she also called that tiger out of the wood, and I thought it was all over for me. The truth is, she positively enjoys scaring me. If I met her on the road ahead, how terrible it would be! I'd better return to the Eastern Capital. He went back.

Eterna, who had conjured up a tiger to appear and scare him, said to herself, he won't dare come this way again. I'll go on to Zhengzhou by myself, walking nice and slowly. But then her feet began to ache, and she had to rest beneath a tree. While sitting there, she heard the rumble of a cart, and saw a carter with a Fanyang felt hat on his head and wearing a cloth traveling gown tied with a towel around the waist, trousers fastened with leg bindings, and eight-grommet hemp shoes. He was pushing a cart toward the tree, intending to take a rest there. Eterna got to her feet and said, "Greetings!" He bowed in return.

"Where are you heading, miss?" he asked her.

"I want to go to Zhengzhou to seek refuge with my parents, but I have sore feet and can't walk, so I'm taking a rest here. But what valuable goods are you carrying and where are you taking them?"

"I'm from Zhengzhou, and I'm on my way back there after delivering a load of honey locust pods to the Eastern Capital."

"If you're going through the city of Zhengzhou and can take me in your cart, I'll give you three taels to spend on wine."

The carter considered the offer: I've sold all my goods, Zhengzhou is on my way, and I stand to make three taels. "All right," he said. He told Eterna to climb up and sit in the cart. He then applied all his energy to pushing it and neither spoke to her nor looked at her. This carter is a truly honest man, thought Eterna. How rarely one comes across such people! She recalled how the young man she had met tried to seduce her, and how she had used a little magic on him. Although she hadn't taken his life, she had certainly put a good scare into him. This carter, on the other hand, would be the right sort of person to convert, she thought. One day they would have a use for him.

The carter pushed his cart as far as the East Gate of Zhengzhou. "Where do your parents live?" he asked Eterna.

"I don't know what the place is called, but I'll know it when I see it."

The carter pushed the cart through the East Gate and as far as the crossroads, when Eterna called out, "Here we are!"

Setting down the cart, he looked up and saw an empty house, all locked up. "But miss, this is an empty house that's locked up. How can it be your home?"

Leaping down from the cart, she shouted, "Presto!" and the lock came off. She pushed the gate open and went inside.

The carter waited there for a good four hours, but no one came out. It was getting toward evening, and still he kept looking inside. Then someone shouted at him, "You there! Carter! You've been standing around for a long time. Why do you keep looking in here?"

The carter saw that it was an old man who had asked the question, and he hastily bowed and said, "Sir, let me explain. Not long ago I met a young woman about twenty miles outside of town. She said she had sore feet and couldn't walk anymore and would pay me three taels if I brought her here. Then she went inside and didn't came out again. She's kept me waiting half the day."

"This is the official residence of Deputy Prefect Diao, and I'm the caretaker."

"In that case, would you please go inside and tell them what I've told you and get them to give me the money."

"This is an empty house, all locked up, where nobody lives—you must be out of your mind! The authorities have lately put up notices ordering the arrest of Eterna Hu. Anyone who knows anything about her and doesn't inform them will be found as guilty as she is. If you know what's good for you, you'll go."

"But that doesn't make sense! I brought your young lady to her house, and she promised me three taels but never handed them over—and all you do is give me this claptrap! Let me just go in and have a look around. I'm prepared to face a lawsuit, if necessary."

"Well, you said it yourself! If you can't find her, don't try to run away." He opened the gate and let the carter in.

The carter went first to the front hall, then along a portico leading to the back hall, at the end of which he found Eterna, sitting down. "Miss, why didn't you come out and give me my money?" he called out. "That was most unreasonable!"

Seeing him come in, Eterna got up and went further back. The carter strode after her, and she saw him close behind her. At the back of the hall there was an eight-sided well, and she walked up to it and jumped in.

"Oh, no! How terrible!" shouted the carter, aghast. He was about to leave the scene when the old caretaker seized him and said, "In a secure, peaceful time like the present it's unforgivable to do what you did just now—force someone down a well!" He dragged the carter to the front of the residence and called to the neighbors to come and tie him up and deliver him to the Zhengzhou yamen.

The prefect happened to be in the courtroom hearing criminal cases when the local headman and others brought the carter in and made him kneel down. They testified that he had been in front of Deputy Prefect Diao's residence and had chased an unidentified female down the well. Under the prefect's interrogation, the carter testified as follows: "I am a native of this city, Bu Ji by name. I was returning from delivering a load of honey locust pods to the Eastern Capital when under a big tree twenty miles outside Eight Corners Village of Plank Bridge I met a woman whose name I don't know. She said her feet were sore and that she couldn't walk any further. She wanted to pay for a ride in my cart as far as her parents' home at the crossroads and was prepared to give me three taels. I took her to the house, and she opened the gate and went in but never came back again. After I had waited there a long time, an old caretaker came out. He said the house was the residence of Deputy Prefect Diao and that no one lived there, and he refused to give me my money. Shortly afterward, I went in with the caretaker to look for her. She did appear, but then she jumped down the well. I never forced her to do it."

The prefect had Bu Ji held in jail. The following day he was to be taken under guard to the Diao residence for the recovery of the body. The prefect appointed a deputy to go to the prison and fetch Bu Ji, then take him together with the neighbors to the Diao residence. People lined the street to watch, saying, "We often hear spirits singing and ghosts wailing from that place. None of us would ever dare stay there." Some of them said, "I wonder how they're going to recover the body."

The deputy took a seat in an armchair and had Bu Ji kneel before him, then asked the old caretaker and the neighbors how Bu Ji had driven the girl down the well. "She jumped in," declared Bu Ji, "I did *not* drive her down that well."

He called forward the divers engaged in the recovery. They bowed before him, then put on their water jackets.

The deputy said, "On the authority of the prefect of Zhengzhou, I order you to go down the well. You are to take great care with the recovery."

"Sir," said one of the divers, "I inspected the well just now. It's several hundred feet deep, and it would be pointless to go down as we are now. We need a windlass, as well as some means of calling for help in an emergency."

"Tell me what you need, and we'll get it for you as quickly as possible."

"We need a windlass with a three-hundred-foot rope, a large bamboo basket, a large brass bell, and twenty men. If there's an emergency, the diver will ring the bell and the men on top will haul him up."

Before long all the equipment was in place. The men wound the rope onto the windlass and prepared the bell and the basket.

"Sir, you may now order a man down to start the recovery."

"Divers, choose a first-class swimmer to go down."

Four or five men held the windlass while one man sat in the bamboo basket. Two or three others lowered him down the well, while four or five more let out the windlass. After more than two hundred feet of rope had been paid out, they heard an urgent ringing of the bell. The deputy told the spectators to stand back and had the basket hastily raised. But when the spectators saw it, they let out a great cry.

Looking in the basket, they saw a sight never seen before. Never in their lives had they laid eyes on anything so strange.

If the facts were told, Mount Hua would split asunder
And the Yellow River flow backward to its source.

What did they see? Turn to the next chapter to find out.

7

BU JI ENCOUNTERS PRIESTESS PIA DOWN THE EIGHT-SIDED WELL;

HE PRESENTS A GOLD TRIPOD AND IS EXILED TO MIZHOU.

POEM:

Despite the load of sin on his conscience,
Disasters are sent by heaven, he'll say.
But for every sin that he's committed
Reversal of fortune begins this day.

The men on the windlass wound up the bamboo basket and then let out a great cry. When the diver went down the well, he was in the pink of good health, but now, as they looked at him, they saw that his face was as yellow as a sheet of wax and his hands and feet were as stiff as boards—he lay dead in the basket.

The deputy ordered the body carried off to one side and told the man's family to take it home and see to the laying in. And there we shall leave them.

"We can't give up just because one man went down and failed to complete the task," said the deputy. "Send another man down!"

"But sir!" protested the other divers. "We all have families, and you saw yourself what happened just now. How can you throw men's lives away as if they were pebbles you were skimming on the water? We don't *dare* go down! If you insist, we're prepared to go before the prefect and get a beating for refusing. At least we'll die on dry land. We truly *cannot* go down there!"

"I can't say I blame you," said the deputy, "but how are we going to recover that woman's body? You men stand guard over Bu Ji while I go and report to the prefect." He stepped into his sedan chair and was taken directly to the yamen and then to the main hall, where he told the prefect what had happened. However, the prefect had no more idea than he did of how to proceed.

"The local people say that the Diao residence has always been haunted, and now with the death of a diver no one dares to go down the well," added the deputy. "But if we can't recover the woman's body, how can we wind up the Bu Ji case? It might be best to consider it as Bu Ji's responsibility and order *him* to go down and recover the body. Even if he died in the attempt, it could still be considered a life for a life."

"Good idea," said the prefect. "See to it."

The deputy took leave of the prefect and returned to the wellhead, where he had Bu Ji brought out. "You were the one who drove her down the well," he said. "Now go down yourself and recover her body, and when I've reported it to the prefect, he'll absolve you of any crime."

"I'm willing to go down," said Bu Ji. "All I need is a short sword to defend myself with."

"Quite right," said the deputy. He ordered Bu Ji's cangue and manacles removed, gave him a short sword, and had him seated in the basket. The rope on the windlass was then let out for a long time without reaching bottom. "When that man went down before," the men on the windlass cried out, "he rang the bell after only about two hundred feet, but this time all the rope will soon be paid out. This is amazing! We've let out all that rope and he still hasn't touched bottom!" As they were speaking, the windlass stopped turning, but the bell did not ring.

Let us leave the men on top of the well and tell of Bu Ji at the bottom. When he looked up, the wellhead appeared to him a mere speck of light. He felt all around him and found no water, then stamped his feet and discovered that he was on solid ground. Feeling his way along, he had gone about half a mile when he saw ahead of him a place that was all lit up. He groped—it was the door of a cave, which opened easily at his touch. Slipping inside, he found himself once more in broad daylight. Where can this be, he wondered. Then, sword in hand, he went on until he came upon a tiger that was crouching down, blocking his way. "I expect it's this creature that's been killing people," he said. "Well, rather than have you eat me . . . I'll die anyway!" He dashed forward with giant strides and slashed at the tiger, shouting, "Take that!" A sound rang out, sparks flew, and his hand went numb from the shock. When he looked more closely, he found that he had struck a tiger made out of stone.

There must be other places inside, he thought. He walked ahead a few steps and found a path paved with pebbles between two rows of pine trees. Since it's a path, it must lead somewhere, he thought. Sword in hand, he followed the path for a hundred yards or more, when a place suddenly loomed up that struck such fear in him that he dared go no closer. As he looked intently at it, this is what he saw:

A vermilion gate studded with gold,
Figured eaves tiled in green;
Flying dragons, toying with pearls, coiled around the columns,
Twin phoenixes, proclaiming the morning sun, pictured on the
  screens;
Walls of red plaster,
Palace flowers thick among the willows;
Terraces in blue-green mist,

A faint light suffusing the shadows;
Window lattices of brocade,
A scented breeze filtering through the yellow silk;
Curtains of shrimp barbels,
A bright full moon hanging on the purple damask.
If not the abode of immortals in heaven,
It must surely be the palace of some emperor on earth.[1]

What *is* this place, he asked himself. With its closed gate, could it be an abode of the immortals? He wanted to push the gate open, but he didn't dare. He was about to turn back, but then he thought, I have nothing to show that I was here. The prefect is scarcely going to believe me if I just tell him I saw a stone tiger.

As he hesitated, the gate creaked open, and a maidservant dressed all in black came out. "Bu Ji, the priestess has been waiting for you for a long time!" she called.

What priestess is she talking about, Bu Ji asked himself. And how does she know my name? And why is the priestess waiting for me? He had no choice but to follow her. She brought him to a place from which he could see a palace building. Two celestial pages were standing there, as well as another maidservant. In the middle was an old woman sitting in an armchair. Bu Ji stole a glance at her:

Gaunt and gray with an innocent face,
Pure-white hair with a youthful complexion;
Eyes opaque as a mist-wreathed autumn moon,
Brows pale as sunlight on the morning frost;
With embroidered garments and a jade-studded belt,
She looks like the Goddess of the Nine Heavens;[2]
With a phoenix chignon and dragon hairpins,
She resembles the Queen Mother of the West;[3]

An ethereal face that defies depiction;
An awesome presence impossible to paint.

This must be an abode of the immortals, thought Bu Ji, and it is surely my destiny that has brought me here. He stepped forward, saying, "O veritable immortal, the carter Bu Ji bows reverently before you," and gave four deep bows.

"This is no ordinary place," she said. "You have been blessed with the destiny to come here, so you must surely be a man with a great future. Please come up the steps and sit beside me."

He declined several times, until she said, "You're a man of destiny; please take a seat," and he plucked up the courage to take a seat beside her. She ordered tea, which the maidservant brought. After he had drunk it, the priestess said, "It wasn't easy for you to get here. Why did you come?"

"Priestess, I had delivered a load of honey locust pods to the Eastern Capital and was pushing my cart back to Zhengzhou when I came upon a woman sitting under a tree by the roadside. She said, 'I want to go to Zhengzhou to seek refuge with my parents, but my feet are too sore and I can't walk.' She promised me three taels. I brought her as far as the Diao residence inside East Gate, and she said, 'Here we are.' She got down from the cart, pushed the gate open, went inside—and jumped down a well. I was seized by the local authorities and taken to court. The prefect sent a diver down the well to recover the body, which resulted in another death, that of the diver. The prefect had no choice but to send me down. At the bottom of the well I found a path but no water, and I walked aimlessly along until I arrived here."

"And what did you see at the bottom of the well?"

"A stone tiger."

"That creature has proved his worth over many years, killing a good number of people. When ordinary mortals come here, they meet that tiger and end up being devoured by it. You, however, slashed at the beast, which means that one day you will make a great name for yourself. Bu Ji, there is someone here that I should like you to meet." To the maidservant she said, "Tell her to come out."

After a little while the woman who had jumped down the well walked out and curtsied to Bu Ji. "Carter, I gave you a lot of trouble yesterday."

Anger welled up inside Bu Ji at the very sight of her. "You accursed little trollop!" he roared. "You vile creature! You told me you had sore feet and couldn't walk, and out of the goodness of my heart I let you ride in my cart for many miles. Not only did you fail to pay me anything, you went into the house and jumped down a well, which led to my being arrested, clapped in a cangue, and forced to wear manacles while suffering miserably in jail. How can you possibly find an excuse for such an injustice? I never expected to see you again, but here you are!"

When enemies meet, they glare. "I'm going to give you a taste of my sword!" said Bu Ji. He drew his sword, went up and grabbed hold of her, then brought it slashing down.

She gave a shout that suddenly paralyzed his limbs. "I'm allowing for the fact that you gave me a ride, you blackguard—otherwise I'd make mincemeat out of you! I saw how upright and dependable you were, and I intended to convert you, but this behavior of yours is simply too much for me to bear! You had the gall to try and cut me down, but you couldn't do it!"

The priestess rose to her feet and pleaded with her. "Don't kill him! One day we'll have need of him." She blew a puff of air into Bu Ji's face, and he was able to move his limbs freely again.

"What sort of person is she?" he asked.

"If I hadn't been here, you'd have lost your life. Don't be so wild in future."

"I was blessed with the destiny to meet you, Priestess. If you can save me from prison and get me out of the well without further trouble, then every day after I get home I'll burn incense, set up a spirit tablet, and worship you."

"Since your destiny brought you here, don't go just yet. Come and drink a few cups of wine with me before I send you back."

He went in with her and was staggered by the sight that met his eyes. "I'm just a simple countryman," he said. "I've never seen anything so lavish as this!" The feast was exquisitely arranged:

Incense burning in precious vessels,
Flowers arranged in golden vases,
Blue-green curtains all around of the finest silk,
Gold and silver dishes set out for him alone.
A crystal beaker
Filled with the nectar of the immortals;
An amber goblet
Brimming with wine from the Jade Pool;
Tortoiseshell dishes
Heaped with faerie peaches and exotic fruit,
Glass bowls
Offering bear's paw and camel's foot;
Morsels of game sliced thinner than silver filigree;
Tea as delicate as if with jade flowers made.[4]

She invited Bu Ji to take a seat, but he didn't dare. Only when she said, "Do sit down, Master Bu. You're destined to become rich and famous" did he do so.

First came the wine, then the food—and he had never seen such a display! The two maidservants kept pouring wine and serving it to him, cup after cup filled to the brim, goblet after goblet drained to the dregs. Half intoxicated, he thought, I've come miles from that well, I've seen such a place as this, I've encountered a female immortal, and I've also met that woman again—I wonder if she's an immortal or a demon. But this is no place to linger in. He rose to his feet and said to the priestess and the young woman, "I need to go back up the well to see to my cart and other belongings. I'm afraid someone may take them."

"What can your belongings be worth?" asked the priestess. "If I were to give you something to take back with you that would make you indescribably wealthy and eminent, what would you say?"

"Thank you, Priestess, for your kind intentions, but even if it were worth nothing instead of a great deal, I would take it back to the wellhead as proof that I was here in order to clear myself of crime."

The priestess told Eterna to approach and whispered something in her ear. She was gone a little while, and then a maidservant brought out an object that she handed to Bu Ji. As he took it, he noticed that it was rather heavy and thought, what can it be, this thing that's all wrapped up in yellow silk?

"Priestess, why are you giving me this?" he asked.

"Don't open it, and don't give it to anyone when you get to the wellhead, either. Just say that the goddess of this prefecture has had this in her possession for a thousand years and it must now be given to the prefect so that he can absolve you of any crime. And I have another piece of advice to give you, too. Whenever there's an emergency, just call out, 'Priestess Pia,' and I'll come to your rescue." Bu Ji made a mental note of what she had said.

The priestess told a maidservant to escort Bu Ji out of the palace and back along the path and through the cave to where the bamboo basket was lying. He took a seat in the basket and shook the cord. The bell rang, and the men at the wellhead heard it and hauled him to the surface. When they looked inside the basket, however, they found no woman's body, only Bu Ji clutching a yellow silk bundle to show the deputy. "No one is to touch this," he said. "It's for the prefect from the goddess of this prefecture, and it has to be taken directly to him and opened only in his presence." The deputy stepped into his sedan chair, and a squad of his men escorted Bu Ji to the yamen.

The prefect was at his tribunal, his runners arrayed along both sides of the chamber. "Bu Ji was gone a long time before we heard the bell ring and quickly hauled him up," reported the deputy. "We found him clutching something wrapped in yellow silk that he claimed was for Your Honor from the goddess of this prefecture. I didn't dare touch it. I've brought it here to await your wishes."

The prefect ordered Bu Ji to be brought out. "What's in this yellow bundle? And how did you happen to come by it?"

"Your Honor, when I got to the bottom of the well, I didn't find any woman's body, but there was also no water anywhere. However, there was a path, and after following it for half a mile or so, I found myself in broad daylight. Then I saw a tiger and almost lost my life, but I slashed at the creature with my sword. Sparks flew everywhere, and when I looked more closely, I found that it was only made of stone. A path through the pine trees brought me to a palace. A maidservant who was waiting outside invited me in, and I met an immortal. She said she was the goddess of this prefecture and gave me food and wine and brought out this object, which she told me to give to Your Honor. She forbade me to reveal any heavenly secrets."

The prefect took the object in both hands and placed it on his tribunal. It felt heavy. When a precious article makes its appearance in the world, it's only right and proper that it should come into contact with me, he thought. After telling his subordinates to withdraw, he opened the bundle. "No wonder it was so heavy," he said. It proved to contain a gold tripod vessel with two ears. On the tripod were engraved the words "Whosoever cometh in contact with this object is bound to enjoy both riches and honor." After he had finished admiring it, the prefect wrapped it up again, summoned a personal servant from his household, and told the man to take the vessel away and give it pride of place in his personal collection.

The prefect's subordinates then stepped forward. "Sir, Bu Ji is waiting for you to dispose of the case," they said.

Suppose I release him, pondered the prefect. Everyone in the prefecture knows that he drove a woman down a well and that the attempt to recover her body cost a diver his life. Under those circumstances, if I simply let him go, people in the prefecture are bound to criticize. On the other hand, if I make him pay with his life for the woman's death, well, the body has not been recovered, and he did present me with that gold tripod. So what *should* I do? All of a sudden he picked up his brush and passed sentence on Bu Ji, a sentence that led to certain consequences: before long the prefect died an untimely death, and the people of Zhengzhou found no peace.

When his luck runs out, he can get wine on credit;
When disaster strikes, he encounters a friend.[5]

But what disaster did the prefect cause? Turn to the next chapter to find out.

8

ZHANG LUAN RESCUES BU JI IN WILDERNESS WOODS;

ZHANG LUAN ENJOYS TWIN MOONS IN A SPIRIT'S SHRINE.

POEM:

Diamond Chan[1] has the strongest magic;
Twin orbs up above cause a hue and cry.
A mighty arm from the heavens shoots forth
And plucks from danger one condemned to die.

The prefect sentenced Bu Ji to be branded and exiled to the Mizhou prison camp in Shandong. He ordered him to receive twenty strokes on the back and summoned the tattooist to brand him with two lines on the face. He then signed a warrant and appointed two escorts, Dong Chao and Xue Ba. They took custody of Bu Ji, collected the warrant, and brought the prisoner out to the front of the yamen.

Once outside, Bu Ji stopped short and turned to face the yamen. "I, Bu Ji, am the victim of a terrible wrong!" he shouted. "That woman leaped into the well of her own free will—I never forced her to do it. What's more, she's none other than the goddess of this place, and she made me go down the well and obtain that precious object to give to you. After you received it, you ought to have cleared me of all charges, but instead you have unjustly branded me and exiled me to Mizhou. If I ever manage to get back alive, I'll beat the drums of injustice before the palace walls and denounce you for secretly withholding a treasure for your own use. I'll definitely settle accounts with you!"

Hearing these ugly threats, Dong Chao anxiously pushed Bu Ji on his way. "If you start saying things like that around here, you'll get us into terrible trouble!" said Xue Ba. They hastily left the yamen and walked as far as an inn, where they went in and sat down.

"Bring us two dippers of wine!" ordered Dong Chao. He turned to Bu Ji. "Although Xue and I have been officially ordered to escort you to Mizhou in Shandong, it's a long journey and you'll have to pay your own expenses. We're not bringing any money for you, just accompanying you there. Do you have any relatives or friends from whom you can raise some money for use along the way? We're not asking for any of your money for ourselves."

"I did have a little money, officers, but when I was charged, somebody took it along with my cart. Who can I possibly turn to for more? I'm all alone, without any relatives, and there's no way I can raise any money."

"We've escorted many hardened criminals, and we've never yet come across anyone with that sort of attitude!" snapped Xue Ba. "You say you have no travel money? Why, even Li the Heavenly Prince[2] would have to leave a weapon behind! Even green ginger can be squeezed of a little juice! You're our property—you don't think we're going to let you go lightly, do you?" After this outburst, he paid for the wine, and the two men escorted Bu Ji through the West Gate and out of Zhengzhou city.

As they walked along, they heard a shout from behind them: "Officer Dong!" Dong Chao told Xue Ba to go on escorting Bu Ji while he turned back. "I'm in the prefect's confidence," said the newcomer to Dong Chao. "Just now, after that wretch was sentenced to exile, he put on a disgraceful display in front of the yamen, and I'm under orders from His Honor to tell you and your colleague to find some means of finishing him off in a remote spot along the way. You'll be richly rewarded on your return."

Dong Chao agreed and hurried after Xue Ba to convey the message. "Let's finish him off in those woods up ahead," he said. The two men escorted Bu Ji to some lonely woods, where Dong said, "I was up so early this morning, I think I'll take a nap in these woods."

"We haven't gone ten miles from the yamen," said Xue Ba. "Why do you need to rest?"

"I got up too early this morning, and I do need a rest. My only worry is that if you were to escape, Bu Ji, we couldn't just go to the herbalist's shop and get a replacement. Let's tie you up first. Then I'll be able to go off to sleep with an easy mind."

"If you want to tie me up, go ahead. I'm certainly not going to run away."

Dong Chao took a long rope and tied Bu Ji to the branch of a tree, then slung the end of the rope over a large branch on another tree and hoisted him upside down. Then, gripping his cudgel, he said, "Bu Ji, we're under orders from the prefect to kill you—this has nothing to do with us. This time next year will be the first anniversary of your death!"

"Oh, no!" cried Bu Ji. "I'm a dead man!" Then he suddenly remembered something: that immortal who gave me the precious object told me that in an emergency I should call out the name of Priestess Pia. "Priestess Pia, help!" he cried.

The words were hardly out of his mouth when he heard someone shouting from outside the woods: "Escort officers, stop what you're doing! I've been listening to you for some time now."

Startled, Dong and Xue rushed out of the wood and found a priest who was six feet tall and had a face like purple jade and eyes like strange stars.

> With his fiery scarlet gown,
> He's as brave as Zi Lu.[3]
> With his iron-frame Daoist cap,
> He looks just like Zhuan Zhu.[4]
> Lions' bones serve as hairpins on his head;
> Dragons' tendons form the sash at his waist.
> His eyes are red from feasts of tiger flesh,
> His fingers black from stabbing unicorns.

The priest came charging into the wood with his fists cocked, ready for a fight. "The prefect told you to escort him into exile. What do you mean by hanging him upside down and preparing to take his life?"

The two escorts trembled with fear. "Master, we're under orders from the prefect. He told us to do it."

"Utter nonsense! Officials nowadays are perfectly just. Why would he want you to kill an innocent man? As a priest, I ought not to meddle in other people's affairs, but just now I heard someone in the wood calling out, 'Priestess Pia,' and I wondered why. Let that man down. I want to ask him about it."

Dong Chao had no choice but to release Bu Ji.

"Master, let me tell you," Bu Ji began. "I had sold the load of honey locust pods I took to the Eastern Capital and was making my way back again when I came upon a woman beside the road. She complained that she couldn't walk because her feet were too sore and promised me three taels if I would carry her in my cart. When we came to an empty mansion inside the East Gate of Zhengzhou, she leaped down from the cart and ran inside. I didn't see her come out again, and when I went in to look for her, she jumped down a well. The local people claimed that I had driven her to it, and they seized me and took me to court, where the prefect ordered me to go down the well myself and recover the body. When I got down there, I found there was no water, only a path, which I followed until I came to a palace. There I met a female immortal, who gave me a precious object. I was to give it to the prefect so that he would clear me of the charge against me. As I was about to go up the well again, she told me that if ever I found myself in danger, I should call out the name of Priestess Pia."

"I see," said the priest. Turning to the two escorts, he said, "This Bu Ji was not destined to die—he met up with me. Please come out of the woods, and let's all go to a village inn where we'll have a few drinks. I'll also help you with a little travel money, to see that he gets to his destination."

"Thank you, Master," they said. The four men left the woods and after walking a few hundred yards came to an inn. They went in and sat down.

"Master Zhang, how much wine would you like?" asked the innkeeper.

"Give us four dippers," said the priest. "And bring us a chicken as well."

"It's a long way to the village, and there's nowhere else I can get a chicken."

"But if we have nothing to eat with the wine, how are we going to drink it?"

The innkeeper brought the wine, and each of them drank a cup.

"I meant to invite you for a drink," said the priest, "but there's nothing to go with it." Looking about him, he spotted a water pitcher over by the wall that he saw was full of pure water. He took a gourd from his sleeve, removed the stopper, and shook out a white pill that he dropped into the pitcher. He then returned to his seat on the bench and called to the innkeeper: "We can't just drink weak wine. I put something to eat in your pitcher just now. Take it away and cook it for us."

"I didn't see anything when you people came in."

"Take a look now."

The innkeeper looked in the pitcher and saw the water moving. Plunging both hands in, he brought out a three-foot-long carp. "Amazing!" he exclaimed. He had to fillet the fish, put it in a pot, and boil it until it was tender, then add salt, soy sauce, pepper, and vinegar and put it on a plate and serve it to his guests.

As they drank, Dong Chao said, "Let me thank you, sir, for your generosity."

"This fish is wonderful," said Xue Ba. "If only we could get another!"

"But this isn't true hospitality," said the priest. "I like to eat and drink, and I've had the rare good fortune to meet you two gentlemen. Since all men are brothers within the four seas, so long as you don't reject me, let's go to my monastery and really drink our fill there. You can set off again in the morning. Would you like to do that?"

With his young man's temperament, Xue Ba responded promptly, "It's so kind of you to invite us! It's getting late, and we'll go to your monastery and sleep there the night. But we oughtn't to be giving you all this trouble!"

Dong Chao was the older and wiser of the two escorts, and he called Xue Ba aside so that they could not be overheard. "This priest is a strange character. Why go to his monastery with him?"

"Brother Dong!" exclaimed Xue Ba. "Have you lived all those years without learning *anything*? This innkeeper *knows* him! If something goes wrong, we would just have to ask the innkeeper to find him."

"You're right," said Dong Chao.

The priest paid for the wine, and the four men left the inn, chatting idly as they walked along. After they had gone some distance, the priest pointed up ahead and said, "There it is." Dong Chao looked; it was a fine thatched cottage, small, of circular construction, with no houses in front or behind, and the two escorts began to feel a trifle uneasy. The priest opened the door and invited them to come in and sit down. "Don't worry. There's plenty of room to sleep. Get a good night's sleep and then set off in the morning." He carried out a table from the inner room, then went back and prepared some meat and fish dishes, which he brought out and placed on the table. "Just now in that inn I didn't treat you gentlemen with the proper hospitality, but now you'll have to drink up until you're really drunk."

The two escorts looked at each other and whispered, "This priest invited us to drink in the inn, and now we've come to his cottage and he's prepared a whole lot more food and drink. If we don't accept his invitation, we'll go hungry, but if we do, I wonder what he has in mind."

"It's a big responsibility we've been given, escorting this convict," said Xue Ba. "We were only a little way out of Zhengzhou when we ran into this extraordinary priest. Should anything go wrong, we both have families at home, and we'll be in serious trouble."

"Let's drink what he offers us, then see what happens," said Dong Chao.

The priest brought out the wine, and after downing ten or more cups each of them had drunk his fill. "Thank you for all the food and drink, sir," said the escorts, "but we just can't take any more. We'll go to bed, if we may, and then set off in the morning."

"Serving weak wine to one's guests isn't true hospitality. There's no need for any thanks. Please just sit there a moment longer." He got up and went inside again. Before long he was back with two ingots of silver, each weighing fifty ounces. "There is one for each of you. I hope you won't think it too little."

Xue Ba said nothing, but Dong Chao replied, "You were so kind as to offer us wine and food, but now you're offering us money, which is something we definitely cannot accept."

"Just take it for now, as a token of my regard." Unable to resist his urging, they each accepted an ingot.

"There's one thing I'd like to ask of you. I don't know if you'd agree."

The two escorts thought to themselves, we've drunk his wine and accepted his money; how can we not agree? "We'd gladly agree to ten things, let alone one. Please tell us what it is."

"You have each received fifty taels as support for your families. Now spare a thought for Bu Ji, who has been wrongly condemned. He's not someone I knew before; I'm acting solely out of sympathy for him. He maintains that he is an innocent man who was falsely charged and convicted. I hope that you'll find it in your hearts to do me a favor and let him stay here with me. My name is Zhang Luan, and if the prefect should ask, just reply that he was rescued by Zhang Luan. Well, gentlemen, what do you say?"

Dong Chao didn't dare say anything, but Xue Ba cried out, "Master, you simply don't understand! 'All the land belongs to the ruler, and all the people are the ruler's subjects.'[5] You may belong to a religious order, but you live within the boundaries of Zhengzhou, and so you, too, come under the prefect's jurisdiction. This man was sentenced by the prefect, and no one would dare to take him in. You think that because we've received money from you, you can put pressure on us, but the money is still here, untouched. Please take it back!"

"There's no need to get upset," said the priest. "If you're willing to let him stay with me, by all means do so, but if you're not willing, well, you've already accepted the money. Here, have another cup of wine."

"We've drunk your wine and eaten your food, and you've also given us money," said Dong Chao. "Why are you pressing us to drink more?"

"I'm not just offering you wine. I also have a little trick that I'd like to show you. Tonight I'm going to let everyone enjoy the moonlight, from the prefect down to the common man. He took a piece of paper from his breast pocket, and with a pair of scissors cut out the shape of a full moon. He then sprinkled some wine on it and cried, "Up you go!" The paper moon drifted up into the sky.

"Marvelous!" cried the three men in admiration, as two moons appeared in the sky above them.

"Let's drink a toast," said the priest. All four of them drank.

In Zhengzhou the two moons in the sky caused a sensation. From the prefect down to the common people, all the inhabitants both inside and outside the city walls saw the two moons in the sky. The more knowledgeable ones said, "There's only one moon; how can there be two? One of them has to be a demons' moon!"

Let us put aside the sensation that the moon caused and tell how when the priest and his guests had drunk a toast to the moon and were about to part, the priest said, "Gentlemen, do me a favor, will you? Give Bu Ji to me!"

"Unlike you, we have families at home. If the prefect ever got wind of it, we'd have a very hard time explaining what happened."

"The prefect ordered you to arrange his death, and there's a perfectly simple solution. I'm going to give you a piece of evidence that you can show him." He tied the sleeves of his gown together and slung the knot to his rear, then laid hold of Bu Ji with both hands, trussed him from behind with a rope, and secured him to the cottage.

"Master!" exclaimed Xue Ba. "This morning you wanted to rescue him. Why are you tying him up?"

"To give you something of his to take back and show the prefect."

"I wonder what that would be," said Dong Chao.

"Since the prefect wanted him killed, I'm going to cut out his heart for you to take back and give to the prefect. That will show him what capable fellows you are."

"But you can't *do* that!" said Dong Chao. "He's a convicted criminal. If the prefect wants to have him killed, that's his business. If we take his heart back, people in the know will say that it was you who killed him, but those not in the know will say that we murdered him for his money. It would be a false charge, but it would be too much for us to face."

The priest laughed. "So you're frightened of facing a charge, are you? I was only making fun of you just now." Releasing Bu Ji, he arranged their sleeping quarters for them. "If you go back to the city, say that Zhang Luan wanted to rescue Bu Ji. Don't forget, now!" The three men said good night and slept in the outer room, while the priest went into the inner room.

Dong Chao and Xue Ba slept until dawn, when they opened their eyes and received a great shock. There was no Bu Ji beside them, nor any cottage, nor any priest. Instead they found themselves lying on a heap of paper money offerings inside the shrine of a mountain spirit. They looked at each other and began to moan, "Oh, no! We've made fools of ourselves and let our convict get away. Now what are we going to do?"

"We mustn't panic," said Dong Chao. "We'll go and see the prefect." They went straight back to Zhengzhou, where the prefect was just mounting his tribunal for the noon session. They went forward and knelt down before him.

"You two were escorting Bu Ji to Shandong. Why are you back so soon?" asked the prefect.

"Your Honor, we were escorting Bu Ji yesterday when about ten miles outside town we came upon a priest who invited us to his monastery. He wanted to take Bu Ji away from us, but we refused. However, that priest was a magician; he cut out a paper moon and blew it up into the sky, where two moons appeared together."

"How very strange!" said the prefect. "Last night the whole city was in an uproar over the two moons in the sky. Well, what happened next?"

"The priest told us to sleep that night in his cottage, but when we got up early this morning and looked about us, we found we were lying on a pile of paper money inside the shrine of a mountain spirit. We have no idea where the priest and Bu Ji went, but the priest did say, 'My name is Zhang Luan.'"

"Since we have the demon's name, it shouldn't be too difficult to catch him," said the prefect. He called in his detective inspector, but before he had finished giving him orders, a priest appeared in court, a priest with an iron-frame cap and straw sandals, wearing a crimson robe with a black border.

The priest came right up to the prefect and shouted at him, "Prefect! Zhang Luan stands here before you!" He gave no bow of any kind.

The prefect flew into a rage. "You're a demon! How dare you be so rude!"

"You're the head of the prefecture. How could you condemn an innocent man? Bu Ji committed no crime, yet you branded him and exiled him to Shandong. You also told the escorts to murder him along the way. And on top of that, you took away his priceless treasure. What do you mean by it?"

"Don't talk such nonsense! What priceless treasure did he have?"

"The golden tripod in your treasury. I'm now going to call it forth. Golden tripod, why don't you come out?" The prefect and all those in the audience were struck dumb as the golden tripod came flying down from the sky and into the chamber.

"Amazing!" exclaimed the prefect. "Amazing!" The words were scarcely out of his mouth when Bu Ji came leaping out of the tripod, a sword in his right hand. With his left hand he seized hold of the prefect and right there in the chamber cut him in two with a single sweep of the sword.

When the people in the chamber saw the prefect dead, they were stupefied. Then from all parts of the chamber there arose a chorus of voices: "We can't ignore the prefect's murder!" They rushed forward to seize Zhang Luan and Bu Ji, but the two men, seeing the crowd coming for them, ducked behind the mounting stand—and then vanished altogether, taking the golden tripod with them. The crowd of pursuers looked at one other. "We've never seen such an extraordinary thing in all our lives!" they exclaimed. The subprefect was asked to take charge. The officials of the six departments bought a coffin and laid the prefect's body in it, then sent out constables to search for Zhang Luan and Bu Ji. At the same time they consulted together about drawing up a memorial for the emperor.

Certain consequences followed from this incident: The whole of Hebei province[6] was thrown into uproar, and the Eastern Capital descended into chaos. The court mobilized troops and sent them forth, but they failed to arrest the men concerned. The end result was that an honest and upright official came to the country and brought peace to the people.

For the time being with their heresy and witchcraft
They deceive the dragons and tigers among men.

What happened when the officials sent their memorial to court? Turn to the next chapter to find out.

9

LAME PRIEST ZUO TRICKS REN QIAN IN BUYING CAKES;

REN, WU, AND ZHANG FOLLOW HIM IN FURIOUS PURSUIT.

POEM:

Steamed cakes blackened, a fire that wouldn't burn,
A pig's head winking—such magic shows finesse.
Out of their desire to catch Lame Priest Zuo,
Three men come face-to-face with a demoness.

Let us tell how the Zhengzhou officials prepared a memorial and sent it to Emperor Renzong. The emperor opened and read it at his imperial desk, then declared before the assembled civil and military officials, "The prefect of Zhengzhou has been murdered by demons! You must arrest them and rid us of this menace."

He had barely finished speaking when an officer of the Imperial Observatory stepped forward and reported, "Last night a demons' moon appeared in the sky and shone directly in the Double Fish Constellation before setting in the area of Wei. It indicates a demons' revolt. I entreat Your Majesty to give this your august attention so that proper precautions may be taken."

"That other incident has only just occurred in Zhengzhou, and now you report the appearance of a demons' moon! Both involve great danger. You must all take steps to deal with them ahead of time."

The officials declared, "At present South Yamen, Kaifeng prefecture, has no prefect. It is important to select an upright, incorruptible man for the post, in the hope that he will serve as an example to the whole country in removing the evil the demons present."

"Who would be best fitted to serve?" asked the emperor.

"Bao Zheng,[1] style Xiren, edict attendant of the Longtu Pavilion, who is from Hefei in Luzhou. It is vital to appoint him to the position." The emperor agreed to the suggestion and summoned Bao to the palace. Following the audience, Bao was told to take up his duties that very day.

After expressing his gratitude for the emperor's grace, he left the palace. His subordinates in the prefecture escorted him to the yamen, where, needless to say, he was handed the seals of office. Ascending his tribunal that same day, he issued a written directive to the Eastern Capital and all its subprefectures and counties that every five families should form a unit and every twenty-five families a group, all of which were forbidden to give overnight lodging to idlers and vagrants. People from other parts of the country should have their backgrounds checked. Inns were forbidden to admit guests traveling alone, and explicit instructions to that effect were posted on all twenty-eight city gates. The populace burned incense and bowed in gratitude. "What a good man His Honor is!" they exclaimed. Bao governed in such a fashion that all the inhabitants of Kaifeng prefecture were pleased with him. Truly

The runners stood on thin ice;
The people lived in a mirror.[2]

Passersby stepped aside to make room for others. People were happy and well nourished. No one picked up anything that was dropped on the road or locked his door at night. The entire Eastern Capital was at peace.

In Backwater Alley there lived a vendor named Ren Qian. As the eldest male in his generation he was known as Number One, and he worked in the "five ready-to-eat foods" business. What was that business?

> The vendors of noodles were known as boilers;
> The vendors of wheat cakes were known as bakers;
> The vendors of salt fish were known as salters;
> The vendors of steamed cakes were known as steamers;
> The vendors of stuffed dumplings were known as fryers.

Ren Qian was a good vendor, and he strove to be the best in terms of sales. He would cook a day's supply of food at home and then load it onto a rack, neatly arranging the steamed cakes, wheat cakes, steamed buns, and vegetable rolls. With his carrying pole over his shoulder, he would then go to the crossroads on Horse Market Street and there lay down his pole, set up his stand, and greet the other vendors. On this occasion he had no sooner brought out a three-legged stool to sit on from behind his rack when he heard a jangling sound, and someone came rushing up beside his stand—but not to buy cakes. Ren Qian saw that the object making the jangling sound was a *suisu*, known in temples as a set of Daoist rings, which are used by exorcists to call attention to themselves. This exorcist was shaking his rings as he approached Ren Qian's stand. "Riches! Profits! Good fortune! Give me cash!" he called out to Ren Qian.

Ren Qian couldn't help laughing. "Out with the bad smell!" he retorted. He saw that the exorcist was short and slight, that his Daoist cap had lost its brim, and that the crown was torn and allowed tufts of hair to poke through, hair that looked like matted straw. Wearing a cloth gown with a tattered collar and well-worn cloth trousers, he resembled nothing so much as a lion.[3] He wore torn leggings and hemp sandals with the grommets shorn off. Around his waist he had a sash without tassels. "Look down without fail," said Ren Qian, "lest you tread on a mouse's tail. To come out and start exorcising at this hour of the morning[4]—you can't have any idea of time!"

"I know it's early. I've only collected six cash so far."

"Why didn't you wait and come out a bit later?"

"You mustn't blame me, brother! I live with my mother in a tumbledown cave, and so far today we haven't had anything to eat. Give me just one cash. I'll put it together with my six and buy some rice to make a gruel that will fill both of us up."

Hearing his tale of woe, Ren Qian was going to give him a cash, but when he felt in his waist pocket, he found there was nothing there. "If I had any change on me, I wouldn't begrudge you the one cash, but I haven't yet done any business today."

Realizing Ren Qian had no cash on him, Lame Priest asked, "How much are your wheat cakes, brother?"

"Seven cash apiece."

Lame Priest took six cash from his pocket and spread them out on the dish. "Brother, sell me a wheat cake for my mother," he said.

Ren Qian accepted five of the cash and gave the sixth back to Lame Priest. "I'll consider this my first sale of the day," he said. Lame Priest tucked the cash in his pocket. Ren Qian took one large and one small wheat cake from the steamer and gave them to him. As the priest reached out to receive them, Ren Qian noticed that the man's hand was black with filth. I wonder how long it's been since he had a wash, he thought to himself.

Lame Priest took the wheat cakes in his hand, looked at them, and began to knead them with his fingers. "Brother!" he cried. "My mother's eighty. How can she eat *wheat* cakes? Exchange them for a dumpling."

"You've made them all filthy," said Ren Qian. "No one else will want them now." He put them in the bamboo basket in front and went back to the steamer, picked up a dumpling, and gave it to him. Lame Priest took it in his hands and began kneading it as before. "Brother, what's the filling?" he asked.

"Nothing but the finest meat."

"But brother, my mother's a vegetarian! She can't eat this. Exchange it for a red-bean dumpling."

I've still not made a sale, thought Ren Qian, and I have to run into this wretch! He was on the point of refusing when he noticed that a number of customers were milling around his rack, and he was forced to restrain himself and exchange the steamed dumpling for a red-bean one. Lame Priest took the latter in his hands and squeezed it. "This will never be enough to satisfy *her*!" he exclaimed. "Exchange it for a steamed cake."

"No wonder you're starving!" Ren Qian cried out in anger. "You've paid me only five cash, and you've ruined three items. This time I'm *not* going to exchange it!"

"Now, don't get all upset, brother," said Lame Priest. "Two steamed cakes will never be enough to satisfy my mother and me. I'd rather buy some rice to make gruel with." He went up to the rack, snatched back the coins, and then blew on the rack as he left.

"You swine!" shouted Ren Qian. "You've ruined three orders! And *now* where do you think you're going?" He rushed forward and was about to strike Lame Priest when a sudden thought made him stop: from the way he looks, I wonder how many blows and kicks he could actually stand. If something went wrong, I'd be charged with murder, so I'd better let him off. He turned around, but when he looked at his rack, he let out a cry of anguish—all his dumplings and cakes were as black as charcoal. He was furious. That swine has been plaguing me all this time, he thought, and now he's gone and ruined my entire stock. Well, so far as I'm concerned, business is over for the day, and now I'm going to have it out with him! He told the other vendors to mind his stand while he went off after Lame Priest with his fists cocked. Full of youthful hotheadedness, he pursued his quarry for a long time without catching sight of him and was on the point of turning back when he heard a jangling sound up ahead. That must be him, he thought, and rushed off in pursuit, but still did not manage to catch sight of his quarry. After many twists and turns, his pursuit brought him to the tower of Anshang Gate, where he found a crowd of people gathered around the doorway of a butcher's shop.

That's my friend Butcher Zhang's place, he thought. I wonder what brings all these people here. He stopped, pushed his way through the crowd, and found an old woman lying on the ground and a young man helping her to her feet and crying, "Mother!" over and over again. After he had been calling her for a long time, she came to her senses but still kept her eyes shut tight. "Relax, Mother!" the young man said. "Open your eyes!"

"Quick! Take me home!" she cried.

"Open your eyes!" he repeated.

"I can't, I'm too afraid." The young man helped her away.

I wonder why she fell down here, thought Ren Qian. At this point Butcher Zhang called out to the crowd, "Come on, break it up, everyone! There's nothing here for you to see."

Ren Qian knew the butcher as Zhang Qi, the first in his family line. "It's a long time since we last met, Number One," he said.

"Brother Ren! What are you doing here?"

"Oh, I had some odds and ends I needed to see to."

"Come on in. There's something I want to tell you."

Ren Qian went inside. "What was all that excitement about beside your door just now?" he asked.

"Never in all my life have I seen such an extraordinary thing! Just now someone wearing a tattered cap and a well-worn cloth gown and holding a set of Daoist rings in his hand came by chanting, 'Riches! Profits! Good fortune! Give me cash!' I said to him, 'Lame Priest, you can't have any idea of time! I expect you live in a house without windows.' He replied, 'If you don't have any cash, that's one thing. But why do you have to go and make fun of me?' To my astonishment, he looked at the pig's head hanging above my bench, felt it with his hand, moved his lips and said something that I didn't quite catch, then went off shaking his rings. I thought nothing of it, but Zhai Erlang, who makes artificial flowers in the courtyard across from here, had ordered this pig's head, and he sent his mother over to collect it. I took it down and gave it to her, and the pig gave a wink, then opened its mouth and bit the old woman, which caused her to collapse in fright. I at once sent my assistant over to call the son, and luckily he managed to bring her around. If anything had gone wrong, I'd have been charged with a crime. When the son picked up the pig's head and looked at it, nothing happened, and he concluded that the old lady had been seeing things—after all, who has ever seen a dead pig wink?—and took her home."

On hearing this account, Ren Qian told him the whole story of how Lame Priest had bought the steamed cakes. "Incredible!" exclaimed Butcher Zhang. The word was hardly out of his mouth when the two men heard rings jangling.

"That swine is still up there ahead of us!" exclaimed Ren Qian.

"Ruining your steamed cakes, that's not so serious—it didn't do a great deal of harm. But I came close to paying with my life for the death of that old woman. You don't need to do a thing, but when I get my hands on that swine, I'm going to give him a good thrashing!"

"I'm going with you," said Ren Qian. They rushed off after Lame Priest.

For a long time they pursued him without even catching sight of him. "What shall we do now?" asked Butcher Zhang. "If we'd caught him, we'd have shown him no mercy, but since we can't catch him, we'd better turn back." Just as they were about to do so, they heard the sound of the rings once more. They pursued the priest for a couple more miles, to a point several miles outside Anshang Gate. They continued to hear the rings but could never catch up with him. Just as they were about to turn back again, they saw someone beating a man with a stick in front of the noodle shop at the far end of the market. Butcher Zhang recognized the one doing the beating as Wu Three, owner of the noodle shop.

"Hold it, Brother Wu!" said Butcher Zhang. "Let him off, for my sake."

Wu stopped his beating. "My shop was full of people who wanted to eat their noodles and be on their way. I told this fellow to make a fire, but no matter what he did, the fire wouldn't start, and for a long time he couldn't get the cauldron to heat. Meanwhile all the customers left. I'm going to flay him alive!"

"Stop, for my sake!" urged Butcher Zhang.

"This is hardly the time of day for you to be strolling around town, is it?" asked Wu Three.

Butcher Zhang then told him all the things that Lame Priest had done, and Wu Three was dumbfounded. "In that case, I was wrong to beat that fellow. Let me tell you what happened. I was at my stove when I saw a lame priest approach my door, shaking his rings and calling out, 'Riches! Profits! Good fortune! Give me cash!' I was busy, and I said, 'You can't have any idea of time, coming out in the middle of the day like this to exorcise evil spirits. Were you afraid that, if you came later, the ghosts would carry you off? I don't have any change on me, and I'll have to send you away empty-handed.' He peered into my cauldron, blew a breath of air into it, and then left. As soon as he had gone, I told my assistant to light the stove, but he couldn't get it to start. After a long time, when it still wouldn't start, many of my customers left because they couldn't wait any longer for their noodles. That's why I was beating him. If you two hadn't shown up, I'd never have known about any of this. What a vicious character that priest is! He's ruined my entire business for the day!"

As he said this, they heard the sound of the rings once more. Wu Three peered and saw Lame Priest up ahead of them, shaking his rings as he walked along. "Let's go after him!" chorused the three men. Seeing them coming, Lame Priest dashed off.

Because of their pursuit of Lame Priest, certain consequences followed: the three men arrived at an isolated Buddhist temple and saw an extraordinary sight

> Unheard of since the world began,
> Unseen in all the expanse of time.

Where did the three men pursue Lame Priest, and what did they see? Turn to the next chapter to find out.

10

IN MOPO TEMPLE LAME PRIEST ENTERS BUDDHA'S BELLY;

IN A DREAM REN, WU, AND ZHANG RECEIVE ETERNA'S MAGIC.

POEM:

Chunyu dreamed that he traveled to Nanke,[1]
While Zhuang Zi dreamed he was a butterfly.[2]
All manner of things in this world are a dream;
Gain, loss, rise and fall go so quickly by.

Lame Priest saw Ren, Wu, and Zhang coming after him and dashed off. When they quickened their pace, he quickened his; when they slackened their pace, he slackened his; and when they stopped altogether, he stopped, too. They simply could not catch him.

"Let's find out where he lives and then deal with him," said Butcher Zhang after they had left the capital several miles behind. Their pursuit brought them to a place called Dragon Mopo, where the road was utterly deserted. There was a temple there named Mopo, and Lame Priest went straight inside. "Good!" said Butcher Zhang. "It's a dead end. I wonder where he's heading. Let's split up and go after him from three different directions."

"Good idea!" said Ren Qian. Wu went straight ahead, while Zhang took the left portico and Ren the right. When the lame priest saw the three pursuing him from different directions, he raced into the Buddha Hall, scrambled up onto the altar, planted his foot on Buddha's hand, then clambered up onto Buddha's shoulder and took Buddha's head in both hands.

The three men came rushing up to the Buddha Hall. "You'd better come down," they said. "If you don't, we'll go up there and drag you down!"

"Help! Buddha save me!" exclaimed Lame Priest, throwing Buddha's head down. It clattered on the floor and rolled away, while Lame Priest crawled into the belly.

"What a strange thing to do!" exclaimed Butcher Zhang. "There's no way out of that belly! Why crawl in there? But we're not going to let you off!" He scrambled up onto the altar, planted a foot on Buddha's hand, clambered onto Buddha's shoulder, and, holding on to Buddha's neck with both hands, peered down into the chest, where everything was pitch-black. Then a hand reached out from inside the chest and grabbed him by the topknot, and down he tumbled into the belly of the statue.

"Oh, no!" cried Wu and Ren in alarm. They were at a complete loss. "What shall we do?" they asked each other.

"No problem," said Ren Qian. "I'll climb up and find out what's going on."

"Be careful, brother. Mind you don't go in, too."

"I won't do what Zhang did." Ren Qian scrambled onto the altar, planted his foot on Buddha's hand, clambered onto Buddha's shoulder and out onto his chest and looked inside, but saw nothing there but pitch-black darkness. "Zhang!" he called. "Where are you?" There was no response, but a hand reached out and seized hold of him. In his terror Ren Qian cried, "Dear Master! Living Master! Have pity on me, forgive me. I won't dare pursue you anymore. I've come here specially to ask if you'd like any steamed cakes, steamed buns, or red-bean dumplings.

If you would, I'll bring them to you." At this point his head went down, his feet went up, and he plunged headfirst into Buddha's belly.

"Oh, no!" moaned Wu in horror. Both of them have fallen into Buddha's belly, he thought, but I can't go back without them. He was afraid that, if he looked inside, he would tumble in himself. On the other hand, if he went back, he wouldn't know if the other two were alive or dead. He simply had to go up and take a look. He scrambled onto the altar, but his limbs were numb with fright, and he was shaking like a leaf—he didn't dare go any further. But after thinking it over for some time, he felt that there was nothing else for it—he had to plant a foot on Buddha's hand and clamber onto Buddha's chest. He wanted to look inside, but he was too afraid of falling in. He was at an impasse, unable to go forward or back. How stupid of me! he thought. All I need do is find some hard object to break Buddha's belly with, and then I'll be able to rescue them both. He was just about to step down onto the altar when he felt as if someone behind him had seized him around the waist and thrown him down into the belly, where one of his feet came to rest on Ren Qian's head.

"You're treading on me!" yelled Ren.

"Who are you?" asked Wu.

"I'm Ren Qian!"

"Where's Zhang?"

"I'm over here!" said Zhang.

"Wu, how did *you* happen to get in?"

"I went up onto Buddha's chest and tried to look for you two, and then I felt as if someone were throwing me down into the belly."

"I felt as if someone had stretched out a hand and grabbed my hair and pulled me in."

"It was the same with me," said Butcher Zhang. "It must be Lame Priest. He's been having a high old time with us. Let's feel our way around. If we find him, let's not beat him up, just get him to help us out of this belly. If he refuses to help, we'll have no choice but to beat him up." The three men set about feeling their way all around, but they failed to find Lame Priest.

"I never realized that Buddha's belly was so huge. Let's take it one step at a time."

"But how can we walk anywhere when it's so dark in here?" asked Zhang.

"I'll help you along," said Ren.

"And I'll go behind," offered Wu.

They made their way slowly along for several hundred yards, when Butcher Zhang said, "This is all very strange! How can the Mopo Temple hall be so large? We've already gone a long way inside the belly."

As they were speaking, they suddenly saw a speck of light up ahead. "There's a way out, after all!" said Wu.

A few more steps brought them to an ill-fitting stone door with a shaft of light shining through one of its cracks. Butcher Zhang stepped forward and pushed the door open, then focused his eyes and looked inside. "Wonderful!" he exclaimed in astonishment.

An unearthly scene presented itself,
With exotic blossoms of dazzling hue,
Pairs of swallows flying hither and thither,
A splendid bridge one hundred paces long,
And green waters wending their way around.

"Out of this world!" exclaimed Butcher Zhang.

"I never imagined there'd be scenery like this inside Buddha's belly in the Mopo Temple!" marveled Wu.

"But if there's no one living here," said Ren, "how are we going to get back?"

"That's all right," said Butcher Zhang. "Since there's a path, there must be somebody living here. Let's start out."

After walking another half mile, they came to a manor house:

Brilliant flowers fill the garden,
Verdant bamboos line the hedgerows.
A vivid blue stream, cold and fresh,
Shines brightly, crystal clear.
A thatched lodge, quiet and secluded,
While nest-building swallows hovered in the wind;
A compound, empty and deserted,
As chattering orioles flit through warm sunlight.
A young boy returns on his buffalo
Singing a mountain song;
A swarthy villager comes back from his plow
Listening to a village tune;
A lean and hungry dog
Barks at passersby through the hedge;
And a solitary bird
Speeds the traveler on his way from an old tree.

"Let me go and call out to them," said Butcher Zhang. "We're travelers passing through and we've lost our way!" he shouted.

From inside came a response: "Coming! Coming!" Then the door opened, and an old woman walked out. The three men greeted her, and she returned the greeting.

"Where have you three come from?" she asked.

"We're from the city, and we've lost our way. We'd like to ask you for directions, and also whether you have any food in the manor that we could buy."

"We're country folk—how could we have food for sale? If you're travelers who are just passing through, you might as well stay and have a meal here. Come on inside."

They followed her into the thatched hall and sat down on some wooden benches. The old woman brought a table over and placed it in front of them. "You look hungry," she said. "I'll just prepare some food for you. If you can drink wine, have some before you eat."

"Thank you, ma'am," they said. She went inside and soon returned with a pot of wine and set out three cups. She then brought out a meat dish with a mouthwatering smell and poured them three cups of the wine.

"This wine doesn't compare with what you get in the city," she said. "Here it's all homemade. Just drink it up as if it were tea."

After their pursuit of Lame Priest, the three men were both hungry and thirsty, and even before they had tried the hors d'oeuvres or tasted the meat, they cried out, "Oh, this is so good!" Each of them drank two cups of wine. The old woman then brought out some rice, of which they ate their fill. "Thank you, ma'am," they said. "We'll pay the usual tariff."

"What! For a little bit of food and wine? I can't ask anything for that!" she said, gathering up the dishes and taking them inside. The three were just about to thank her and take their leave, asking for directions out of the area, when someone walked in from outside. It was none other than Lame Priest!

"You tormented us all morning," said Butcher Zhang, "and here you are!" The three men flew down the hall like eagles swooping on a sparrow, seized hold of Lame Priest, and were about to beat him when he cried out, "Mother, help me!"

Emerging from the inner quarters, the old woman called out, "You three, stop that wild behavior this minute! He's my *son*! If you have an issue with him, you need to show some consideration for me." She came down the hall and told them to let him go, then invited them to sit down. "Just now out of the goodness of my heart I offered you some food and wine," she said. "Why do you want to beat my son the moment you set eyes on him? You're being *most* unreasonable!"

"We're sincerely grateful for your hospitality, your ladyship" said Butcher Zhang. "We truly had no idea that Lame Priest was your son. If we had known, we would have put up with his unreasonable behavior. It's only out of consideration for you that we're not beating him to a pulp right now!"

"What has my son done that you should want to beat him?" she asked. Butcher Zhang, Ren Qian, and Wu Three told the old woman the things the priest had done that morning. "From what you tell me," she said, "he was at fault in all these cases. Let me get him to beg you for forgiveness."

Lame Priest came before her, and she said, "Gentlemen, do forgive him, for my sake!"

"Ma'am, we no longer have any desire to fight with him. Just get him to show us the way back."

"Stay a little longer, why don't you? I believe it's only because you are men of destiny that you were able to come here in the first place, but now that you *are* here, you're surely not going to go straight back? We all know some magic, and we'll tell each of you how to do one trick, which will be something you can take away and make use of for the rest of your lives."

To Lame Priest she said, "You mustn't go out anymore. When you did go out, you caused a lot of trouble and brought these three men here. Now, show them what magic you know." To the three men she said, "My son has learned a few tricks that he's going to demonstrate to you."

"Thank you, ma'am," they replied.

"As you wish, Mother!" said Lame Priest. He brought out a gourd from his waist pocket, recited a formula, and shouted, "Presto!" A stream of water gushed from the mouth of the gourd.

"Bravo!" cried the three men.

"Now let me show you how I bring the water back again," said Lame Priest.

Little by little he brought the water back into the gourd. Then he recited another formula and shouted, "Presto!" A tongue of flame shot forth from the gourd.

"Bravo!" cried the three men. Little by little Lame Priest also brought the flame back inside the gourd.

"Lame Priest, would you be willing to give me that gourd?" asked Butcher Zhang.

"Son, give the gentleman that water-and-flame gourd," said the old woman. Lame Priest didn't dare disobey. He handed the gourd to Butcher Zhang, who thanked him.

"I have another trick that I'll show you," said Lame Priest. He took a sheet of paper, cut out the shape of a horse, then laid it on the floor and shouted, "Presto!" The paper horse, as white as snow, seemingly made of cotton, shook itself, got to its feet, and showed that it could both walk and gallop. Lame Priest mounted it, gave a shout, and the horse slowly rose up into the sky, and then after a considerable time sank gradually down to earth again. Lame Priest stopped it and dismounted, and the horse turned back into a paper cutout.

"Which of you gentlemen would like to have this?" he asked.

"I'd like to have the paper horse magic," said Wu. Lame Priest handed him the horse cutout, and Wu thanked him.

"Now two of the gentlemen have their magic," said the old woman to Lame Priest. "What about this one?"

"I would never disobey your instructions, Mother," said Lame Priest, "but I'm afraid my magic is too limited." As they spoke, a woman came walking out.

The newcomer was none other than Eterna Hu. After curtsying to everyone, she said to the old woman, "Just give me the word, Mother, and I'll teach this gentleman a magic trick."

"I'm looking forward to a superb performance."

Eterna brought out a wooden bench and placed it in the front of the hall. Then, sitting astride the bench, she recited a formula, shouted, "Presto!" and the bench turned into a slant-eyed, white-browed tiger.

A short neck, a barrel chest, tiny ears,
Chiseled brows, white forehead a pile of silver;
Claws lightly spread, as swift as in flight,
Leaping over ravines like level ground;
The sweep of its tail terrifying deer,
Its roar scaring foxes half to death;
How could Bian Zhuang,[3] brave as he was, prevail?
Even Zi Lu would have been sorely pressed.

Riding on the tiger's back, Eterna called out, "Up!" and the tiger soared into the sky. She shouted, "Halt!" and it sank gradually back to earth. She shouted, "Presto!" and it turned back into a bench.

"Did you see that, Master Ren?" asked the old woman.

"Yes, ma'am, I did," said Ren.

"Daughter, you must teach that magic to Master Ren," she said. Eterna passed the magic formula on to Ren Qian, who thanked her.

"Now, I want all three of you to perform your magic once," said the old woman. They practiced until they could do it successfully.

"Now that you know some magic," she said, "there's something I want to ask you. I don't know if you'd be willing to agree."

"Ma'am, I wonder what it is you want us to agree to," said Butcher Zhang. "Do tell us."

"You must commit this to memory: One day in the future you are to come to Beizhou and help us. You mustn't fail to come."

"Since you're giving us an order, we'll certainly go there to help you," said Butcher Zhang. "But just now we ask you to guide us to the road that will take us back home."

"I'll have my son escort you into the city."

"As you wish," said Lame Priest.

The three men took leave of the old woman, who said to them, "Today I'm having my son take you back, but tomorrow you must all come and wait for me at the Mopo Temple."

The three men took leave of the old woman and Eterna. Lame Priest then led them a distance of a few hundred yards before they came to a high mountain, which they duly climbed. "Gentlemen, can you see the city from here?" asked Lame Priest.

They looked and saw that the city was close at hand. As they did so, Lame Priest gave them a sudden shove, and they tumbled down and awoke with a start in what they realized was the Buddha Hall. In a state of complete bewilderment, Butcher Zhang watched as the other two also came to their senses.

"What did you two see?" he asked.

"Lame Priest taught us some magic," said Wu. "Do you have your gourd with you?" he asked. Zhang felt for it—it was there in his breast pocket.

"I have my paper horse here, too," said Wu.

"What I learned was the formula for tiger transformation," said Ren.

"We seemed to be living in a dream. Lame Priest, the old woman, and Eterna Hu are surely all supernatural beings. They insisted that one day we should go to Beizhou to help them. I wonder what they have in mind."

The three men were puzzling over this question when they saw Lame Priest come walking out from the back of the Buddha Hall. "Go on home," he said. "Don't forget your skills and the magic that you have learned, and come back here tomorrow and wait for us." They took leave of him and went to their separate homes.

Nothing else of significance happened that day. The next morning, after they had had their breakfast, they made their way to the Mopo Temple and went up to the top of the Buddha Hall, where they found the Buddha head intact and in place. Then they went to the rear hall to look for the old lady and Lame Priest, but could not find them.

"Let's go back!" said Butcher Zhang.

As he said this, they heard someone calling out, "Now, don't have a change of heart, you three! I've been waiting for you for ages!" They turned to look and saw someone coming out from the back of the Buddha Hall—the old woman they had met the day before. They bowed low before her. "Why are you so late?" she asked "I want you to demonstrate the magic that you learned yesterday, so that you'll be able to use it in future."

"I'm the one with the coordinated fire-and-water gourd,"[4] said Butcher Zhang. He recited the formula, shouted, "Presto!" and a stream of water shot forth from the gourd. He shouted, "Back!" and little by little the water went back into the gourd. Again he shouted, "Presto!" and a tongue of flame darted forth from the gourd. Again he shouted, "Back!" and little by little the flame went back inside the gourd. "I've mastered it!" he said gleefully.

Wu Three then took the horse cutout from his breast pocket, put it on the floor, and recited the formula with a shout of "Presto!" It turned into a white horse, its hooves going clippety-clop as it trotted along. Wu rode it for some time, then leaped off, and it turned back into a paper cutout.

Ren Qian then went to the rear hall and fetched a bench and sat astride it. He recited the formula and shouted, "Presto!" and the bench turned into a tiger that roared as it bounded along. Ren Qian shouted, "Halt," and the tiger gradually stopped and turned back into a bench.

As the men were demonstrating their magic, they heard someone call out, "In these idyllic times of peace and good order, here you are, practicing the demonic arts! The authorities have recently put up notices calling for the arrest of any demons. If they learn about this episode, I'm bound to be implicated!"

When they hastily turned to see who it was, they found a priest wearing a fiery red cassock and gold earrings. "I've been watching you from the portico for some time," he said.

"Please forgive me, Master," said the old woman. "I was just teaching them a little magic."

"Teach them well, and you will not have labored in vain; teach them badly, and you will have wasted all your efforts. You should get them to give me a demonstration."

The old woman told them to demonstrate their magic, and they did so. "Well, Master," she asked, "what do you think of my disciples?"

"In my opinion," he said, "they are none too good."

The old woman bristled. "I daresay that you, as a priest, have stupendous talents. Well, if you know some magic, show it to us!" The priest stretched out a hand, spread his fingers wide, and each of his fingers gave forth a ray of golden light in the midst of which there appeared a buddha figure. The three men prostrated themselves at the sight.

As they did so, they heard a voice crying out, "This temple was built by imperial order. Why are you practicing the black magic of Diamond Chan in here?" The priest retracted the golden light, and they saw that the speaker was a Daoist priest mounted on a wild beast who was coming up the hall. At the sight of the old woman, he jumped down and, raising his fists, kowtowed to her, saying, "Your disciple has come especially to bow down before you."

"Master, please sit down," she said. The Daoist and the Buddhist bowed to each other, and the three vendors came forward and bowed to the Daoist.

"Do these three men know any magic?"

"Yes," she said.

"I, too, have converted a disciple, and I have him here with me."

"Where is he?"

The Daoist said to the wild beast, "Withdraw your miraculous powers." The beast shook its head, waved its tail, and disappeared from sight. What stood up in its place was a man! The onlookers were flabbergasted. The old woman recognized the man as the carter Bu Ji.

Bu Ji bowed low before her.

"Bu Ji, how do you come to be here?"

"Madam, if my teacher, Master Zhang, had not come to my rescue, I would probably never have seen you again."

"How did you happen to save him?" she asked the Daoist.

"I was in a wood a few miles outside Zhengzhou when I heard someone cry out, 'Priestess Pia, help!' I thought to myself, that's your name, ma'am. Why is someone calling on you? I rushed over to see and found Bu Ji, who had been hung up in a tree by some men who were about to murder him. I asked him the reason, and he told me the whole story. I then employed a little magic and rescued him from danger."

"I see," she said. "In that case, I suppose you also taught him some magic?"

"Yes, he did," said Bu Ji.

"Have any of you ever seen *my* magic?" she asked.

"We would like to see your superb performance."

She took a gold hairpin from her head, shouted, "Presto!" and it changed into a precious sword. She slashed her chest with the sword, then put the sword down. With both hands she pulled the skin of her chest apart. The others came forward to look. This is what they saw:

A vermilion gate, gold studded,
Eaves with emerald tiles;
Blue-green cypresses grown together against the gate,
A ring of green pines surrounding the hall;
A seraphic boy beating a drum
And a flock of white cranes listening to scripture;
A cherubic girl tolling a bell
And several green gibbons brewing a magic potion;
The image of the Penglai paradise,
Exactly like the immortals' abode.

"Bravo!" cried the onlookers in amazement. As they watched, they heard shouts from in front of the door, and a group of men trooped in.

"What shall we do now?" cried the vendors in alarm.

"Don't panic! Everyone, just follow me inside," said the Buddhist priest. They took refuge in a secret hideaway.

The newcomers, over twenty in number, had crossbows at their waists and falcons on their wrists. Five of them were falconers, and the rest of the party included both officials and private citizens. Among them was a eunuch on a horse. He rode up to the front of the hall and dismounted, then opened up a folding chair and sat down, while his followers formed up on both sides. The eunuch was Marshal Goodman Wang. He was not on duty at court that day, and he was using his free time to take a number of men outside the city to play games and enjoy themselves. They had chanced to come to this Mopo Temple, where they played a little football and practiced some archery, and also enjoyed some wine and food. The eunuch himself drank several cups of wine before remounting his horse and riding off escorted by his men.

The old woman and the others returned to the Buddha Hall, where she said, "I thought they were going to start something, but instead they came here to amuse themselves. Still, it gave us quite a shock."

"We know him as a court eunuch by the name of Marshal Goodman Wang. He lives in Baitieban,"[5] said Zhang, Ren, and Wu. "He's an extremely generous man who donates to Daoist and Buddhist priests alike."

Hearing this comment, the Buddhist priest said, "Just watch me torment him tomorrow."

Then they dispersed.

Precisely because the priest wanted to torment Marshal Wang, thirty smart, sharp-eyed constables and a clever, capable inspector were given no peace. When they did find the priest, they were unable to arrest him. He roiled the Eastern Capital and threw the whole of Bianzhou into chaos.

Common vendors joined the Double Adepts;[6]
Good-looking fools enrolled in Diamond Chan.

Truly,

They studied the art of demonic magic—
And consigned their manly bodies to the grave.

How did this priest torment people? Turn to the next chapter to find out.

11

PELLET PRIEST SPIRITS AWAY MARSHAL WANG'S MONEY;

SEVEN SAINTS DU CUTS OFF HIS SON'S HEAD WITH MAGIC.

POEM:

Varied is the magic of the Dark Goddess;
Study it—you'll have an epiphany;
If anger, greed, and lust you can forswear,
A minor immortal in this world you'll be.

After Marshal Wang returned from his excursion outside the city, he had no other activity planned for that day, and his followers dispersed. The following day they all—officials, private citizens, and idlers alike—called on him to pay their respects. "Yesterday we spent the day outside the city," he said. "but today I'm not going out. Instead I've arranged a drinking party in the back garden." He told them not to go home but to join him there to watch plays and other diversions. Now, this garden of his had not just a single pavilion but a large number of places for enjoying oneself. The pavilion they went to on this occasion was called Four Views. After his men had arranged his food and drink, the marshal sat alone in the pavilion, while all the others, from officials to private citizens to mere attendants, demonstrated their talents in front of him.

As they drank, they heard a sudden sound from one of the uprights in the pavilion, and everyone was startled, from the marshal himself down to the lowliest servant. When they looked, they found that someone had fired a pellet into the garden.

"What a scoundrel!" said Marshal Wang. "It's lucky he hit the upright. If he'd struck me, it would have been a disaster!" He ordered his staff to find out who had fired the pellet. They searched all around, but how could anyone fire a pellet into such a large garden with such high walls? As they debated the question, the pellet itself rolled along the pavilion floor, made a few skips, and then spun around hundreds of times like a jade bobbin.

"Incredible!" exclaimed the marshal. At this point a loud pop was heard from the pellet, and out shot the tiny figure of a man. Although small at first, once it met the first breath of terrestrial wind, the figure gradually grew until it became a six-foot-tall priest wearing a fiery red cassock and gold earrings. The marshal and all the others present were dumbfounded.

The priest stepped forward and addressed the marshal: "I bow before you."

Although he said nothing, the marshal thought, what a fine priest this man is! I must treat him with all due respect. He rose to his feet and returned the bow, asking, "May I ask what brings you here, Reverend Master?"

"I'm an itinerant monk from the Manjusri Temple on Mount Wutai in Yanmen county of Daizhou, and I've come here especially to visit you, sir, and to beg for a vegetarian meal."

The marshal had always venerated Buddhist doctrine and regularly donated to the Three Buddhist Treasures,[1] and so now, on seeing this kind of priest coming to beg for alms and arriving in such an extraordinary fashion, how could he be anything but delighted? "Please take a seat," he said.

The priest sat down opposite. "I'm afraid I'm interrupting your drinking party," he said.

The marshal sent orders to the kitchen to prepare a vegetarian meal. "Master, would you be willing to join me in a few cups of wine before you eat?" he asked.

"Thank you very much," said the priest. A set of gold cups and gold plates, the gift of the emperor, were placed in front of him. "You wish to give me a vegetarian meal," said the priest, "but how can these tiny cups bring me any pleasure?"

The marshal responded by promptly ordering a large gold tankard to be set before the priest. He himself drank from a cup, while the priest used the tankard. The marshal told his servants to keep on pouring the wine. The priest never demurred, and altogether drank over thirty tankards. If he weren't a holy man, he could never have drunk so much, thought the marshal happily.

The kitchen then reported that the vegetarian food was ready. "Since it's ready, let me invite you, Master," said the marshal. He had the dishes brought out and placed before the priest. He ate a little himself in order to keep the priest company.

At sight of the food, the priest picked up his bowl and chopsticks and never put them down again. The marshal told his servants to keep on bringing more, and the priest finished everything that was set before him—rice, broth, and wine. The waiters couldn't keep pace with him, and the marshal's servants were all agog. The marshal, too, was stunned to see what a trencherman the priest was. He must be a holy man, he thought, he eats and drinks so much. I can't imagine where he puts it all!

Just then the priest laid down his bowl and chopsticks, and the servants exclaimed among themselves, "Thank goodness! There *is* an end to his eating, after all!"

"Now I'm full!" exclaimed the priest. The dishes were gathered up, and tea was ordered. After he had drunk his tea, the priest got to his feet and thanked the marshal.

"Master, there's no need to thank me for the plain fare that I've given you," said the gratified Marshal Wang. "But may I ask where you are going now that you've finished your meal?"

"I'm in charge of raising funds for the Manjusri Temple on Mount Wutai, and the abbot has ordered me to come and solicit donations. The temple gate is dilapidated, and three thousand strings of cash will be needed to rebuild it. Today I have met you, sir, and been given a meal. If you could spare three thousand strings to accomplish this glorious task, I would wish you increased good fortune and longevity as well as a rich harvest of future blessings."

"That's a small request to make. I wonder when you intend to bring the subscription book around?"

"We don't need a subscription book. It's more convenient without, and more beneficial to the temple."

"What if I were to give you the money in gold or silver, Master?"

"Gold and silver are less convenient for buying materials. It would be best if I could have three thousand strings of cash."

The marshal chuckled to himself. "But master, you're here on your own! You'll need a great many men to carry three thousand strings."

"I know how to do it, sir."

The marshal told his steward to open up his treasury, and had his followers, officials, and private citizens alike, as well as his staff, move the strings in relays and pile them up outside the pavilion. In all there were thirty piles, each with a hundred strings in it.

"Master, the three thousand strings are all here, but it's a long way that you have to travel, and you'll need a lot of money for porters. How can you get the cash to Mount Wutai?"

"That's no problem!" said the priest. He got up, stepped down from the pavilion, and thanked the marshal for his generous contribution. "There's no need for you to trouble yourself, sir. I have my own men to transport it." He took a sutra scroll from his sleeve.

The marshal said nothing, but he thought to himself, let's see what he does.

"A priest possesses the vast power of the faith," said his visitor. He glanced at the sutra, told the marshal's men to step aside, and in the blink of an eye flung the sutra up into the heavens, where it opened out to form a golden bridge. The priest then beckoned skyward and called out, "Monks, acolytes, hired hands of Mount Wutai! I have received a contribution of three thousand strings from Marshal Wang. Now come and transport it!" Before long all the monks, acolytes, and hired hands of the temple came tumbling down out of the sky to Four Views Pavilion, then proceeded to go back and forth across the bridge as they hauled, shouldered, or simply carried the strings of cash away. In no time they had removed them all.

The priest came forward and addressed the marshal, "I am grateful to you, sir, for providing me with a meal and also for your generous contribution of three thousand strings of cash. If you should ever come to Mount Wutai, I shall welcome you by assembling the monks, tolling the bells, beating the drums, flying the flags, and displaying our regalia. I shall now return to Mount Wutai." Taking leave of the marshal, he ascended the golden bridge, and his figure grew steadily smaller until, as he went further and further away, he disappeared entirely from view. A wind then sprang up in the heavens, and when it had passed by, the bridge, too, had disappeared.

The marshal was jubilant, and he told his retainers to burn incense and pray. "For over fifty years I've been offering meals and giving alms to priests. Today I've met a holy man, an arhat." Everyone present came forward and congratulated him.

Nothing else of significance happened that day. The following day the marshal was on duty at court. He rose early, washed and combed, and was met by his subordinates, who escorted him to the front of the imperial palace. There he alighted from his sedan chair and went inside. He had arrived a little early. Walking past the waiting room, he met an official and bowed to him—it was none other than Prefect Bao. Ever since Bao had begun administering Kaifeng prefecture, the populace had been delighted with him.

Upright and honest his whole life long,
Wise and intelligent by nature,
Constantly evincing loyalty and piety,
Always filled with humanity and kindness.
Under him the population had increased
And new land been brought under the plow;
The common people laud his virtue in the streets and lanes.
Lawsuits have decreased,
And robbers and thieves lie low;
Old men sing his praises in the marketplace.
People would surround his carriage and cut his stirrups;[2]
His name in history will last a thousand years;
His achievements will be carved in stone;
His fame will shake the prefecture and be transmitted to the ages;
In truth his spirited writing outshines that of Li and Du,[3]
Just as his virtue and integrity outshine the merits of Gong and Huang.[4]

Prefect Bao was at court waiting for the early audience, and on seeing Marshal Wang he invited him to sit with him. The marshal was an upright man, while Prefect Bao was an incorruptible official, and each had heard of the other's virtuous character. Although the marshal was a eunuch, he liked this Prefect Bao, and Bao liked him.

"During our lives we all receive rewards or retribution for our good or bad deeds," said the marshal, as they sat together in a side room.

"I've had the same experience in my position," said Prefect Bao. "For example, in Kaifeng prefecture I have decided many cases, and the criminals had to be sentenced before they would repent their ways and reform their lives. As for people like you, though, who love to do good deeds, I wonder what reward you would get."

"To take just one instance, yesterday I was enjoying myself in a pavilion in my back garden when we were struck by a pellet from out of nowhere. A holy man popped out of the pellet and said he was soliciting donations for the Manjusri Temple on Mount Wutai. He asked for a vegetarian meal, and after I'd fed him, he had a second request, for three thousand strings of cash. He didn't need anyone to transport the cash, he said. Instead he flung the scroll of a sutra up into the sky, where it opened out to form a golden bridge. He then summoned monks, acolytes, and hired hands from Mount Wutai, and in no time at all they had moved the money away. He also went back over the bridge himself. And so it's a proven fact: buddhas and arhats really do exist in our mortal world."

Prefect Bao said nothing in response, but he thought to himself, what an odd story!

Gradually the dawn came, and the civil and military officials attended the imperial audience and afterward went back to their yamens.

Bao went back to his but not to decide cases. Instead he asked who the police officer on duty was that day. Below the steps a man bowed in response—Detective Inspector Wen Dianzhi. "Today at the morning audience I was sitting in the waiting room when Marshal Goodman Wang spoke to me," said Bao. "He told me that he was drinking in the pavilion in his back garden yesterday when someone shot a pellet in from outside. A priest popped out of the pellet who said he was a mendicant friar from the Manjusri Temple on Mount Wutai. He asked for and got three thousand strings of cash. The marshal thinks he was a holy man or arhat, but I believe that if he were a holy man or arhat, he would scarcely be in need of the money. In my judgment, he must have been a demon priest. Recently the prefect of Zhengzhou has been murdered by the demons Zhang Luan and Bu Ji, and notices have been posted for their arrest, so far without any success. Under no circumstances can we allow such demonic figures near the imperial palace in the capital city." Pointing at Inspector Wen, he said, "You must arrest this demon priest at once and bring him here before me."

Inspector Wen had no choice but to accept the order. He left the yamen, walked along Sweet Spring Lane to the police headquarters, and took a seat at the head of the chamber. The constables arrayed on each side saw him with locked brows and a worried look on his face, his eyes cast down, not saying a word. Among them was a man named Ran Gui, known as Saturn, who was a particular favorite of Wen's. One of his eyes was always closed, but he could do things that no one else in the world could do, and in cooperation with Wen he had solved many difficult cases, which was the reason Wen liked him.

Ran Gui now stepped forward. "Sir, I wonder what could be giving you so much concern."

"If I told you what it is, Ran, you'd be concerned, too. Just now the prefect called me in and said that before the morning audience Marshal Wang of Baitieban had spoken to him. He told the prefect that yesterday he was drinking wine in a pavilion in his back garden when someone shot a pellet in from outside. A priest popped out of the pellet and asked the marshal for a donation of three thousand strings of cash. The marshal thought he was a holy man or arhat, but the prefect said that if he were a holy man or arhat, what need would he have for the money? He had to be a demon priest. I've been given until today to arrest the man. I'm afraid that, having gotten three thousand strings of cash, he will naturally have gone off somewhere else by now, so how am I going to arrest him? His Honor is not like other officials, and though this is a difficult task, I had no choice but to take it on. But that priest is never going to step forward and confess, and I frankly don't know what to do. That's why I'm worried."

"What's so difficult about that?" asked Ran Gui. "You order a large number of constables to take great care as they split up and go to all twenty-eight city gates to arrest the man. If we delay any longer, I'm afraid he'll be gone."

"You're right. You're older and more experienced than I am." To the constables he said, "Split up and go and do your job. See you take great care, each one of you!" They left to carry out his order.

Wen himself took Ran Gui and two capable, highly trusted assistants with him. Departing from the police offices, they left Sweet Spring Lane and hurried along to the highway. Wen was hiding his face under a winter hat, while Ran Gui dressed up as a servant and with both eyes open scanned the passers-by. If they came upon anyone in a tea shop or tavern who looked a little suspicious, they promptly investigated him.

"That fellow's vanished into the Eastern Sea. We're *never* going to find him!" said Wen.

"Don't despair, sir," replied Ran. "Let's go on until evening and then reconsider." They walked to the front of the Xiangguo Temple, where they found a crowd of men gathered beside the wall. "Wait here a moment, sir, while I find out what's going on," said Ran. He set off, and in the center of a crowd of a hundred or two people he found a man wearing a turban that sported a brocaded peony flower, while at the back of his head he had a pair of gold rings the size of saucepans. He was wearing a half coat with an embroidered waistband and hemp shoes with grommets, and he displayed a body decorated with brilliant tattoos. Behind him a silver spear was stuck in the ground. Several banners stood there, as well as a pair of gold-lacquered bamboo baskets. The man was a magician, and he had attracted this crowd of people to watch him.

The magician, Seven Saints Du by name, enjoyed a great reputation in the capital. Clasping his hands together, he began: "I am a native of the Eastern Capital. This is a place visited by officials and travelers from all parts of the country. Some of them know me, while the others don't know me but have heard of me. Every year I make a pilgrimage to the Eastern Sacred Mountain, where I compete with others and always carry off the honors. Someone asked me, 'Seven Saints! Seven Saints! What skill do you possess?' and I said, 'Beneath the sun and the moon, throughout the entire cosmos, in heaven above or on earth below, apart from my teacher I have yet to meet an opponent who can compete with me in this kind of magic!'"

Turning around, he called out, "Shoushou, my boy, come on out!" The boy who came out was stripped to the waist, and his skin was as white as a jade bobbin.

The audience roared their approval. "What a fine-looking lad!"

"Of all the people in the Eastern Capital, from the highest to the lowest, only a few have seen this magic during the past year," said Seven Saints. "It was handed down by our patriarch. Flames heat the oil, a hot pan warms the bowl.[5] It's known as Head Restoration Magic. I have my son lie down on this bench and cut off his head with a knife, cover him up with this cloth, and then join the boy's head back on again. Now, gentlemen, let me begin by selling you these hundred charms, after which I'll proceed to demonstrate my magic. The charms cost only five cash apiece!" He struck the gong, and the spectators crowded even closer, but although there were two or three hundred in the audience, he managed to sell only forty charms. Exasperated at his inability to sell more, he addressed the audience: "Perhaps there is some knowledgeable person among you who would dare to step up and compete with me in magic?" He asked the same question three times, then three more times, but no one stepped forward, and he went on: "With this magic of mine, I have the boy lie down on the bench. I then recite the magic formula, and he enters into an apparent state of sleep." He was just about to demonstrate the magic and perform the trick.

Unfortunately for him, there was a priest in the crowd who was familiar with this particular magic. Offended by Seven Saints' boasting, he recited a formula himself, cried, "Presto!" and caught the boy's soul before anyone else could do so. He tucked the soul in his sleeve, and then, seeing a noodle shop across the way, said to himself, I'm hungry. I'll go over and have a bowl of noodles. There'll be time enough afterward to restore the soul to the boy's body. He entered the shop and went upstairs, where he sat by the window and watched Seven Saints. The waiter set out chopsticks and side dishes and asked how he wanted his noodles done, then went downstairs. While waiting for his noodles, the priest took out the boy's soul and covered it with a saucer.

To return to Seven Saints. When he recited the formula, raised the knife, and cut off the boy's head, the crowd swelled even more. He put the knife down and covered the body with a sheet, then picked up the charms and circled the boy's body several times, reciting the formula. "Gentlemen," he said, "don't blame me for harping on this, but once the boat leaves the shore, I'm afraid there won't be another one. When I've shown you this magic, I'll sell off all these hundred charms!" He lifted the sheet with both hands to look and found that the head had still not joined. The crowd cried out, "When you pull off the sheet, the boy jumps up, but today the head hasn't joined—you've bungled it!"

Seven Saints hastily covered the body with the sheet again and tried to talk his way out of trouble: "Gentlemen, you thought this was going to be easy, did you? Well, I guarantee that this time the head *will* join up!" Once more he clicked his teeth and performed his magic, reciting the formula, but when he pulled up the sheet to look, the head had still not joined. Panic-stricken, he addressed the audience: "Gentlemen! We may be in very different walks of life, but we have one thing in common: we have families to support. I was distracted just now by concerns about money and I failed to use the proper wording—I hope you'll forgive me for it. Let me join up the head, and then I'll come down and share a drink with you—we're all friends within the four seas." Full of remorse, he continued, "It was all my fault, but this time I *will* join it up." He concentrated his mind on reciting the formula, but when he pulled up the sheet to see, the head had still not joined.

In a sudden flash of anger, he cried out, "You're stopping my son's head from joining! I'm pleading with you again; several times I've admitted my faults and asked for your forgiveness, but you *will* insist on this bad behavior!" He took a packet from the bamboo basket behind him, opened it, and picked out a bottle gourd seed. Loosening the earth around him, he planted the seed, then recited a formula, spat out a mouthful of water, and shouted, "Presto!" Lo and behold, a vine appeared and grew steadily larger, branching out with foliage and bursting into flower. Finally it withered, leaving behind a small bottle gourd.

As the crowd applauded, Seven Saints picked the gourd and held it in his left hand, while in his right hand he gripped a knife. "You've behaved most unreasonably. You took my son's soul, preventing me from joining his head to his body. Well, don't hope to go on living in this world any longer!" Taking aim at the gourd, he slashed it across the middle, cutting it in two.

Meanwhile, the priest in the noodle shop was picking up his bowl of noodles and just about to eat them when his head tumbled down from his body. The other people eating noodles in the upstairs room were shocked; the more timid among them abandoned their noodles and fled downstairs, while the bolder ones stood their ground and watched. The priest hastily put down his bowl and chopsticks, got up from his seat, and felt around on the floorboards until he came upon his head. Gripping the two ears with both hands, he replaced the head on his shoulders, setting it in the proper position and then feeling it with one of his hands. I was so preoccupied with my noodles, he thought, that I forgot to return his son's soul to him. He reached out a hand and lifted up the saucer. At the very moment that he did this in the restaurant, Seven Saints' son sprang to his feet outside it, to the applause of the spectators. "I've been practicing this magic all my life," said Seven Saints, "but today I've met my master!"

Among the customers in the noodle shop a lively discussion broke out. One gossipmonger in the crowd said to Seven Saints, "The one who ruined your magic is a priest who's upstairs in this shop." Among the crowd at the time were Inspector Wen and Ran Gui, and when they heard this, Ran Gui said, "Sir, perhaps that priest is the one who cheated Marshal Wang out of his money."

"That may very well be."

"If you see a hare and don't release your falcon, you miss your chance," said Ran Gui. He tipped his turban as a signal to the constables, who let out a roar and burst into the noodle shop. When they saw the priest coming downstairs, they went to seize him, but the priest pointed a finger at them, which led to certain consequences—tumult in the Eastern Capital, uproar in Kaifeng prefecture. Seeing the priest but finding themselves unable to arrest him, the constables were enraged, and a young man avid for wealth died an untimely death.

He yielded to one of the temptations,
And lost that upstanding body of his.

Did the constables manage to catch the priest? Turn to the next chapter to find out.

12

JUDGE BAO ORDERS THE ARREST OF A DEMON PRIEST;

LI TWO INFORMS ON THE DEMON AND FALLS TO HIS DEATH.

POEM:

Content yourself with virtuous poverty;
To unrighteous profit try not to yield.
When the moth strikes the flame, its life is lost;
When the bat meets the pole,[1] its fate is sealed.

When Inspector Wen and his constables burst into the noodle shop, they found a priest descending the stairs. Wen pointed with his iron-jointed whip and ordered his constables to arrest the man, but when the priest saw the constables coming after him, he pointed at them. Lo and behold, the proprietor behind his counter, the waiters scurrying to and fro, and the customers eating their noodles—all of them turned into priests, as did Inspector Wen and his constables. They gazed at one other, stupefied. The constables surveyed the scene before them but didn't know whom to arrest, and in the ensuing commotion, all the customers dispersed. Then Inspector Wen noticed that although the proprietor and the rest of the people had reverted to their original forms, the priest was nowhere to be seen. He told his men to split up and give chase, and also dispatched messengers to each of the city gates with orders that any priest found trying to leave the city should be arrested.

He returned to the yamen just as the prefect was holding his evening session. Wen bowed, and Bao said, "I told you to arrest the demon priest. What happened?"

"Sir, I acted on your order to arrest Pellet Priest," said Wen. "Just now I saw a magician in front of the Great Xiangguo Temple, a magician called Seven Saints Du, who cut off his son's head with one stroke of his knife. Upstairs in the noodle shop opposite was a priest who caught the boy's soul, thus preventing Du from joining his son's head back onto the body. Du became furious, and after planting a bottle gourd seed in the ground, cut the gourd in two—and upstairs in the noodle shop the priest's head rolled off as he was eating his noodles. He groped about on the floor until he found the head, and then fitted it on again—and down below the boy's head also joined up. On seeing this extraordinary sequence of events, I sent my men in to arrest the priest. But he pointed at us, and all the people in the noodle shop, including my constables and me, turned into priests, rendering us utterly helpless. Sir, I beg to report that this kind of demon is indeed truly difficult to arrest. I await Your Honor's further orders."

"With demons of this sort about in the capital, I fear that the court will blame me, as prefect of Kaifeng, if there's any further trouble," said Bao. He ordered the duty clerk to write out proclamations to be hung on all the city gates, informing the personnel of religious establishments that if they could catch Pellet Priest, they would receive a thousand strings from the public purse; if, on the other hand, they took in any priests of dubious background and harbored or hid them without informing the authorities, they as well as their neighbors would be held collectively responsible. The order threw the capital and its environs into an uproar.

In the market district of the Eastern Capital there was a fruit seller named Li Two, who lived with his wife at an inn. Only recently recovered from an illness, he had no capital left to carry on his business. He was accustomed to visiting friends and trying to borrow two or three hundred cash for his daily expenses, but on this particular day he had not managed to borrow anything, and he returned home utterly dejected.

"How did you get on?" his wife asked.

"I tell you, I didn't manage to borrow so much as a single cash. There's such pandemonium in the streets that the vendors can't do any business. They say that yesterday a priest was eating noodles upstairs in a noodle shop when his head suddenly rolled off and fell to the floor. He groped about until he found it, and then, holding it by the ears, planted it back on his neck, where it joined up again. The constables saw these weird goings-on and rushed forward as one man to arrest him, but the priest pointed at them, and everyone in that whole shop changed to look like the priest. Now the prefecture is offering a reward of one thousand strings of cash for the priest's arrest. It turns out that this same man, who's known as Pellet Priest, cheated Marshal Goodman Wang out of three thousand strings just a few days ago."

"Are you telling me the truth?" his wife asked.

"I saw the notice just now. Why would I lie to you?"

"You and I have no food left. Wouldn't it be wonderful if by some lucky chance we were able to catch this priest, claim the thousand strings, and set ourselves up in business?"

"Nonsense! If the authorities heard what you're saying, it'd be no laughing matter, I assure you."

"I guarantee that you can claim that thousand strings."

"And just how are you going to do that?"

"Let me tell you. He could be here, there, or anywhere, but he happens to be right in front of our eyes."

"Where?"

"In the room next door."

"What is it about him that gives him away?"

"He's been living next door to us for three months now, and I've never once seen him go out begging for alms or reading sutras for people. He sleeps until breakfast, then gets up and goes out. Only after dark does he return, and he's always dead drunk. Half a month ago, I ate something that was too cold for me, and I had indigestion and a stomachache. I wanted to go to the back, but I was afraid the room would be too small and I'd leave too much of a smell, so I had to go to the privy behind the inn. As I went past his room, it was midmorning, and I could see a light flashing from inside the room. I thought he must have left a lamp on from the night before, so I peeped through a crack in the wall and saw him lying on his bed with his whole body giving off sparks. He raised his head, and his body soared up from the bed until it was pressing against the rafters. I was so terrified that I didn't dare go to the privy but returned to our room. He simply *has* to be the demon priest."

"Is that true?"

"When have I ever told you a lie?"

"Keep your voice down, then. Don't let this get out."

After giving instructions to his wife, he left the inn and without telling anyone went straight to police headquarters. Once there, however, he did not dare go in but walked to and fro in front of the gate. A constable saw him and called out, "What do you want, Li Two? You keep going to and fro."

"Officer, I have something confidential that I've come specially to tell the inspector about."

"Wait there by the gate while I give him the message."

Inspector Wen was at his tribunal when the constable came in and reported: "Sir, the fruit seller Li Two was walking to and fro outside the gate, and when I asked him why, he said he had something confidential he wanted to tell you."

"Send him in."

The constable went out and brought Li Two into the lower part of the chamber, where he gave a deep bow.

Inspector Wen was afraid of frightening the man, so he adopted a genial tone. "Well, Li Two, what did you want to see me about?"

"Sir, recently I've been ill and unable to work. This morning I went out to do some errands and saw an official proclamation. I can read a little, and I saw that the notice was offering a thousand strings of cash as a reward for the arrest of the demon priest. I went home and told my wife about it, and she said, 'That priest living next door to us is the demon priest.'"

The inspector did not dare show his astonishment. Affecting a smile, he said, "Li Two, in a case such as this we have to be extremely careful. In your and your wife's opinion, what was it about this priest that gave him away?"

Li Two repeated the story that his wife had told him.

"We shall need to follow the correct procedure. Go off and file a formal accusation."

Li Two went out and asked the constable on duty to draft an accusation for him. He then asked for a sheet of paper, copied out the accusation in regular script, and brought it back to the chamber and handed it to the inspector.

"Is the priest at the inn now?" asked Wen.

"He goes out every morning after breakfast and doesn't return until dusk."

"You sit here while I get someone to buy you some wine." Before long the wine arrived and was offered to him. Wen then called in the constables and told Li to act as guide. They left police headquarters and moved to a tea shop beside the inn. After taking a seat in the tea shop, Wen told Li to walk to and fro outside, watching for the priest.

It was not yet dusk when the priest was seen lurching and staggering down the street, dead drunk. Li Two rushed into the tea shop to report to Wen: "Sir, he's here!"

The priest was just passing by the door of the tea shop at the time. Wen pointed him out to the group of constables and gave the order, "Arrest the demon priest." With a roar they rushed forward like eagles swooping down on a swallow or tigers devouring a lamb. Pulling the priest to the ground and trussing him up with a hemp rope, they escorted him under close guard to police headquarters in Sweet Spring Lane.

"Thank goodness!" said Inspector Wen. "We've solved the case and relieved His Honor of his concern." Although the constables trussed the priest up like a stuffed dumpling, he did not awaken from his drunken sleep but continued his snoring.

Wen went directly to the yamen and reported to the prefect. "The demon priest has been arrested. Properly speaking, he should have been brought before you, but he's drunk and unconscious. He's in police headquarters at present. I await your instructions."

Bao told him to see that the priest was held securely and to bring him over in time for the morning session the following day. Wen left and went back to police headquarters, where he saw that the priest had still not awakened. He told the constables to guard him with the utmost care.

Around midnight the priest sobered up, feeling highly uncomfortable. He opened his eyes to find lamps blazing as bright as day and constables sitting on both sides of him. "Where am I?" he asked.

"You're in police headquarters," said the constables.

"What crime have I committed that I'm tied up in here?"

The constables knew well enough that he was a demon priest and they did not dare to provoke him. One of them, an older and more experienced hand, said, "Reverend, you mustn't make the mistake of blaming us for this—we're just doing our job. We all have families at home, and we don't want to bring any trouble down upon ourselves. According to Li Two, the fruit seller who lives next door to you at the inn, in the three months that you've been there you've never once gone out to read sutras for people or beg for alms. Every day you've just gotten drunk. He said you had a suspicious background, and that's why we came and arrested you."

"But I haven't done anything since I received some alms in an official's compound!"

"There's nothing to be done about that now. Wait until tomorrow morning, when you go before His Honor and can argue your case with Li Two."

Toward the fifth watch, Wen told the constables to bring the priest under close arrest to the yamen to await a hearing. As the prefect entered the chamber, his subordinates stood before him. The court was in perfect order, and as for the prefect, he was "a crystal lantern, a brilliant candle lighting up the sky."[2] "Silence in the court!" shouted the runners as Wen escorted the priest into the lower part of the chamber and bowed before the prefect.

The prefect read Li Two's accusation and angrily berated the priest: "You scoundrel! You became a priest, but you weren't content with your lot; you had the gall to cheat someone out of his money!" He ordered the jailers to bring out the long cangue and lock the priest in it, then ordered two strapping jailers to come before him: "Give this priest a hundred strokes. When you've done that, I'll examine him."

The jailers bowed their assent, but they had struck the priest's legs no more than two or three times before an uproar broke out among the audience. "Silence!" shouted the doorkeeper, without producing the slightest effect. The prefect could see the cangue, but he could not see any priest—there was a broom tied up in his place. "How could there *be* such a demon?" he asked. "A moment ago we had him arrested and locked up in the cangue. How is it there's a broom in his place?"

As he spoke, shouts were heard from outside the yamen gate, and the prefect asked in surprise, "What's going on out there?"

"Sir, there's a priest outside the gate who's clapping his hands, roaring with laughter, and calling out, 'Good old Bao Longtu! He can't touch me!'" said the gatekeeper.

Bao was furious. "How dare he insult me like that?" He immediately ordered his men to arrest the man. "Whoever catches this demon priest will get the stipulated reward of one thousand strings!"

The constables rushed out of the yamen gate and went to seize the priest, but he saw them coming and promptly walked to the city market, as casual as you please, the sleeves of his cassock swinging from side to side. The constables spotted him, but when they quickened their pace, he quickened his; when they slowed their pace, he slowed his; and when they stopped altogether, he stopped, too. They pursued him until they were exhausted and came to a halt. They could get within a few dozen paces of him, but they could never quite catch up. They chased him all the way to the front of the Xiangguo Temple. The priest was standing on Yan'an Bridge, and when he saw them coming, he ran into the temple.

"He's cornered," said Wen. "One way or another we'll catch him now." He ordered half his men to surround the front and back gates of the temple and the other half to split up and go through the Buddha Hall and the two porticoes. At this point the abbot of the temple came out, and after greeting Wen, said, "Inspector, this is a court temple. Why are you causing all this disturbance, leading a group of armed men into the temple?"

"I'm under orders from His Honor the prefect, and I have pursued a demon priest into your temple. Don't hide him. If you're wise, you'll tie him up and bring him out."

"My temple has hundreds of priests, all with proper certification," said the abbot. "As for itinerant priests who call at the temple, the monk in charge of reception has never dared let any of them stay the night. If you have pursued someone into the temple, you must know him by sight. In that case, why didn't you arrest him before, instead of coming in here to get him?"

"This demon priest has cheated Marshal Goodman Wang out of three thousand strings of cash and plagued everyone in the prefecture, giving them no peace. If you don't send him out, I'll report that to the prefect, and your temple will be held responsible."

This threat so alarmed the abbot that he said, "But inspector! All our priests have clean records—none is a demon priest. If you don't believe me, I'll call them out so that you can inspect them one by one."

"Very good!" said Wen.

The abbot tolled the bell to summon the hundred or more priests, and then had Inspector Wen examine them. He and his men did so, and found that none was the demon priest. "Abbot!" said Wen, "I pursued him into your temple myself. How could he have disappeared? You will have to let us search the temple."

"I'll lead the way, and you can search." From the monks' cells to the kitchens, the latrines and the storerooms, Wen and his men searched through the temple without success. Turning to the Buddha Hall, they found a statue of a six-spirit Buddha with three heads like mountain peaks and six arms like mountain ranges, each arm holding one of the six items of a monk's possessions.

"You don't have any buddha images in the temple," said Wen. "Why is there a statue of Prince Nezha here?"

"Prince Nezha is the Royal Buddha Aryacalanatha," said the abbot. "He reforms people by rewarding the good and punishing the bad."

Wen and his men saw that the hall was completely empty save for the statue of Nezha. Just as they were leaving, they heard someone from the upper part of the hall shout out, "Inspector Wen! Prefect Bao told you to arrest me. Now that you've seen me, why don't you do it?" Wen and his men turned to look and realized that the sound was coming from Prince Nezha's statue, a plaster work decorated in multiple colors that stood over fifteen feet high. The statue's six arms were shaking, and the middle one of his three heads had its mouth open, with the four canine teeth dripping blood as he called out, "Inspector Wen! Come and arrest me!"

The onlookers were terrified. "A ghost! A ghost!" they cried. They wanted to rush forward and arrest Nezha, but Nezha was a plaster statue. How do you arrest a statue?

"Why don't you get your men to come and arrest me?" Nezha continued.

They consulted together. "Perhaps the plaster statue of Nezha has turned into a malevolent spirit and come out to plague us? Let's go and report to the prefect. We'll need to smash the statue to stop it from coming out and causing trouble."

"Inspector, you can't *do* that!" said the abbot. "The molding and coloring both cost money, and if the statue is smashed, it will be very hard to restore."

"If we don't do away with it now, I fear it will cause disaster in the future!"

From the ranks of the priests one man of notably virtuous character brought his hands together in prayer over his chest and said in front of Buddha, "May the dragon kings and devas and the Three Precious Ones[3] protect the Buddha truth and drive the demon priest out; otherwise, I fear that the god's statue will be destroyed." After he had finished his prayer, they heard someone outside clapping his hands and roaring with laughter: "Here I am, Inspector! Why waste your energy?"

The constables looked—it was the priest. With a roar they surged forward to arrest him. But although they could manage to get within a dozen paces of him, they could never quite catch him. The priest led them out of the Xiangguo Temple and onto the main street. The vendors were prevented from doing their business; their stands were overturned and their tables and chairs knocked over as the number of spectators grew and grew. The constables pursued the priest back and forth and then right out of the city. Passing the Reception Pavilion,[4] they had nearly reached the end of the market when the priest called out, "Don't chase me anymore! I'm going home of my own accord." He gave a glance at the River Bian and leaped. There was a sudden splash. He had leaped into the river.

"We've done it!" said the constables. "He's saved us endless trouble by drowning himself!"

The river had a swift current, and the men said, "I don't know how far his body will be carried before it comes to a stop."

Wen had to go back and report to the prefect, who was in court hearing cases at the time. Bowing deeply, Wen proceeded to give a full account of the arrest of the demon priest.

Prefect Bao listened and said, "Confound the man! I feel so frustrated that I couldn't do anything to him, but at least he's jumped into the river and drowned."

The words were hardly out of his mouth when he heard a woman's voice below the steps protesting an injustice. "What are you protesting about?" the prefect asked.

"Your Honor, because my husband, Li Two, informed on him, the demon priest has been arrested, but my husband is being held in jail. At this point I'm not hoping for any reward money, I just want my husband home so that we can try to make ends meet. I beg Your Honor to rule on the matter."

"Li Two gave us the correct information," said the prefect, "and he deserves to receive the reward. Why is he being held in jail?"

"We haven't put him in jail," said Wen. "He's being held at police headquarters and given food and wine morning and night pending Your Honor's instructions."

The prefect ordered him released, and Wen went straight to police headquarters and told Li Two to appear before the prefect. "Since we posted the notice *before* he gave us the information, it's only right that he should receive the thousand strings reward," said the prefect. At that time in the capital a string of cash was worth one tael of silver, and for an impoverished vendor like Li it was a wonderful boon to receive a thousand strings out of the blue like this. He and his wife accepted the reward money in court, thanked the prefect, and returned to the inn.

From ancient times to the present, storytellers have told the same old story: if you have no money, that's that, but once you acquire some, you have Master A and Master B urging you to spend it and even volunteering to help. Li Two rented a house in front of the Xiangguo Temple itself and set up a large fruit shop. He and his wife enjoyed a comfortable existence.

One winter day about noontime they were sitting before a charcoal stove. They had poured a few cups of wine and were drinking when a man walked in. "Li Two," he said, "if you have any fruit, I'd like to buy some."

Recognizing Pellet Priest, both Li and his wife were struck dumb with fright.

"Li Two," continued the priest, "if it weren't for me, you wouldn't be enjoying the life you lead today. I've come specially to ask for a vegetarian meal." Now, if either Li or his wife had had a grain of sense, they'd have come forward and thanked the priest. Even if they had given him a meal, how much would that have cost them? Surely he didn't really want their food? Perhaps he just came to test them. Alternatively, they could have gracefully declined his request and gotten him out of the house. But Li and his wife were not so sensible, and never in a million years should Li have said what he did say.

"You demon priest!" he said. "We heard you'd been caught by the constables and had leaped into the river and drowned. Why have you come back to our place to cause more trouble? If you have any sense, you'll go away as quickly as you can. If you delay a moment longer, we'll raise the alarm. Don't blame us if the local patrol arrests you and takes you to court!"

"If they could do anything to me, they'd have arrested me a long time ago. You informed on me, and I was accused, whereas I helped you to earn a thousand strings of reward money and live a comfortable life. I came here to visit you, and you ought to have thanked me. Instead you have this wicked idea of calling the constables in to arrest me. You're behaving *most* unreasonably, and I'm going to make you suffer for it!" He pointed and shouted, "Presto!" The fire pan beside Li Two flew up in the air and struck him full in the face, and he fell to the floor screaming. When his wife rushed to his aid and lifted him up, she saw that the charcoal had singed his face, which was now covered in blisters. But when she looked around for the priest, he had disappeared.

Li's burns were unbearably painful. In the days before he had any money, he would have been forced to endure the pain, but because he had all those strings of cash, he called in a doctor to treat him. However, the medicine that the doctor prescribed stung even worse than the burns. Li cried out in agony for three days and nights, and his wife was at her wits' end. Then, just at that point a Daoist priest appeared at the door in a black turban and yellow gown and approached the counter. "Seeking alms!" he called out.

"If we weren't in so much trouble, I wouldn't think twice about giving you two or three cash, but a man's life is in danger here, and I simply don't have the time to give you anything."

"What's the trouble, madam?"

"Let me tell you, Master. A demon priest flung hot coals all over my husband's face, leaving him with a great many blisters that hurt even more when the medicine is applied to them. He's been screaming with pain for three days and nights now, and I fear he's going to die."

"Madam, I have obtained some burn medicine that stops the pain when it's applied and then causes the scabs to fall off. It has proved successful in many cases and has saved numerous lives."

"Even if it doesn't cure him, so long as it stops the pain, I'll give you a handsome reward."

"Then ask him to come out here. And do get me some water." She went in and helped her husband out, and also handed the master a cup of water. He shook some medicine from a packet into the water, then steeped a goose feather in the mixture and spread it over the sores.

Li Two cried out in delight. "What marvelous medicine! My burns have stopped hurting, just as if ice and snow had been applied to them."

"You can hardly call that marvelous! What would you say if I made the scabs fall off and cured you altogether?"

"If you could do that, I'd be everlastingly grateful, Master."

"You're suffering from what's called 'evil heat.' You need to go outside and face the breeze in some cool spot, and the scabs will fall off."

Li Two followed the priest's directions and went out to the street. The master told him to sit on a stool, and then said, "Now say, 'Off with the scabs' three times, and they'll fall off."

Li was more than delighted to hear this, and he yelled out the words at the top of his lungs, at which the stool soared up into the sky and came to rest squarely on top of the hundred-foot-tall flagstaff of the Xiangguo Temple. The people on the street below set up a great commotion, and when Li's wife came out to see what the matter was, she received a terrible shock. "Oh, no!" she cried. "Master, how can my husband get down?"

"Don't panic! I'll get him down. Let me show you who I really am." He took off his yellow robe and black turban, and when she looked more closely, she let out a cry of horror—it was the demon priest.

"Your husband was most unreasonable," said the priest. "He set his heart on destroying me, but he couldn't do it. And now I'm going to make him sense a little fear on top of that flagpole!"

A vociferous crowd had gathered in the street below to watch what was happening. Among them were some constables, who said, "The authorities have just posted notices offering tons of money for capturing the demon. This priest is up to his old tricks again, and we'll surely be held responsible." The constables and bailiffs[5] rushed forward to arrest the priest, but he slipped into the crowd and was lost to sight. "We've never seen such a fantastic thing in all our lives!" people cried.

Li Two clung tightly to the top of the flagpole. There was no way he could possibly get down. The spectators discussed how to rescue him, but there was no ladder long enough to reach him, and the entire population, soldiers as well as civilians, was thrown into a state of alarm. "How terrifying that priest is!" they said. "That fellow will *never* be able to get down!"

The local patrolmen raced off to tell Prefect Bao, who came immediately by sedan chair. He stepped out, opened up a folding chair, and sat down in front of the temple. On looking up, he saw Li Two sitting on a stool on top of the flagpole, shouting for help. Concluding that there was no way to get him down, Bao summoned Li's wife and questioned her.

She prostrated herself before him. "How did your husband happen to get up there?" he asked. "Tell me the truth, now." She told him the whole story in detail of how the priest had asked for alms and then burned her husband's face, and how the Daoist master had treated him.

"That confounded demon priest has behaved outrageously! The next time we catch him, we'll show him no mercy whatsoever!" The words were hardly out of Bao's mouth when a priest approached from the side of the Buddha Hall and bowed deeply before him.

Prefect Bao glared at him. "Well, priest, what business do you have with me?"

"I know how to get Li Two down."

"If you can rescue Li Two, I'll reward you with a vegetarian meal."

The priest then shinned up the flagpole, threw both arms around Li Two, and proclaimed in a loud voice, "Bao Longtu! You're an honest official, and I wouldn't have dared to upset you. But what did my begging three thousand strings from Marshal Wang have to do with you, that you should try to arrest me? I have nothing else to repay you with, so I'm returning Li Two to you instead!" From high up in the air he flung Li Two to the ground. The crowd let out a horrified cry, and when they looked at Li Two, they saw

His frame was like the moon at dawn, sunk below the hills,
His life was like a midnight lamp, its oil run dry.

Did Li Two lose his life in the end? Turn to the next chapter to find out.

13

ETERNA SELLS MUD CANDLES AND SEDUCES WANG ZE;

PRIESTESS PIA TEACHES WANG ZE HOW TO PLAN A REVOLT.

POEM:

The demonic magic works its wonders;
The immortals' wisdom it can outdo.
Consider these candles Eterna makes—
From dusk to dawn they last the whole night through.

Li Two should never have informed on the priest for the sake of a thousand-string reward. However, after obtaining that reward and using it as capital to open up a fruit shop, he should have repaid the favor the priest had done him. Instead of which he deliberately offended the priest when the latter came begging for a meal.

That day he was thrown down from the top of the flagpole directly in front of Prefect Bao, who saw that he had fallen head-first and that the force of the impact had driven his head right into his chest. How tragic! Might his spirit partake of the sacrificial offerings! Li's wife burst into a loud sobbing. Needless to say, she had to get people to carry the corpse back home for the laying in. And there we shall leave her.

Meanwhile, as the priest sat on a stool on top of the flagpole, the sea of spectators grew larger and larger. Many of them started to clamor, and Bao's men could not quiet them down. Bao surveyed the situation, but he had no idea how to arrest the priest. He would have had the flagpole chopped down, but whereas the flagpoles in all the other temples were made of wood, this one was cast in bronze—hard though it is to imagine how a hundred-foot-long pole could ever have been cast.

As it happens, this Xiangguo Temple had three famous historical sites. There was a well in front of the Buddha Hall that was three hundred feet deep. It was equipped with a rope woven of human hair and a bucket that was painted black with these characters on it in red: "For Public Use in the Great Xiangguo Temple." One day the rope broke, and the well bucket could not be retrieved. Later, someone returning from a voyage overseas came to the Xiangguo Temple and said, "I was a passenger on a ship traveling in the Eastern Sea when I saw a well bucket floating on the surface of the water. The sailors pulled it out, and on it were the characters 'For Public Use in the Great Xiangguo Temple.' As we gazed at it, the waves sprang up and almost capsized our ship. I at once took a vow to return the bucket to the temple, and the waves promptly subsided. I am now fulfilling that vow." This incident shows that the temple well is directly connected to the Eastern Sea.

In front of the temple gate there is a bridge called the Yan'an Bridge. From it the temple appears to be down at the bottom of a well, but viewed from the temple, the bridge appears to be a hundred yards or more lower than the temple's own foundations.

Together with the bronze flagstaff that was impervious to axe and saw, these were the temple's three famous historical sites.

As the priest continued to taunt him from the top of the flagpole, Prefect Bao became highly indignant, but there was nothing he could do about it. Then suddenly an idea occurred to him, and he ordered a hundred archers to be summoned from the camp. A messenger promptly called the men, and Bao told them to surround the flagpole and shoot at the top. Among the archers there were some good marksmen, and they shot at the priest, but he managed to protect himself with his sleeves. Then just as Bao was at a loss as to what to do, a Daoist priest came to see him. "What do you have to tell me?" asked the prefect.

"I saw how offensive that demon priest was, and I've come specially to offer you a plan to capture him."

"And what plan do you propose, Master?"

"He's a demon priest, so you should dip your arrowheads in a mixture of pig's and sheep's blood, horse urine, and garlic before you shoot at him. That way he won't be able to use his black magic." The priest gave a bow and departed.

Prefect Bao ordered that pig's and sheep's blood, horse's urine, and garlic be procured, and his staff went off in different directions to get it. The prefect had them mixed together and told the archers to dip their arrowheads in the mixture. Then at the sound of a clapper, all one hundred bows let fly. Had they not done so, nothing untoward would have happened, but one hundred arrows sped toward their mark, and a great roar arose among the thousand or more people watching from inside and outside the temple as they saw both priest and stool come tumbling down out of the sky.

"If he's not killed, he's bound to be crippled for life!" they cried.

However, there was a pond on the west side of the temple, and the priest fell fair and square into the middle of that pond. The constables dragged him out and at the pond's edge poured a bucket of pig's and sheep's blood over his bald head before they tied him up. Prefect Bao then took a sedan chair back to his yamen and gave orders that the priest be brought before him under guard.

"Confound you, demon priest! You had the gall to come here to the imperial capital and use your demonic arts to harm the people. What do you have to say for yourself, now that we've caught you?" He ordered that the Number 1 cangue be brought out and the priest placed in it, then had him taken under guard to the interrogating officer of the Right Army, who should find out his name and place of origin. In case he had followers, a thorough investigation must be made and the followers arrested. Having given these orders, the prefect went off to rest.

Because of the urine and blood covering his body, the priest could not employ his demonic arts. He was escorted by a squad of constables from the prefect's yamen to the interrogation department of the Right Army. The officer in charge said to the priest, "On the orders of His Honor the prefect, I am going to question you about your activities. You must have been staying in a monastery. How many others are in league with you? Very well then, since I can't get anything out of you . . ." He told the warders to pull the priest down and thrash him. They tied his feet to the end of the cangue bar so that he couldn't budge and subjected him to three hundred severe strokes of the rod. However, the priest did not utter a word, nor did he cry out in pain, and when the officer took a closer look, he found that the man was asleep and snoring. "That's incredible!" he muttered, and called on the jailers to lock the priest up in prison and bring him out later for interrogation. From then on he was beaten three times a day, until the jailers themselves reached the point of exhaustion. The priest, however, continued to act unconcerned and refused to say anything. Whenever they beat him, he would go off to sleep. After the officer had interrogated him for over ten days, he felt utterly frustrated and had to report as much to the prefect: "Sir, I received your order several days ago to interrogate the demon priest. He has been beaten three times a day, but whenever he's beaten, he goes off to sleep. This sort of demon priest is truly difficult to interrogate, but if we keep him in jail, I am afraid we shall face serious trouble in the future. I respectfully await your order."

"What's the point of keeping a demon priest like that in jail?" asked Bao. He promptly issued a written order setting the appropriate sentence according to the law: the priest was to be taken out to the marketplace and beheaded. The officer on duty had him escorted out of the jail and rushed to the execution ground. The placard stating his conviction read as follows: "For deliberately murdering Li Two and practicing the demonic arts in the Eastern Capital, for harassing and harming the public, the criminal known as Pellet Priest is hereby sentenced to be beheaded according to the law." People living both inside and outside the capital heard that a demon priest was about to be executed, and all the vendors shut down their businesses and went to watch. The spectators were packed together all along the route as the executioners, with the placard carried in front and the armed guards following behind, escorted the demon priest out of the offices of the Right Army.

When they arrived at a point not far from the center of the marketplace, the priest halted. "Be a good fellow and keep going," said the executioners. "Why have you stopped?"

"Gentlemen, it was wrong of me to upset the prefect, and I am now paying the penalty. But officers! Just up ahead there's a tavern that sells wine! Get me a cupful before I depart this life!" The executioners could hardly refuse his request; they asked for some wine and brought a dipperful back for him. He put his lips to the dipper and drank most of the wine, after which the escorts urged him to start walking again. However, the priest had retained some of the wine in his mouth, and when they approached the execution ground, he spat it up into the sky. It was a clear day, but out of nowhere a storm sprang up, and as the gale raged, a black fog blanketed the execution ground, and stones and pieces of tile pelted down on the spectators' heads, causing them all to flee. Before long the gale subsided and the fog lifted, but when the jailers and executioners and the official in charge looked at the priest, they found that he had burst his bonds and disappeared. Although they searched for him everywhere, they found no trace of him. From the officer in charge down to the jailers and executioners, they were all desperately worried: "I'm afraid the prefect will blame us for letting that priest get away, and we'll all suffer for it." But they could not avoid their duty to report the incident. When Bao heard, he mounted his tribunal, and the officer in charge along with the others who had escorted the priest admitted their error and asked to be punished. But Bao, who realized that with the appearance of demons the court would need to use armed force, was reluctant to subject people to indiscriminate prosecution, and so he freed them all. That night he wrote a memorial to the court stressing that if the problem were dealt with at an early stage it would be comparatively easy to solve, but that if the demons were allowed to multiply, they would be a great deal harder to suppress. The court duly issued an imperial order that inspections be carried out throughout the country, in all districts and villages, and that great care be taken to investigate and suppress the demons.

The order reached Beizhou in Hebei province, where the proclamation was hung up in front of the prefectural yamen, a particularly busy area. There was a young woman there wearing mourning dress and carrying a basket who walked to and fro in front of the yamen some five or six times. Had she been plain looking, no one would have followed her, but although she was not dressed up, she was strikingly beautiful. There were idle characters standing about, and one of them said to her, "Sister, I've seen you walking to and fro half a dozen times. Why are you doing that?"

"To be honest with you, brother, I lost my husband and have no way of making a living. I possess just this one skill with which I can earn three or four hundred cash to live on."

"And what skill might that be, sister?"

"Unless I have an empty space, I can't show you. I can only do it if I have a space."

The man chased away the musicians and gamblers. "Here's a good spot," he said. "The buskers have been using it. You'll do well here."

She sat herself down on the ground and crossed her legs, while twenty or thirty men stood around, drawn first by her beauty and second because she was about to put on a show. "I wonder what she's selling," they said to themselves.

They watched as she took a bowl out of her basket and said to them, "Gentlemen, I'm no street performer, nor can I sell medicines or tell fortunes. Since I lost my husband I've been at my wits' end, and I need to come out and earn twenty or thirty cash every day. Would one of you brothers like to take this bowl and fill it up with water for me?"

"I'll go!" said one youth. He was back in no time with a bowl of water.

"I wonder what she's selling that she needs water for," said the spectators.

The woman opened the basket and took out a glistening knife.

"Perhaps she knows how to do magic tricks," said one of the spectators. They watched as she dug up some soil with the point of the knife, loosened it, poured half the water into the middle of the soil, and made a lump of mud. From the basket she took several bamboo strips and, kneading a piece of the mud, worked one of the strips into the form of a candle. Then she kneaded another piece of mud and worked another strip of bamboo into a second candle. Before long she had made ten candles, all arranged on the ground. The spectators pressed closer and began scoffing at her efforts. "For no earthly reason we've let ourselves be deceived by this woman! She's taken all this time, shown no skill whatsoever, and stupidly produced a few mud candles. What good are they?"

"Shut up!" said someone else. "She looks as if she knows what she's doing."

They watched as she washed her hands in the water left in the bowl and said, "After I lost my husband, I had no way to get by, but I don't want to be too greedy, just to make three cash on a candle. Here are ten candles, which I'll sell for thirty cash. If you light one of them in the evening, it will last you until dawn."

The spectators laughed. "She's making fun of us Beizhou locals! How can you light mud candles when they're freshly made and the mud's not even dry? She's obviously making fun of us!" No one came forward to buy any of the candles.

When she saw that no one wanted to buy her candles, she said, "How suspicious you Beizhou people are! Do you really think I'd tell a lie just to cheat you out of three cash? Which one of you will go and get me a light?" A certain Master Shen, an idler from the city morgue,[1] offered to go to the tea shop for an ember, which he handed to the woman. She took a sulfur taper from her basket, lit it from the ember, and then lit the tops of the mud candles.

The audience burst into applause. "What a wonderful trick! A damp mud candle that can be lit, and it costs only three cash! Of course we'll buy one!"

One enthusiastic customer took out three cash and gave them to her. She accepted the money, picked up one of the candles, blew it out, and handed it to him. In no time at all the ten candles had been sold. She got to her feet, gathered up the knife and the bowl and put them in her basket, curtsied to the spectators, and left the scene.

The following day she was back at the same space, and people crowded around to watch. "Yesterday thanks to you I managed to sell thirty cash worth of candles, and I had enough to live on for a day. Now I've come back to impose on you once more."

"Truly amazing!" they said. "Yesterday we bought a candle for three cash, and it really did last all night. The light was brighter than that of any lamp, and we saved ten cash on oil."

The woman asked for water, dug up some more soil, and made another ten mud candles.

"You don't need to light them!" said the crowd of spectators as they competed with one another to buy the candles. When she had made another thirty cash, she packed up and left. From then on she came every day. The candles had barely left her hands before someone bought them, but each day she sold only ten. Within half a month she had created a sensation among the people of Beizhou, who said, "There's a woman in front of the yamen who makes candles that not only last longer than other candles but are brighter as well."

One day she was at the same place and had made half the day's candles when someone came walking out of the yamen. The spectators saw that he was a professional army officer[2] named Wang Ze, assigned as an aide to the prefect. On this occasion he had come to the yamen at the fifth watch to register and now, having finished his day's work, was coming out again when he noticed a crowd of people gathered in a circle watching something. Standing on tiptoe, he saw that it was a woman in mourning dress who was sitting on the ground. When he looked at her more closely, this is what he saw:

In a plain white dress
And mourning skirt;
With neither powder nor rouge
Her naturalness enchants;

Without adornment of any kind,
Her inborn beauty dazzles.
Her hair puffs half in place,
A face to make fish dive and birds fall from the sky;
Starry eyes full of tenderness,
Beauty to humble the moon and put the flowers to shame.
Like Chang'e[3] come down from the Moon Palace,
Like Weaving Maid[4] descending from the Jasper Pool.

"What's that woman doing over there?" Wang Ze asked his attendant.

"She's selling mud candles, sir," said the attendant.

"I've been busy every day in the yamen, but for some time I've been hearing talk of a woman selling mud candles. A fellow officer told me he bought one and lit it, and it gave off a bright light. I meant to ask him why it's called a mud candle."

"It's an amazing story," said the attendant. "She digs up some soil, mixes it with water, kneads it around a bamboo strip until it looks like a candle, and then lights it from a lamp. It lasts from dusk until dawn."

How very strange, thought Wang Ze. I've always enjoyed magic tricks, but this one is truly astonishing. He squeezed his way through the crowd and saw the woman, who had finished her work and was washing her hands. "These candles of mine sell for three cash apiece," she said as the spectators fought with one another to buy them.

"Stop!" shouted Wang Ze. "Don't buy them, any of you!" The spectators knew that Wang Ze was a professional army officer, and when he said, "Don't buy!" they didn't dare disobey.

The woman looked up, saw Wang Ze, and rose to her feet, greeting him and curtsying. He bowed in response.

"You make candles out of mud, but how do you get them to light up?" he asked.

"Sir, I've been selling them here for half a month now, and if they didn't light up, people wouldn't come asking for them. I make only ten a day, but I still wouldn't be able to sell any."

"Now, don't try to fool me!" Wang Ze said. He put his hand inside his lapel, took thirty cash from his wallet, and bought all ten candles. As she handed them to him, he said, "Just a moment! If I buy them and they don't light up, I'll have wasted my money. It's not that I don't believe you, but I haven't actually seen them yet. Light one up and show me."

"That's simple enough. Just send someone for an ember." Wang Ze told his attendant to go and get one and give it to the woman. She used it to light a taper and then lit all ten candles for Wang Ze to see.

He was effusive in his praise. "Splendid! That's truly amazing! But I don't need the ten candles myself. If you people would like them, please help yourselves." The spectators took the candles and went off. Meanwhile the woman got to her feet, gathered up the knife and bowl and put them in her basket, then curtsied to everyone and left the scene.

Wang Ze sent his attendant back and then followed the woman at a leisurely pace. She's not one of us Beizhou people, he thought to himself; I expect she lives in the village market. I think I'll follow her to her place and offer to pay for some lessons in this kind of magic. The woman went through West Gate, past the village market, and kept on walking. If she doesn't live in the market, I wonder where she does live, Wang Ze asked himself. She walked on for another three or more miles, to a place that Wang Ze did not recognize. She really is the strangest person, he thought. I think I'll go back and wait till she comes to sell her wares tomorrow and then ask her where she lives. He turned and was about to go back when he saw that the road before him was different from the one he had come on. Sheer cliffs towered up, and tall mountains blocked all passage; there was no way to return, and there were no people about whom he could ask. In his state of alarm, he heard the woman ahead of him shouting, "Officer Wang! I had a hard time getting you this far. Why do you want to go back so soon?"

He was so terrified that he started to tremble. "Madam, who are you?" he asked, approaching her.

"Officer, Priestess Pia sent me to invite you to discuss certain great issues. There's no need to be suspicious—I'll go with you." How strange, thought Wang Ze. He would have liked to go back, but he had lost his way and had no choice but to follow her. They entered a pine forest and then after a long time wound their way through it and came to a manor house.

"What *is* this place?" asked Wang Ze.

"This is where Priestess Pia lives. She's been waiting for you for a long time."

As Wang Ze arrived at the manor house, out came two maidservants dressed in black. "Is this gentleman Officer Wang?" they asked.

"Yes," said the woman.

"The priestess has been waiting for you for a long time," said the maidservants, leading Wang Ze into the lower part of the hall. "Officer Wang is here!" they reported.

Wang Ze saw an old lady wearing a star headdress and a robe woven of crane's down[5] who was sitting at the head of the hall.

"This is the priestess," said the woman who had brought him. "Why don't you pay your respects?" Wang Ze bowed low, and the priestess called him up to the head of the hall, where the three of them sat down together. She ordered tea to be served, and when they had finished their tea, she told the maidservants to serve him wine. Wang Ze was of an ambitious nature, and he was flattered by all the attention he was receiving.

"It was fate that enabled me to meet you today, priestess," he said, adding, "I wonder what wisdom you care to impart."

"Let me discuss it with you as you drink your wine. The destined moment is now upon us, and you fit the design of heaven—you're bound to make a great name for yourself. Of the thirty-six prefectures in Hebei province, you are destined to become sole ruler."

"You shouldn't say such things, priestess," said Wang Ze. "The eyes and ears of the authorities are everywhere. I'm merely a soldier stationed in Beizhou—how could I aspire to become ruler of the thirty-six prefectures?"

"If you didn't have that particular good fortune in store for you, I would never have sent anyone to invite you here. I'm just afraid that you may let this opportunity slip, which would be a great pity! And there is one other thing. I've been worrying that you'll be all on your own and will need someone else's help in order to succeed." She pointed toward the woman who had sold the mud candles and said, "I have this daughter named Eterna, a virgin, who is your predestined lover from five hundred years ago. Marry her now, and she'll help you in your task. What do you say?"

Wang Ze was secretly thrilled. My own wife died last year, he reflected. If today the priestess gives me this beautiful girl in marriage, it is surely a heaven-sent destiny. "Thank you, priestess, for your kindness," he said. "I wouldn't dare to decline. A few years ago I met a holy man who predicted that I would eventually make a great name for myself; he even tattooed the word 'Blessed' on my back. The favor you are doing me now confirms his prediction. There is one problem, however. The prefect of Beizhou, confound the man, asked me to buy him a lot of articles of gold and silver, silk and satin but then refused to pay the shopkeepers for them. All the trades and professions suffered, and they're seething with resentment. The officers and men of the two battalions stationed in Beizhou have served for three months, but this prefect has refused to issue even one month's pay. If they opposed him, they wouldn't stand a chance—he has far too much influence at court. My fellow officers and I have suffered countless wrongs at that man's hands, but if we don't have the strength to drive out one tyrannical official, how can we hope to succeed in the great enterprise?"

The priestess smiled. "You can't act on your own, you know. You would need to rely on your wife. She has a hundred thousand men and horses under her command to help you, and together with her you could certainly succeed in rebelling."

"I've heard that an army on the march needs a thousand in gold every day," said Wang Ze with a smile. "And when they stop anywhere for even a little while, all the rivers and lakes run dry. With so many men and horses, you would need a vast amount of provisions. And no matter how large this manor house is, where would you quarter a hundred thousand men and horses?"

The priestess smiled. "Our men and horses don't need provisions or quarters. When there's an urgent need for them, they're put to use; otherwise, they're put away."

"It would be all very fine, if that were the case."

"Let me show you our men and horses." She told Eterna to go in and fetch two small baskets, one full of beans, the other full of snippets of rice straw. Eterna took some beans and some straw between her fingers and scattered them around, shouting, "Presto!" as she did so. The beans and straw turned into two hundred or more mounted men at the front of the hall.

Wang Ze applauded. "Since you have the skill to turn straw into horses and beans into soldiers, we need have no fears about the great enterprise."

As he said these words, shouts were heard from outside the manor house. "Such fine goings-on in there! The authorities have just put out notices calling for the arrest of demons, and here you are making horses out of straw and soldiers out of beans, preparing to start a rebellion!" Terrified by the shouts, Wang Ze felt as if his cranium had been opened up and half a bucket of ice and snow poured inside it.

Before the plot was hatched, how was it heard outside?
With the plans barely made, trouble breaks out at home.

Truly,

You may draw up plans of cosmic scope,
But eavesdropping you cannot prevent.

Who was this newcomer? Turn to the next chapter to find out.

14

LAME PRIEST DISTRIBUTES MONEY AND RICE TO RAISE AN ARMY;

WANG ZE IS CHARGED WITH A CRIME AND THROWN INTO JAIL.

POEM:

The false doctrines[1] lack the real art, they say,
Fearing its secrets exist no more.
But if you know them, and your heart is true,
Why need you seek the immortals' lore?

Wang Ze was watching the mounted men when, in the midst of his conversation with the priestess, someone could be heard shouting, "Are you plotting a rebellion in there?" and he began to tremble with fright. When he looked up, however, he saw a person of wonderfully bizarre appearance wearing an iron-frame Daoist cap, straw sandals, and a scarlet robe with a black border. His complexion was a purplish red, his eyes were like strange stars, and he rode into the manor house on the back of a tiger.

"Master Zhang!" exclaimed the priestess. "I was in the middle of a discussion with Officer Wang. Come in if you want to, but why make such a to-do about it?"

The master jumped down from the tiger's back, shouted, "Off with you!" and the tiger ran outside. He then paid his respects to the priestess. Wang Ze bowed to the master, who returned the gesture and took a seat.

"Master Zhang," said the priestess, "this is Officer Wang of Beizhou. In five days' time you will all be going to his aid."

"I'm Zhang Luan," said the master to Wang Ze. "I've often said to the priestess that you could make yourself the sole ruler of this area. Several times I've thought of visiting you, but I was afraid you might not be willing to see me, so I didn't dare. But priestess, how did you get Officer Wang to come here?"

"I sent Eterna to Beizhou to perform a little magic in front of the yamen and lure him into coming. We were just discussing what to do when you arrived."

"When is he going to rebel?"

"Very soon now. Once the mood of the army units changes, he'll spring into action, and you and the others will go and help." She had barely finished saying this when a strange beast came in. Wang Ze looked—it was a lion, which entered the thatched hall and prowled around, roaring as it did so. Wang Ze was both terrified and elated. This is a celestial creature, he thought; how could there be one like it on earth as well? It must be my destiny to meet it."

He was about to ask the priestess, when she started shouting at the lion: "You wretch! Since you've come to help Officer Wang, why do you need to play these tricks on him? Put your magic powers away!" The lion shook its head and vanished. In its place stood a man.

"Who is this?" Wang Ze asked the priestess.

"His name is Bu Ji." She told Bu Ji to pay his respects to Wang Ze. After he had done so, he took a seat in the upper part of the thatched hall. "Officer Wang, did you see Zhang Luan's and Bu Ji's skills?"

"Those two are so remarkable I don't doubt that we'll succeed."

"There's one other person we need to get, to make sure that you succeed."

"Who is that?" As he said these words, a celestial crane flew down from the sky and landed in the thatched hall. A man jumped off its back, and Zhang Luan, Bu Ji, and Eterna all bowed before him. Wang Ze saw that the man was not more than four feet tall, and that he was wearing a tattered turban, a coarse cloth gown, torn leggings, and hemp shoes with the grommets shorn off. A black sash was tied around his waist. Noting these things, Wang Ze did not get up to greet him. I wonder who this could be, he thought.

"Officer Wang!" called the priestess. "This is my son, Zuo Chu. If you had his help, you would certainly succeed in your great enterprise. Why don't you get up and greet him?" Wang Ze scrambled to his feet and bowed.

Zuo Chu came up to the head of the thatched hall, bowed to the priestess, and sat down beside the others. "Madam," he said to the priestess, "has the date been set for Officer Wang's rebellion?"

"Son, the sooner the better, given the circumstances. We were just waiting for you to arrive in order to set the date."

"It's too late today," said Zuo Chu. "Let's take Officer Wang back." To Wang Ze he said, "Tomorrow I'll come to Beizhou with Zhang Luan and Bu Ji and help you with the rebellion."

Wang Ze thanked Priestess Pia and the others, and Eterna led him out of the manor house and through a forest, then pointed to the road he should take. When he turned back to look at her, however, she had vanished. He walked a few steps further and was astonished to find that he had arrived at the gates of Beizhou. How very strange, he thought. A while ago I had to walk for ages to reach the priestess's manor house, but now I've arrived at the city gates after just a few steps. Those people must all be supernatural beings who can practice magic. If they come to my aid, I shall certainly make a name for myself.

He entered the city and went to his house, where nothing of significance happened that night. He was not on duty the next day, but when dawn came, he received a shock. This is another strange thing, he thought: Why has all my furniture disappeared? And where did this roomful of rice come from? He had scarcely finished asking himself these questions when he saw three men coming in the door—Zuo Chu, Zhang Luan, and Bu Ji. "Since you're my guests, I ought to offer you some tea," said Wang Ze when they had greeted one another, "but I don't have any servants. I wonder if you'd be willing to accompany me to the tavern next door for a few cups of wine?"

"Don't say a *few* cups," said Zuo Chu. "Let's drink until we're really drunk!"

"I'm off duty today, so it's a good time for a long session," said Wang Ze.

The four men moved to a table near an upstairs window in the tavern and were drinking there when a squad of soldiers came marching by with banners flying. "This isn't scheduled as a day for drill," said Wang Ze. "Why have all these soldiers come out from the two battalions?"

"Officer Wang," said Zuo Chu, "go down and ask them."

Wang Ze went downstairs and out the door. The soldiers all knew him, and they came forward and greeted him. "Where have you men been?" he asked them.

"Officer Wang," the battalion commander said, "the prefect is grinding us professionals down! We've served for three months, and he's not even issued us with money and rice for the first month. We went to the granary this morning, but he drove us away."

"Well, what do you plan to do about it?"

"If he won't issue the money and rice tomorrow, we'll have to mutiny!" The commander and his men went off, while Wang Ze returned upstairs and reported to Zuo Chu what he had said.

Zuo Chu sprang to his feet. "Rush after them and tell them to come back and you'll give them a month's supply yourself! That should bring them over to your side."

"But Master!" protested Wang Ze. "Where are we going to get all that money and rice?"

"You just bring the soldiers back. I know how to provide it."

Wang Ze rushed after the commander and asked him to bring his men to a halt. If they came back, he said, he would give them a month's supply of money and rice. The commander ordered a large number of men to Wang Ze's house, which they found piled high with rice.

"Soldiers," said Zuo Chu, "so long as you have the strength, it doesn't matter whether you take one picul or two of rice. Just don't quarrel among yourselves." In groups of three and four, the soldiers came forward and carried the rice away, some taking a picul and a half, others taking two piculs.

"We have less than two hundred piculs," said Wang Ze, "as against the six thousand men in the two battalions. How are we going to provide for all of them?"

"Don't you worry about that," said Zuo Chu. "I'll guarantee that they all get supplied with rice."

The soldiers worked from breakfast until noontime, moving over ten thousand piculs, and still there were four or five left in the house. The commander and his men came to thank Wang Ze.

"Officer Wang," Zuo Chu said to him, "it's still early. Have a word with the battalion commander and tell him to announce to his men that they can come by today and collect one month's wages."

The commander was thrilled to hear this, and he raced back and announced to his men that they could come and collect their pay.

"Master, you've distributed a great deal of rice," Wang Ze said to Zuo Chu, "but where is the money?"

"I have it," replied Zuo Chu, sending Zhang Luan and Bu Ji inside to begin carrying it out. With a thousand strings in each pile, the room was soon stacked full of money. Even before they had finished stacking it, the soldiers were at the door, and Wang Ze allowed them to come in and carry the money away. They went on doing so until evening, by which time every man in the two battalions had been paid. Of the six thousand men and their families, none failed to sing the praises of Wang Ze: "Good old Officer Wang! Who else but he would have been willing to let people come in and take his money and rice away? If you were quick and strong enough, you now have three months' supply of rice and money in your home. So what do we have to worry about?" Zuo Chu, Zhang Luan, and Bu Ji, having distributed all the money and rice, took their leave, arranging to come back the following day.

Wang Ze was on duty that day. At the third quarter of the fifth watch he entered the yamen and attended the prefect, who was mounting his tribunal. The prefect's name was Zhang De, and the inhabitants of the prefecture cursed him as

A beast wrapped up in silks and satins,
A swine fed only on the choicest morsels.

This prefect never paid any attention to his proper duties; he was interested only in acquiring money. Taking his seat at the head of the chamber, he now called on his aide, Wang Ze. From the lower part of the chamber Wang Ze bowed and said, "At your service, sir."

"Wang Ze," said the prefect, "I understand you're so wealthy that yesterday you took my place and distributed money and rice to six thousand soldiers. If you distributed it to them, why didn't you offer me any?"

Wang Ze didn't dare tell him that the money and rice had been magically created by the three men and had to reluctantly agree to the prefect's demand. He was just about to set off when two men stepped forward dressed in purple robes with silk sashes around their waists. One of them bowed and reported to the prefect, "Your Honor! All the rice in one of our storehouses has disappeared, even though the locks have not been tampered with!"

The prefect was shocked. He was at a complete loss until the keeper of the treasury stepped forward, bowed, and reported, "Your Honor! All the money in the treasury has disappeared, even though the locks have not been tampered with!"

"*Now* I understand!" exclaimed the prefect. "Wang Ze, my storehouse has lost its rice and my treasury its money. You have neither storehouse nor treasury, so how did you manage to distribute both rice and money to six thousand men?"

He ordered the jailers to bring out the long cangue and had Wang Ze locked in it right there in the chamber. He was then taken to the jail and turned over to the Office of Public Order for questioning. Because Prefect Zhang sent Wang Ze to jail, certain consequences followed: the prefect's head parted company with his body, all his family died untimely deaths, and the people of Beizhou were prevented from leading peaceful lives. This state of affairs continued until the court raised an army to root out the demons and retake the area. Truly

The corrupt official deserves to die;
Demons are agents of his early doom.

What disaster was it that the prefect provoked? Turn to the next chapter to find out.

15

LAME PRIEST RESCUES WANG ZE BY PARALYZING THE REST;

LIU YANWEI LEADS AN ARMY TO CAPTURE WANG ZE.

POEM:

Winning the empire is easy, they say,
But of ten who rebel, nine are destroyed.
Even if you wield unearthly powers,
Present disaster is hard to avoid.

In his fury the prefect had Wang Ze locked up in a cangue and sent to the Office of Public Order for interrogation as prescribed by law. The official doing the interrogation, a man named Wang Jiang, asked him, "Yesterday you are said to have distributed money and rice to the professional soldiers of both battalions; how did you have room in your house to store it all? And today all the money in the prefectural treasury and all the rice in the prefectural granary are missing; how did you manage to get it out?"

At first Wang Ze denied everything, but eventually the torture proved too much for him and he had to confess: "I was off duty yesterday, and I was relaxing at home when I noticed a number of professionals going past my door full of resentment. 'We've served for three months,' they said, 'and we've not been able to draw a single month's money or rice.' On top of that, three people turned up from I don't know where and, despite my protests, took over my house and started distributing money and rice to the six thousand men. Afterward they simply left, and I truly don't know their names."

"Do you mean to tell me that you didn't know who they were and without asking them anything about themselves you just let them use your house to distribute money and rice?" The official ordered the jailers to pull Wang Ze down and tighten the cangue with all their strength, then give him a beating. Wang Ze couldn't bear the pain and had to confess: "One is Zhang Luan, another is Bu Ji, and the third is known as Lame Priest Zuo Chu." The official had Wang Ze sign his confession and then sent him back to jail before reporting to the prefect. Notices were issued for the arrest of the three men.

Meanwhile the six thousand men of the two battalions, together with their families, were fully aware that the prefect was blaming Wang Ze for issuing the money and rice and had sent him to suffer in jail. In the taverns and teahouses, everyone was talking about the case—and uniformly condemning the prefect for his unreasonable behavior. The discussions were still continuing when Zuo Chu appeared before the camps, clapped his hands, and announced in a loud voice, "Attention, all you professional soldiers in the camps! Officer Wang ought not to have taken that money and rice and distributed it to you! But now that he has been confined to prison by the prefect, you ought to repay his kindness by rescuing him!"

"Out of the goodness of his heart," the soldiers said, "Officer Wang issued money and rice to us, and now the prefect is blaming him for it and has locked him up. The trouble is that we aren't strong enough and don't have anyone to lead us. How *can* we rescue him?"

"You gentlemen are perfectly right," said Zuo Chu. "You do need a leader. Now, if I were to offer myself to you as your leader, would you give me your support?" The men looked at Zuo Chu and said nothing, but what they thought was as follows: This fellow is so small, and he has a game leg—why, even if he jumped down someone's throat, he couldn't stab the man to death! If we were to follow him, not only would we probably fail, we'd be taking part in a farce!

When they remained silent, Zuo Chu asked, "Why aren't you saying anything? Perhaps you think I'm too small and weak and couldn't harm anyone, is that it? Let me change and show you what I'm like!"

With a shout of "Presto!" he demonstrated all his magical powers. Gone was the four-foot-tall priest with the game leg. In his place there appeared an enormous ghost with red hair, green eyes, and a blue face that sported prominent fangs.

The crowd was so shocked that they prostrated themselves before him. "We failed to see Mount Tai when it was right there in front of our eyes!" they said. "You're a *god*! No wonder Officer Wang's house, which isn't very large, was able to distribute all that money and rice to the whole six thousand of us!"

When they stood up and looked about, they found it was actually just Lame Priest, who said, "Battalion commanders, tell your men to get their weapons ready. I am going on my own to rescue Officer Wang and kill the prefect of Beizhou, and you must come along and back me up. If you will support Officer Wang, he will see that you are well provided for and that you live out the rest of your lives in happiness!"

"We'll come and support you!" responded the crowd of soldiers.

Leaving the camp, Zuo Chu made his way slowly back to the yamen. The prefect was in court, and when Zuo Chu entered the chamber, no one noticed him. He went up to the steps and announced in a loud voice, "Prefect! Zuo Chu has come specially to pay you a visit!"

The people in court commented among themselves, "We've just put up notices calling for the arrest of this man, and here he is, sticking his head right into the cangue!"

Noting his visitor's puny physique, the prefect was not greatly concerned about him. "So you're Zuo Chu?" he said. He ordered his men to seize him, bring out the long cangue, and lock him in it and then take him to jail. They were to establish the truth about the money and rice by means of a confrontation with Wang Ze. The jailers brought Zuo Chu to the jail and also dragged Wang Ze along to the examination room.

At the sight of Zuo Chu, Wang Ze asked, "Why are *you* here?"

"How could I rescue you otherwise?"

"You there, confess, starting from the beginning!" said Wang Jiang of the Office of Public Order. "How did you spirit away a granary full of rice and a treasury full of money?"

"Sir," said Zuo Chu, "even you don't understand. The prefect is so stupid that he refused to issue the monthly wages of the two battalions, and the men were simply furious. Why shouldn't I hand out the money and rice in his place?"

At this point Wang Jiang lost all patience and barked out an order to the jailers to beat Zuo Chu as hard as they could. The jailers raised their rods, pulled him over, and beat him until they had broken the skin all over his body. Zuo Chu roared with laughter and gave a shout of "Presto!" which caused his and Wang Ze's bonds to fall apart like rotten shallots and their cangues to open wide.

Wang Jiang was terrified. "The man is a demon!" At once he ordered the jailers and all his other men to advance and seize Zuo Chu, but the latter pointed a finger at them, which paralyzed their legs so that they found themselves rooted to the spot, unable to put one foot in front of the other. Zuo Chu and Wang Ze arrived in the prefectural chamber just as the prefect was checking tax receipts. "Prefect Zhang!" roared Zuo Chu. "You've done terrible harm to the people of Beizhou, and now your retribution is at hand. If I fail to rid the people of Beizhou of this scourge today, I cannot call myself a man!"

The prefect saw that the two meant no good, and he turned and ran behind the screen. However, two other men came rushing out from the back room at that moment—Zhang Luan and Bu Ji, each armed with a sword. Bu Ji went up to the prefect and seized him, while Zhang Luan killed him with a single sweep of the sword, severing arm from shoulder and cleaving him in two.

The people in the chamber were so horrified they were transfixed, unable to move. "Listen to me, all of you!" cried Wang Ze. "Most of you have been victimized by this man. Today I have rid you of the root cause of your distress and brought happiness within reach of everyone in this prefecture. Those of you who have suffered at his hands should now follow me into the yamen. You are free to take his gold and silver and make yourselves rich." The crowd rallied to Wang Ze's support.

Some soldiers from the two battalions happened to come by the yamen, and when they heard that Wang Ze had killed the prefect, they rushed in and massacred the prefect's entire family. Zuo Chu, Zhang Luan, and Bu Ji then led a squad of soldiers in hunting out and killing the prefect's cronies as well as Wang Jiang of the Office of Public Order and a number of constables. They also opened up the prison and released all the convicts, then went to the prefect's private residence and brought out all his gold and silver, silks and satins, which they piled up in big heaps in the lower part of the chamber.

"I don't want to keep a penny of all this wealth for myself," said Wang Ze. "I intend it for the professional soldiers. If there's any left over, it should go to the poorest of the street vendors, to enable them to ply their trade with an easy mind." Taking over the yamen himself, he sent out notices to reassure the public. He also ordered the troops from the two battalions to get their weapons ready, to put on their armor, and to man the four gates and mount a strict guard over the walls and moats.

We have now come to the end of the episode. From this extraordinary event only two officials escaped, Controller-General Dong Yuanchun and Judicial Commissioner Tian Jing. Abandoning their families and taking with them only their seals of office, they raced to the capital to inform the court. When Emperor Renzong heard their report, he immediately issued an imperial decree that the prefect of Jizhou should take the troops under his command and go directly to Beizhou to capture Wang Ze. The prefect's name was Liu Yanwei, and he came from a long line of military officers; he was a man in whom the civil and military virtues were perfectly joined. On receiving the decree, he selected five thousand troops from his own command and dashed to Beizhou.

Because of this action, certain consequences followed: Wang Ze declared himself king and created havoc in Beizhou, resulting in numerous extraordinary events and costing thousands of lives.

Because the five thousand fierce horsemen came,
Demon magicians were provoked to act.

Was Liu Yanwei victorious in the end? Turn to the next chapter to find out.

16

WITH WANG ZE LEADING THE THRONG, BEIZHOU REVOLTS;

ETERNA HEADS TROOPS IN RAIDING NEIGHBORING TOWNS.

POEM:

He declared himself king without much thought—
What royal virtues could he exemplify?
It's so easy all of a sudden to lose
And, cut to pieces among the swords, to die!

When the Beizhou spies found out that Liu Yanwei had mobilized his troops, they raced back to report to Wang Ze, and the whole population of the prefecture was thrown into panic. Wang Ze himself was so shocked that he didn't know what to do. He hastily asked Zuo Chu, Zhang Luan, and Bu Ji for their advice.

"Have you heard how many troops he has?" asked Zuo Chu.

"Five thousand—that's what scares me. How are we going to deal with this?"

"Don't panic! I'll need only three thousand men to counter him. You're about to see what I'm capable of." He at once selected three thousand mounted men, rewarded them with money and gifts, and told them that they were to do battle the following day.

The following morning he marshaled his troops, then left Beizhou city and arrayed them in battle formation. Liu Yanwei, in full armor, with a lance of tempered steel and riding a horse that could go like the wind, came out in front of the battle lines. The three thousand troops saw how formidable he looked and quailed inwardly. Liu pointed his lance at them and declared, "If there are any men of good sense in Beizhou, they will tie Wang Ze up and hand him over to the court, thus sparing the city from wholesale slaughter!" Wang Ze, who was scared out of his wits, didn't dare say a word.

Zuo Chu, wearing a tattered cloth gown and gripping a sword, pointed with the tip of his sword at Liu Yanwei and declared, "If *you* have any sense, you'll take your troops straight back to Jizhou and save your own life! The slightest delay, and all your men will die at my hands!"

"You're one of Wang Ze's accomplices, and without even wearing any armor you have the nerve to challenge me! Why, I'll run you through with a single thrust of my lance!"

"I'm not going to fight a war of words with you. Instead let me show you what I can do!" As Liu Yanwei demonstrated his lance technique in front of the lines to intimidate him, Zuo Chu pointed with the tip of his sword. The center of his battle line opened up, and a pack of tigers and leopards burst forth. Liu Yanwei's horse reared up in fright, throwing him to the ground. Although his troops rushed forward to help him back onto his horse, when they saw the strange animals, they fled for their lives, leaving their weapons behind. Wang Ze led his three thousand men in pursuit of the enemy, killing them as they ran. Liu Yanwei had suffered a grave defeat, with the loss of fully half his men. He returned to Jizhou, which is where we shall leave him.

Having won one battle, Wang Ze felt reassured and emboldened. When the people of the prefecture saw how he had defeated the government troops, they rallied to his side. The men under his command, impressed with Zuo Chu's magical powers, gave him their wholehearted support. Wang led the Beizhou troops in attacks on neighboring prefectures and counties, while Eterna commanded the demon soldiers in raids on the local towns and villages. They recruited the troops who surrendered to them and obtained large quantities of money and provisions, and Wang's power grew even greater.

In the Eastern Capital, when the butcher Zhang Qi, the steamed cake vendor Ren Qian, and the noodle seller Wu Sanlang heard that Eterna was now Wang Ze's wife, they fled to Beizhou to join him. Impressed by the way people had transferred their loyalties, Wang proclaimed himself King of Dongping and named Eterna his queen, Zuo Chu his strategist, Pellet Priest his state mentor, Zhang Luan his first minister, and Bu Ji his field marshal. His lesser followers also received official appointments. And his power continued to grow.

The neighboring prefectures and counties prepared urgent appeals for help and submitted them to the emperor. A shocked Emperor Renzong addressed his assembled civil and military officials: "Beizhou is in revolt, and Wang Ze has gathered a large number of demons about him. They have raided the neighboring prefectures and defeated Liu Yanwei of Jizhou. We find this setback extremely distressing and wonder whom we could best appoint as commander to overcome Wang Ze."

The assistant director of the left, Lü Shun, stepped forward holding his tablet: "I recommend Wen Yanbo from Fenzhou in Hedong. He performed a meritorious service in subduing the Xi Xia. He has now given up his official post and is living in retirement in the Western Capital. If he is appointed, I am confident that he will be able to retake Beizhou and eliminate Wang Ze."

"But why should we appoint Wen Yanbo ahead of other men?" asked the emperor.

"Yesterday, when I heard the reports," testified Lü Shun, "I felt that Wang Ze was such a formidable rebel that no strategy would succeed in capturing him, but at midnight it suddenly occurred to me that if you add the character 'wen' to that for 'bei,' they make up the character for 'defeat.' That is why Wen Yanbo is the only suitable appointment. I specially waited up for this dawn audience so that I could make the proposal in person. I am prepared to guarantee Wen's success with the lives of my entire family."

Emperor Renzong was delighted with the proposal and immediately issued an order sending emissaries to the Western Capital to summon Wen Yanbo to court. The emissaries traveled posthaste to the Western Capital, where Wen and all the local officials came out of the city to receive the order. Once it had been read out publicly in the yamen, the officials kowtowed in the direction of the imperial palace to express their gratitude. After receiving it, Wen Yanbo parted from his family and left at once for the court. Because he came to suppress the rebellion,[1] certain consequences followed: a band of people responsible for devilish crimes died deaths even more ghastly than the death of Li Cunxiao in the *History of the Five Dynasties* or that of Peng Yue in the *Han History*.

When he points with his whip, the bane of evil is destroyed;
Wherever his horse's hooves go, the deviltry comes to an end.

Was Wen Yanbo victorious? Turn to the next chapter to find out.

17

WEN YANBO LEADS AN ARMY TO SUPPRESS BEIZHOU;

CAO WEI DEFEATS THE DEMONS' MAGIC WITH BLOOD PUMPS.

POEM:

As the mighty force descends on Beizhou,
The demon army will meet its doom, we trust;
When heaven sends the three Sui to crush you,
Valiant though you be, you'll turn to dust.

After receiving the emperor's order, Wen Yanbo raced to the capital at twice the normal speed. He was met by the local officials at the Reception Pavilion and escorted into the city, where the next day he attended the dawn audience and saw the emperor from the ranks of court officials. How shall we describe that audience?

Blessed clouds obscure the graceful pavilions;
An auspicious haze shrouds the splendid towers;
Mist-covered royal willows brush the flags and banners;
Dew-laden palace flowers welcome the swords and lances;
In an aura of heavenly fragrance,
With jade hairpins and vermilion shoes the attendants assemble
before the scarlet palace steps.

Amid the strains of ethereal music,
In embroidered jackets and brocade uniforms the guards escort
    the imperial carriage.
The pearl curtains are rolled up
As the golden chaise appears in the yellow gold chamber;
The phoenix feather shade[1] is opened
As the jade vehicle halts before the white jade steps.
The silence whip[2] raps faintly three times,
As row upon row of officials line the two sides.

Emperor Renzong summoned Wen Yanbo before him and issued this order: "Wang Ze of Beizhou in Hebei has revolted, and I am appointing you as commanding general to subdue the demon rebels. How many troops will you need? And how many deputy commanders? Kindly consider these matters and give me your decision."

"I understand that Wang Ze's entire faction is composed of demons, and if we have too few troops, I fear that we will not prevail. To defeat the enemy I should like to ask for just one man as my deputy but for a hundred thousand troops."

"You shall have the troops you ask for, but I wonder whom you would recommend as your deputy."

"I should like to have Cao Wei."

"Might this Cao Wei be a descendant of Cao Bin's, who was ennobled for his outstanding service in conquering Jiangnan?"

"Yes, he is Cao Bin's grandson."

Highly delighted, the emperor summoned Cao Wei into his presence and proceeded to appoint Wen Yanbo as commanding general to suppress the revolt and Cao Wei as his deputy. He drew gold, silver, cash, and silks from the palace treasury and awarded them to the troops. Wen Yanbo and Cao Wei thanked the emperor for his gracious kindness and withdrew from court, then went the rounds of the various training camps to select men and horses. As soon as they had done so, they left the capital, crossed the Yellow River, and went as far as the boundary of Hebei province, where they set up camp at Jizhou.

Liu Yanwei, the prefect of Jizhou, met the two commanders outside the city and ushered them in, then gave them a full account of how formidable Wang Ze's demon magic was. Wen Yanbo discussed the issue with Cao Wei. "We're now about to attack and subdue Beizhou. I wonder what brilliant strategy you have, Deputy Commander, what tactic that would defeat the rebels."

"As deputy commander, I would not be so presumptuous as to offer any plans. I will carry out any order you care to give me."

"But that's not at all appropriate. You're descended from a famous general who rendered signal service to the late emperor. I may be the commander, but when all's said and done, I'm really just a scholar. I am depending entirely on you to cooperate in carrying out our mission. There's no need to be overly modest."

Cao Wei acceded. "In my humble opinion, it would be advisable to divide our force into three columns and to use the 'long snake' formation in attacking Beizhou," he said. "If one column meets with a reverse, the other two will come to its aid."

"Beizhou is a small area and we know from the spies we've sent out that they have fewer than ten thousand troops as against our hundred thousand. If in addition we have a brilliant plan of yours, Deputy Commander, it should be simplicity itself to destroy the rebels."

"I have also heard that, although Wang Ze and his men have no civil or military skills, they make full use of demonic magic. When Liu Yanwei went to subdue them, Wang Ze used that magic against him, which is why he returned home badly beaten and suffering heavy losses. I would like to suggest that you command forty thousand men in a central column, and allow me thirty thousand for a support column on the left wing and General

Wang Xin another thirty thousand on the right. In addition, you should order General of the Vanguard Sun Fu to carry out inspections of the camps. Wang Ze currently has fewer than ten thousand men and can oppose only one of our columns. If we're victorious, the three columns will join together and take Beizhou; if one of our columns meets with a slight reverse, the other two must come to its aid. It's an infallible plan."

Wen Yanbo was delighted. "With this sort of deployment, there's no doubt that Beizhou will fall!" The next day he divided his force into three columns for the attack on Beizhou, and there we shall leave him.

Meanwhile Wang Ze had learned of the impending attack on Beizhou by Wen Yanbo's hundred thousand men. At once he called Zuo Chu and the other demons together to discuss the threat. "When Liu Yanwei of Jizhou came here with his force, a single battle was enough to annihilate his army," said Pellet Priest. "Even though Wen Yanbo has a hundred thousand men, what do we have to fear? Give me ten thousand troops, and I'll bring you back his head."

Wang Ze was happy to oblige and mustered ten thousand troops for battle. That same morning he opened the city gates and drew his men up in formation beside the wall. Commander Wen, with his troops arrayed in three columns, rode forward from the ranks to speak to Wang Ze.

When he saw Wen Yanbo come forward, Wang Ze bowed and declared, "Because Prefect Zhang was corrupt, I killed him, ridding the people of a curse, and they honored me by making me the temporary leader of this small territory. Why should the court need to send troops here?"

Commander Wen roared at him: "As a soldier of this prefecture, you had the effrontery to kill the head of the prefecture! What's more, you seized Beizhou and slaughtered the government troops sent against you—those are *monstrous* crimes! And now, when by rights you ought to open the gates and surrender, you have the gall to lead your troops against us!"

Wang Ze clapped his hands and laughed. "You may have a hundred thousand men, Commander, but you will never get me to surrender!"

Commander Wen called for a roll of drums, and General of the Vanguard Sun Fu pointed with his lance and ordered his men to charge the walls and capture Wang Ze. Hearing the drums and seeing the cavalry charging toward him, Wang drew the sword at his side and pointed it. At once the battle line opened up and Pellet Priest, Zuo Chu, Zhang Luan, Bu Ji, and others started clicking their teeth and practicing their magic. Suddenly a dark wind sprang up combined with a fierce rain; there were rumbles of thunder and flashes of lightning; fireballs rolled back and forth; and from the army's ranks a sandstorm spiraled upward, darkening the sky. The sandstorm was full of creatures with the faces of spirits and ghosts who led jackals, wolves, tigers, and leopards against the government lines. The troops could only fight humans; how could they contend with spirits, ghosts, and fierce animals? The horses were so panicked that they bolted, throwing their riders to the ground. When Wang Ze saw the front ranks of Wen Yanbo's column in such disarray, he seized the chance to make a surprise attack. Wen Yanbo and General of the Vanguard Sun Fu fled, suffering a major defeat. Wang Ze ordered his men to pursue them, but when Deputy Commander Cao Wei and General Wang Xin saw that Wen Yanbo's troops had been beaten, they brought their forces to his aid, and at the sight of the two columns advancing toward him, Wang Ze feared that he might lose and ordered his troops to return to the city.

Wen Yanbo took his forces ten miles away from the city and set up camp. When he checked his losses, he found that countless numbers of men had been killed or wounded in battle or been trampled to death by their own side. He discussed plans for attacking the city with Deputy Commander Cao and General Wang Xin. "I've fought dozens of battles, great and small, against the western barbarians," said Wen Yanbo, "but I've never seen anything like this deployment of Wang Ze's. It's no wonder our columns lost. Hidden within their ranks the rebels had creatures with the faces of spirits and ghosts, as well as thunder, lightning, and fireballs. They also had fierce animals, and when they came pouring forth, our horses reared up in panic and our whole formation was thrown into disarray. The enemy seized his chance to come after us, and we couldn't fight him off. If the deputy commander and general had not come to my aid, we would certainly have lost even more heavily. What are we going to do in the face of such a defeat?"

"I have heard that, apart from Wang Ze and four or five others, no one else on their side is able to practice demonic magic," said Cao Wei. "If that's the case, I know a way to defeat their demonic magic, take Beizhou, and capture Wang Ze."

Wen Yanbo was jubilant. "May I hear your brilliant plan for defeating their magic?"

"The magic of Wang Ze and the others is called 'Diamond Chan' by the Buddhists and 'Heretical Way' by the Daoists. If you're skilled at both kinds, you're known as a 'double adept.'[3] Both are black magic, and the only things the adepts fear are pig's and sheep's blood, horse urine, human feces, and garlic. If you sprinkle just a drop of that mixture on them, they are no longer able to transform themselves into spirits or ghosts or to make use of their black magic."

Wen Yanbo was delighted, and he ordered his men to dip their weapons in blood whenever they went into battle. Commander Cao had three hundred pumps made, each of which was filled with pig's and sheep's blood. He also selected three hundred tall, strong soldiers as pump hands; in the course of battle, if they saw any spirits or ghosts or fierce animals, they were to squirt this liquid at them.

Wen Yanbo rewarded his men. Next morning he arranged them in three columns as before and took up positions about a mile outside the city.

When Wang Ze saw Wen Yanbo's army close to the city wall, he declared to his men, "Despite the defeat we inflicted on them yesterday, they're still not afraid but have come back today to fight us again. Well, this time we're going to capture Wen Yanbo and all his men, leaving nothing behind!" He mustered ten thousand men to go out and confront the enemy.

The two armies faced off in a full circle with their flags and drums directly opposite each other. Then their drums began to rumble like thunder, their battle cries rose to the heavens, and their arrows fell like rain, stopping the forward ranks in their tracks.

Wang Ze had no great champion under his command; he was dependent solely on demonic magic for his string of victories, and he did not consider Wen Yanbo and his large army a serious threat.

Wen Yanbo ordered the drums and gongs beaten together. General of the Vanguard Sun Fu attacked the top of the enemy line with his lance while Cao Wei, wielding a pair of swords, attacked the bottom. Wen Yanbo led the center column, and the three columns advanced together. As soon as he saw them coming, Wang Ze pointed with his sword, and the center of the battle line opened up and out rushed a horde of spirits, ghosts, and strange beasts. Wen Yanbo shouted an order to open up his own center, letting out the three hundred pump hands, who proceeded to squirt their liquid together. When Wang Ze's spirits, ghosts, and strange beasts came in contact with the filthy matter, the pig's and sheep's blood, they fled back to their own lines, stripped of their magic power.

Wen Yanbo's troops seized the opportunity to make a sudden attack, and Wang Ze suffered a major defeat. His men fled for their lives, abandoning their weapons, and both men and horses were trampled to pieces. Because of this defeat, certain consequences followed: the wicked rebel faction suffered death by the sword, and a woman skilled in the demonic arts was taken to the marketplace and beheaded.

If black arts are used against upright men,
A beneficent spirit will shield them.

What happened when Wang Ze fled? Turn to the next chapter to find out.

18

ZUO CHU TRIES TO STRIKE THE DUKE OF LU WITH A FLYING MILLSTONE;

ARGUS-EYED SPIRIT SAVES THE DUKE OF LU AND OFFERS A PLAN.

POEM:

As strong as Lame Priest's grasp of magic is,
When he meets the blood pumps, his defeat is sure.
As for Ma Sui, Li Sui, and Zhuge Suizhi,
For quelling demons their fame will endure.

Wen Yanbo shouted for the battle line to be opened, which allowed the pump hands and the archers to come forth and either squirt the weird creatures and fierce animals in the face or else shoot at them. Many of the creatures proved to be paper cutouts or snippets of straw, and countless soldiers were shot by the archers. The government army, sensing the possibility of victory, attacked and killed three-tenths of the enemy force, two-thirds of the dead falling victim to Wen Yanbo's column. Having suffered a major defeat, Wang Ze hastily withdrew his men into the city, raised the drawbridge, locked the gates, and made no further forays.

Following his victory, Wen Yanbo withdrew his troops and camped at a point not far from the city wall. From there he gazed at Beizhou like a tiger eyeing its prey—the city could fall within a matter of days. The names of the officers and soldiers who had distinguished themselves were recorded in the honors register, and the army's morale rose even higher. Wen Yanbo ordered five hundred men to go up into the mountains and fell timber for battering rams, scaling ladders, catapults, assault platforms, and flaming arrows. Within a day or two all the equipment was ready, and he ordered an attack on the city wall. The army went up to the moat and began the assault.

In the aftermath of his defeat, Wang Ze illustrated the truth of the saying "When your sword suffers a nick, your prestige takes a loss." He ordered his army to keep their bows at the ready and place a close guard on the battlements, but not to issue forth from the city. He also invited the demons Zuo Chu, Zhang Luan, Bu Ji, Pellet Priest, Ren Qian, Zhang Qi, and Wu Sanlang to the yamen chamber and had them sit there in a circle. "Gentlemen," he began, "Wen Yanbo has seen through our use of magic, and we have lost a great many soldiers. I no longer dare to leave the city and engage him in battle. He has now come right up to our walls and is challenging us to fight. What are we to do?"

He had barely finished speaking when a scout brought in a report: "Commander Wen has ordered his troops to make scaling ladders, catapults, assault platforms, and flaming arrows, and they're under the walls right now attacking the city!"

"With the situation so dangerous, what will happen to all the people in this city?" asked Wang Ze in alarm.

Zuo Chu rose to his feet. "You needn't worry, Your Majesty," he said. "I, Zuo Chu, can perform thousands and thousands of transformations. There's no need for us to fight; I'll merely see to it that Wen Yanbo comes to an unnatural end outside the city. Once they're deprived of their leader, his hundred thousand troops will scatter without a fight. What do you say?"

"What brilliant plan do you have in mind, my dear minister, that would bring about this man's death and make an army of a hundred thousand scatter in all directions, ending the siege?"

"Simple!" said Zuo Chu. He ordered the men under his command to go to a mill and fetch a large millstone. Before long a dozen men entered the lower part of the chamber carrying a millstone on their shoulders. Zuo Chu went down there and wrote a charm on the stone with a vermilion brush. Next, with loosened hair and bare feet, holding a sword in his right hand[1] and an earthenware bowl of water in his left, he chanted a magic formula and took a mouthful of water, then spat the water at the millstone, shouting, "Presto!" At once, to the cheers of Wang Ze and the others present, the millstone floated up into the sky and flew off outside the city.

Commander Wen had just taken his seat in his command tent and invited Deputy Commander Cao Wei, General Wang Xin, and General of the Vanguard Sun Fu in to discuss their plans for taking the city when a millstone came flying down out of the sky aimed directly at his head. An earthshaking crash followed, and the faces of the men in the tent turned pale with horror—they thought that the millstone must have struck and killed their commander. However, Wen had been sitting in an armchair when he was suddenly seized around the waist by someone and pulled a few steps away. As the millstone came down, it missed him but smashed his chair to pieces and buried itself a foot or two in the ground. The other men were overjoyed to find that Wen was unhurt, although he had suffered a considerable shock. Another armchair was fetched. "Who was it who seized me around the waist?" asked Wen.

The words were hardly out of his mouth when someone stepped forward and bowed, a large, tall man with an ugly face. Nobody recognized him; he wasn't a member of Wen's staff, nor was he one of the guards posted at the front of the tent. "You saved my life!" exclaimed Wen Yanbo. "Who are you? Please tell me about yourself. Of course I shall give you a handsome reward."

"I'm not one of your soldiers. Wang Ze of Beizhou was using demonic magic to try and crush you to death with that millstone. I came especially to save your life in order to repay you for a meal that you once kindly gave me."

Wen was delighted to hear this. "I'm grateful to you for saving me, but I wonder where I could possibly have given you that meal. And I would dearly like to know your name."

"If I tell you, I'm afraid you may forget it. Could I borrow a silver bowl as well as some writing materials?"

One of the attendants brought out a silver bowl and some writing materials and arranged them on the table. Then the man said, "Could I ask you to send your staff out of the room?" Commander Wen dismissed his staff, and the man wrote something in the bowl, placed it upside down on the ground, and strode out of the tent. Commander Wen immediately sent someone after him, but he had disappeared.

How very strange, thought Wen. He told an attendant to turn the bowl over. The words "Argus-Eyed Spirit" were written in it in large characters. None of those in the tent knew what to make of them.

Commander Wen puzzled over the name for some time before suddenly realizing what it meant. "Before I graduated, I once stopped for the night at a courier station," he said. "The officer in charge warned me about the room I had. 'This place is haunted by a ghost, and many of the men who slept here lost their lives.' At the time I didn't believe him, and I lit the lamp and the candles, bought some wine, and sat there drinking by myself. Then at midnight a wild wind sprang up, and when it had passed, there was a man standing in front of the table. His hair covered his face and his hands were crossed over his chest. Addressing me as prime minister, he asked me for some food and wine. 'Who are you?' I asked. 'And why don't you show your face?' He replied, 'I'm so ugly that people die of fright when they see me—that's why I don't dare show my face.' When I doubted him, he parted his hair and revealed a blue face with a dozen flashing and flickering eyes. I was frightened, too, but I gave him the food and wine, and when he had finished it, he said, 'Someday you'll be in great danger, sir, and I'll be sure to come to your aid.' And with that he disappeared. It just occurred to me that the man who saved my life just now must have been that Argus-Eyed Spirit." When the others looked at the silver bowl, they found a column of small characters beside the name: "If you meet the three Sui, you'll be able to take Beizhou."

Wen was jubilant. "I never expected that he would not only save my life but also give me a plan to defeat Wang Ze. The trouble is I haven't the slightest idea what 'the three Sui' means. Can any of you think of an explanation?"

"We're completely in the dark," they said, before returning to their own quarters to puzzle over the meaning. And there we shall leave them.

Meanwhile in Beizhou Wang Ze and the other demons had set out some wine in the chamber and were congratulating Zuo Chu while at the same time dispatching scouts to find out what was happening on the front line. One scout returned and reported as follows: "Commander Wen's forces are under strict discipline and arrayed in good order. There's been no change."

"If they'd been deprived of their commander," said Wang Ze, "they'd surely be in disarray and have lost any taste for battle. If there's nothing going on among Wen Yanbo's forces, I wonder if the millstone did actually hit him."

"That magic of mine has never been known to fail," said Zuo Chu. "No one can stop it. He must have been crushed to death."

"If we want to find out the truth," said Wang Ze, "we'd better get someone to go over there and issue a challenge."

"Quite right, Your Majesty," they said.

They wrote out a challenge and sent it by a reliable soldier right to Commander Wen's tent. When the commander saw what it was, he called the bearer in. His staff received the document and laid it on the table, and Commander Wen opened and read it. He quickly deduced what lay behind the challenge: Wang Ze must have thought that by demonic magic he had caused the millstone to crush me to death. How could anyone imagine that I would escape unscathed? When he saw that nothing was going on over here, he decided to use the challenge to find out what really happened. He wrote his reply right on the document: "We'll fight tomorrow," he said, and gave it to the bearer to take back.

After reading the reply, Wang Ze put a question to the bearer: "Did you go right into Commander Wen's tent?"

"Your Majesty, Commander Wen didn't act at all suspicious. He called me into his tent and personally wrote the reply before sending me back."

Hearing that Wen was unharmed, Wang Ze was filled with anxiety and that night invited Zuo Chu and the other demons to devise a plan to counter the enemy. "Since the millstone failed to crush him to death . . ." said Zuo Chu and continued by whispering something in Wang Ze's ear that concluded with the sentence, "In the battle tomorrow we should do such and such."

Next morning, with his plans set, Wang Ze mustered ten thousand men, opened the gate, let down the drawbridge, and drew up his soldiers in formation outside. For a long time the two armies stood facing each other. Relying as before on the pump hands with their pig's and sheep's blood, Commander Wen had someone shout out demanding an exchange of words with Wang Ze. Wang, however, did not come forward but stayed in the ranks. His hair was loosened and his feet bare, he wore no armor, and he was completely naked. Holding a sword in one hand, he led a white horse with the other. Zuo Chu clicked his teeth and worked his magic. He paced out the Big Dipper,[2] then recited a formula and shouted, "Presto!" at the same time thrusting his sword into the horse's neck. When the blood spurted forth, he took it in his mouth and spat it at the front line. Before he spat, it was a fine day with bright sunshine, but after he did so, a dark wind sprang up and a fierce rain fell, with intermittent thunder and flying sand and gravel. You couldn't see the person opposite you or even your own outstretched hand, and the soldiers were so panicked that they cast aside their weapons and fled for their lives. Their flight led to certain consequences: the prime minister in the Eastern Capital lost his way, and Commander Wen chanced to meet someone who suppressed demons.

> If it's your fate, you'll meet though far away;
> If not, you'll never meet though close at hand.

Did Commander Wen survive in the end? Turn to the next chapter to find out.

19

WEN YANBO HAPPENS TO MEET ZHUGE SUIZHI; FISH SOUP LI OFFERS A PLAN TO CAPTURE WANG ZE.

POEM:

He serves by offering plans and strategies;
The demon rebels he must subjugate.
The blessings of the court last forever,
While rogues and villains meet a common fate.

Had Commander Wen not been destined to become prime minister, he might well have lost his life. When the wind sprang up and he was pelted with sand and gravel, he managed to escape from the battlefield, but when he turned and looked back, he saw no one following him—he was utterly alone. In his desolation and despair, he resembled

A phoenix fallen on a barren slope, all its feathers stripped away;
A dragon in a shallow pool bereft of the pearl beneath its chin;
The king of Shu in spring, mournfully crying blood;[1]
Song Yu in autumn, lamenting the vernal hues;[2]
Lü Qian without the dagger in his belt;[3]
Lei Huan after the sword of Fengcheng was lost;[4]

A flood dragon with neither clouds nor rain;
A boat stranded onshore without a wave.

As he rode along, he came to a hill covered in trees and realized that he didn't know where he was. Reining in his horse, he rounded an outcropping of the hill and saw a flagpole and heard a bell tolling—he had arrived at a monastery. I have no choice, he thought; before deciding what to do, I shall need to go in and ask someone which road will take me back to camp. He dismounted in front of the monastery and went in. Coming upon a monk, he told him that he would like to see the abbot, and after the monk had gone in and reported the request, the abbot himself came out. He could tell at a glance that Wen's armor and that of his horse were not those of a junior officer and concluded that he must be a general. Hastily pressing his palms together in greeting, he told a monk to lead the horse away while he invited Wen into his private quarters. He realized that his visitor must be famished and ordered the kitchen to prepare a vegetarian meal, in the meantime serving him tea. When Wen had drunk the tea, the abbot asked, "I wonder if you would tell me your name, General, and what it is that brings you here."

"My name is Wen Yanbo."

"Not the Commander Wen who won such distinction in conquering the Xi Xia?"

"The same."

"I've long heard of your reputation, General. Our monastery is greatly honored by your visit. But why haven't you brought any followers with you?"

"After Wang Ze of Beizhou started a rebellion, the court raised an army of a hundred thousand to subdue the rebels and appointed me as commander. This morning we met them in battle, and to our shock we suffered a major defeat. I fled, and ended up here."

The abbot was astonished. "But with you as general and an army a hundred thousand strong—Beizhou is such a small place, it cannot have many troops—how did you happen to lose?"

"If it came down to fighting, they could never have gotten the better of us. But Wang Ze has a band of rebels with him who are adept at demonic magic. Whenever we fight them, they let loose weird ghosts and spirits as well as fierce animals from within their ranks, and our horses bolt at the very sight. Deputy Commander Cao Wei devised a plan to squirt the creatures with pig's and sheep's blood, horse's urine and garlic. That enabled us to win one battle, and for several days after that the rebels did not dare come out to fight. Then a day or two ago I was in my command tent discussing tactics with my generals when the demons employed their black magic to bring a millstone crashing down out of the sky—fortunately, Argus-Eyed Spirit saved my life. This morning, while engaged in battle with the rebels, we were taken by surprise; a wicked wind sprang up out of the enemy ranks, with thunder and lightning in rapid succession as well as flying sand and gravel that caused havoc in our lines. I escaped alone and ended up here after losing my way. I hope that you will guide me back to the road I came on. Once I return to camp, I'll see that you are handsomely rewarded."

This account brought the abbot to his feet, striking his hands together in fury: "In an idyllic age like ours, with a saintly ruler and wise ministers, that these demons would even *dare* to cause trouble for the court! But Commander, I urge you not to worry. Let me exert myself on your behalf and smash their black magic, wiping out the whole rebel band."

Commander Wen was greatly heartened by his declaration. "May I ask your honorable name?" he said.

"Zhuge Suizhi."

Wen reacted with delight. "Argus-Eyed Spirit wrote these words for me: 'If you meet up with three Sui, you will be able to take Beizhou.' We've been puzzling over what he could have meant, but today heaven has arranged that I should meet you, Master. If you are willing to go back with me, and if we are able to take Beizhou, I shall memorialize the court, and the government's response will be far from insignificant."

"As a Buddhist I have no desire for wealth, honors, rank, or reward, but in a peaceful world like ours there is no place for demons such as these. I shall do my utmost to make a modest contribution by helping you suppress them. Let me invite you to spend the night here, and then tomorrow morning early we'll go together to your camp."

Commander Wen took off his armor, ate his supper, and spent half the night in discussion with the abbot. He slept until the fifth watch, then rose, washed, and ate a little breakfast. The abbot had a monk bring a horse from the monastery for himself, and with three monks holding torches they made their way to the camp. When the officers and soldiers saw Commander Wen coming, they were jubilant and welcomed him into the command tent. Deputy Commander Cao and the others asked, "You've been away all night, sir, and we've been at our wits' end. We are wondering where you went after the rout, and why you brought this priest back with you."

"Yesterday, when Wang Ze employed his black arts, an evil wind caused me to lose my way. I came to a monastery, where I met this holy man, and he told me that he is able to overcome the black arts. I believe he fits that prophecy that Argus-Eyed Spirit left us." Whispering in Cao's ear, he added, "His name is Zhuge Suizhi."

Cao was overjoyed. Sending his staff away, he asked the priest, "Master, may I ask what divine art you possess that would overcome the demons' evil?"

"I once met a person with supernatural powers who taught me the Rectifying Magic of the Five Thunder Gods' Celestial Heart, and whenever I come across any of the black arts of Diamond Chan or the Heretical Way, I quote a mantra and am able to counter the evil and turn it to good. Should you doubt me, Commander, you will be able to see for yourself on the battlefield tomorrow."

After inviting the abbot and the monks to stay in the headquarters that night, Commander Wen wrote out a challenge for the following day and gave it to a soldier to deliver. As soon as Wang Ze saw it, he wrote his reply on the document and sent it back by the same messenger. He then consulted with the demons: "In the battle we fought two days ago, we inflicted heavy losses on them, routing them completely, and yet today they have the nerve to come back and issue a challenge to *us*! We ought to use the same tactics as we used last time, pursuing and cutting them down all the way to the border, leaving not a single man alive out of the whole hundred thousand!"

We need not go into the details. Each side mustered its men and horses and awaited the next day's battle.

On the following day Wang Ze led his troops out of Beizhou and took up battle formations. The two lines were directly opposite, their banners in full view of each other. Beneath the banners Wang Ze was once more to be seen, with his hair loosened and his feet bare, gripping a sword and leading a white horse. Muttering a formula, he stabbed the horse with his sword, caught some of the blood in his mouth, and spat it out. From his lines an evil wind sprang up full of sand, gravel, rain, and hail and advanced toward Commander Wen's troops. Zhuge Suizhi saw it coming. He shook his long-handled bell and uttered a mantra, then pointed with the bell. In a flash the evil wind with all its sand, gravel, rain, and hail turned back and moved against Wang Ze's lines. Wang saw how threatening the situation had become and hastily ordered a retreat. Commander Wen pointed with his whip and the three columns joined together in pursuing and slaughtering the fleeing soldiers. Wang Ze lost most of his force—countless numbers of soldiers were driven into the moat to drown—and he desperately rounded up the remaining men and horses, beaten and injured as they were, and raced into Beizhou, pulling up the drawbridge and locking the gates behind him. He mounted a strict guard on the gates and did not venture forth.

Commander Wen's army brought its pursuit right up to the city wall, cutting off the heads, ears, and noses of the enemy dead and seizing their drums and banners. Commander Wen then ordered the gongs to be struck for withdrawal and set up camp not far from the wall itself.

After inviting Zhuge Suizhi to take a seat in front of him, he bowed and said, "This victory is entirely due to your efforts, Master. If we continue like this, the rebels will soon be destroyed."

"I used right to destroy wrong," said Zhuge, "which is always successful. With me in your ranks, you need hardly fear Wang Ze's gang of demon magicians."

Wen was delighted to hear this. "Wang Ze lost a battle today, and he'll be guarding the walls with particular care," he said, giving orders for a concerted attack on the city. But black clouds and mist covered the walls completely, and ghostly beings appeared in the sky along with venomous snakes and fierce animals. The army failed to seize the walls, losing many men and horses in the attempt, and after two or three days of fighting was still unable to take Beizhou. Wen ordered his hundred thousand men to surround the city and shout their war cries, but Wang Ze would not come out, and Wen was forced to withdraw his troops and return to camp, where his men once more rang their bells, shouted their commands, and observed the watches of the night. He took counsel with Deputy Commander Cao: "You and I have been given command of these hundred thousand troops, costing the court a vast amount in resources every day, and we'll soon have spent two months trying without success to take Beizhou. What are we to do?"

"Don't you worry, sir. Let me think of a plan." He went back to his own troops, while Wen in his tent continued to fret. Slowly the night wore on.

Brightly shines the Milky Way;
Afar off sounds a water clock.
Moonlight floods the camp with icy brilliance;
A chill wind pierces the tents with night air.
At the honking of a wild goose,
The brilliant youth on his lonely bed is startled from his dream;
At the crickets' dismal chirp,
The beautiful maiden, sleeping alone, is brokenhearted.
In the army the war drums' beat goes on hour after hour;
In the distance the pounding on the washing slabs never ceases.
In figured eaves the wind chimes' tinkling
Shatters the mood of the highborn lady;
Above the banners a flashing blue lamp
Reveals the soldiers' deepest sighs.
The hearts of the demons and rebels are full of scorpion venom,
While the spirits of the loyal and righteous blaze forth in
rainbow splendor.

That night Commander Wen tossed and turned, unable to sleep. At about the third watch, noting the utter silence outside, he got up and left his quarters to listen. Then, as the watch was about to be struck, he saw a soldier shaking a rattle as he came to take his turn; the soldier was singing a song in a low voice and keeping time with the rattle. Hearing this, Wen returned to his tent to sleep.

At dawn the following morning, when the officers presented themselves, Commander Wen took his place in the command tent, and the officers duly greeted him and drew themselves up along both sides. After he had issued his orders about military matters, Wen told his staff to summon the soldier who had sounded the third watch the previous night. The man was soon found and brought into Wen's presence. "Were you the one who was singing a song while sounding the third watch last night?" he was asked.

"Sir, I was afraid I would fall asleep and miss the watch, and I sang that song to keep myself from nodding off."

"Nonsense! You broke my army rules and you'll have to be beheaded!" He gave orders to the executioners: "Take him away! Report back to me after you've cut off his head!"

"But sir! If you will forgive my crime, I'll cut off Wang Ze's head and present it to you!"

Wen had the man brought before him. "You're talking rubbish, you knave! Here am I, in command of an army of a hundred thousand, and after two months here I am still unable to take Beizhou! How are you going to cut off his head all on your own?"

"He and I come from the same town, and we've been sworn brothers since we were very young."

"What is your name?"

"Ma Sui."

Wen was secretly thrilled. He definitely fits Argus-Eyed Spirit's prophecy, he thought; if he goes there, he's bound to succeed. "What scheme do you have for killing him?" he asked.

Ma Sui went up and whispered in his ear. "If I go, I'll do thus and thus, and I'm sure to succeed in cutting off his head."

At these words, Commander Wen flew into a rage. "Take him away!" he roared. "You knave! By imperial appointment I command an army of a hundred thousand, and I still have no plan for taking Beizhou. Who are you, that you dare to undermine my army's rules by coming up with this sort of proposal? If I don't have you beheaded, I shall never be able to maintain discipline in the army!"

As the executioners dragged Ma Sui away, the officers knelt down and pleaded with Wen. "Ma Sui deserves to be executed," they said, "but executing him now will only hurt morale. We ask that you show leniency and postpone the punishment till later. There will be time enough afterward, when Wang Ze is defeated."

But Commander Wen's anger was not to be appeased, and the officers had to plead even more urgently before he relented. "If it were not for the sake of the officers, I would certainly have you beheaded," Wen said to Ma Sui. "But since you've broken my rules, I can't let you off entirely!" He ordered his men to give Ma Sui a hundred strokes as punishment. His men pulled Ma Sui over and had administered fifty of the strokes before the officers once more began pleading for mercy. Wen rose to his feet shouting, "Oh, leave off the other fifty, then!" and stalked into his tent fuming with rage.

The officers returned to their own quarters. "What bad luck!" said Ma Sui once he was back in his tent. "I was wrong to sing a song and anger Commander Wen. He would have had me beheaded, but the officers twice interceded for me, and I got fifty strokes instead!" He looked at the other men and heaved a deep sigh. That night he slipped out of the tent and went straight to the Beizhou city wall and shouted across the moat, "You up there on the wall! I have a secret matter of the utmost importance to report to your commander! Open the gate and let me in!" The guards reported to the officer in charge, who opened the gate and ferried Ma Sui across the moat in a small skiff. Needless to say, his men searched Ma Sui carefully but found no metal on him. When they saw the injuries he had suffered, they refrained from binding him but kept a close watch over him until dawn, then escorted him into Wang Ze's presence.

Wang Ze recognized Ma Sui as a sworn brother from the same hometown. "It's been a long time since we met," he said. "So you're in Wen Yanbo's army? What brings you here to see me?"

"May it please, Your Majesty, I had lost all credit, serving in that army, and I didn't *dare* to come and see you. But the night before last I was on duty at the third watch, and for fear of nodding off I was unwise enough to sing a song to myself. Commander Wen said I was undermining army morale and wanted to have me beheaded, but fortunately the officers pleaded for mercy and I received fifty strokes instead. Today I've come especially to offer you my allegiance. I hope you will accept me in your army as a common soldier; I'll serve you with every ounce of my strength!" With that, he stripped off his clothes and showed Wang Ze the extent of his injuries, which were such that Wang could scarcely bear to look at them. He told Ma Sui to dress himself again and then invited him to sit by his side. "But Your Majesty is the ruler of thirty-six prefectures! If you will take me in, it is enough that I serve as your groom. I would never presume to sit beside you!"

"But we come from the same place, and we've been brothers from an early age. You're not the same as other people." Ma Sui had to take the seat that was offered him. Wang Ze called for wine to be brought and invited Ma Sui to drink while plying him with questions about the true nature of Commander Wen's forces.

"Commander Wen had only fifty thousand men, which he misrepresented as a hundred thousand. In those defeats the other day he lost over ten thousand, so now he has no more than forty thousand. Yesterday they held an inventory of their supplies, and from what I hear they have only enough left for another ten days. If Your Majesty holds firm, within a dozen days or so his army will withdraw without a fight." Wang Ze was so delighted with this report that he invited Ma Sui to stay overnight in the yamen. He also brought in a doctor to treat him, and day after day provided him with the best of wine and food, and before long Ma Sui had recovered from his injuries. Wang Ze had no inkling that his guest was employing a "suffer and betray" tactic, but much as Ma Sui wanted to kill Wang Ze, he had so far found no opportunity.

When Commander Wen observed that Ma Sui had been gone a long time and nothing had changed, he issued an order that his troops should approach the walls, beat their drums, yell out their war cries, and try to provoke a fight. Wang Ze came up onto the walls accompanied by a group of demons as well as Ma Sui, and leaning against a parapet and steadying himself on a railing, watched the soldiers below as they moved their scaling equipment close to the walls in order to launch an attack. Lame Priest and the other demons clicked their teeth and employed their magic, Wang Ze uttered his spells, and a host of weird spirits and ghosts, venomous snakes and wild beasts appeared, scaring the soldiers who attacked the walls into withdrawing, afraid to come any closer. Ma Sui was standing at Wang Ze's side, and the thought occurred to him, if I don't do it now, when will I? He saw that Wang Ze was guarded on each side by men armed with swords and broadaxes and would have liked to seize a sword and kill Wang, but he was afraid he might not succeed. Instead he made a tight fist, and just as Wang Ze was uttering a spell, he struck him full in the mouth, knocking out two of his front teeth and forcing him to close his mouth and fall down on top of the wall. Ma Sui was going to seize a sword from one of the guards and cut Wang Ze down, but a rebel officer loyal to Wang named Shi Qing drew his sword and severed Ma Sui's arm with a single sweep of the sword. The other guards came rushing forward and seized him and helped Wang Ze to his feet. Wang was beside himself with rage and ordered his men to behead Ma Sui.

Ma Sui rounded on him: "I had no sword in my hand, and I failed to cut off the demon's head and rid the people of the curse that plagues them. After my death I'll turn into an avenging ghost and come and take your life!" The men pushed him away and carried out the beheading, and there we shall leave him.

Wang Ze's lips had been split open by Ma Sui, and he could neither talk nor eat or drink. His men were greatly concerned about him as well as fearful lest the government troops attack, and they looked at one another in trepidation as they called in doctors to treat him. Wang Ze was in low spirits because of the pain, and nothing could lighten his mood. In the past he had particularly enjoyed one Fish Soup Li, an actor who played the comic role in the drama, and he called him in to raise his spirits. When Fish Soup Li visited, however, he remained silent. "Fish Soup," said Wang Ze, "why aren't you saying anything? What's troubling you?"

"If Your Majesty is troubled, how can I not be troubled? We're both breaking the law, and today even more troops are massing outside the walls ready to combine and attack the city. One of these days we'll both be taken prisoner."

"This odious creature is not merely refusing to entertain me, he's being deliberately offensive!" shouted Wang Ze. He ordered his men to seize Fish Soup, and then had them bind him hand and foot and hang him over a catapult. He was to be shot over the wall and smashed to pieces when he hit the ground. His men bound Fish Soup up, hung him over the catapult, and pulled the lever on the carriage. There was a loud noise, and he shot out over the wall. By great good fortune, however, he happened to fall right into the river that ran alongside the moat.

From his quarters Commander Wen could see someone catapulted over the wall, and he at once sent men to investigate. When they had dragged the man ashore with the aid of a grappling hook, he was still alive, and they removed his bonds and brought him before the commander. "What sort of person are you?" he asked. "What's your name? And why did they catapult you over the wall?"

"Commander, I'm a Beizhou actor named Fish Soup Li. I was unwise enough to admonish Wang Ze and urge him to surrender, and he got furious with me and catapulted me over the wall in order to smash me to death. By heavenly good fortune, I did not die. Instead I have been given this chance to meet you."

"As an actor, how were you in a position to admonish Wang Ze?"

"Wang Ze had his front teeth knocked out by a punch from a man named Ma Sui. His lips were split open, and he could neither recite his spells nor practice his demonic magic, and he called me in to raise his spirits. I got carried away and urged him to surrender; otherwise, I said, he'd soon be taken prisoner. But the rebel refused to see the light and blamed me instead."

Commander Wen was more than delighted to hear this. "You may be an actor," he said, "but you certainly know what's right and proper." He told his staff to reward Fish Soup with wine and food, and when the man had finished, he asked him, "Since you're an actor, you must have lived in Beizhou a long time and have an accurate knowledge of conditions inside the city."

"Commander, ever since Wang Ze, the rebel leader, split his lips, he's been unable to recite his spells—he's quite useless. He has a very dangerous strategist with a game leg called Zuo Chu and also a state mentor, Pellet Priest, as well as others called Zhang Luan and Bu Ji, and three more—Zhang Qi, Ren Qian, and Wu Sanlang. And then there's his wife, Eterna Hu, who's well versed in demonic magic. Wang Ze depends entirely on this band of demons. Although he has over ten thousand troops under his command, they're just a disorganized rabble not worth worrying about."

"What's the population of the city? What are the different wards, canals, and yamens like?" Fish Soup Li gave a full account of the city, and Commander Wen remarked, "This man has been sent by heaven to reveal these facts. Wang Ze can now be destroyed!"

As he spoke these words, an officer came in. "Commander, I can capture Wang Ze alive and bring him before you," he said.

Commander Wen was delighted to see this man come forward. He matches what Argus-Eyed Spirit said, he thought:

"Meet the three Sui and you can take Beizhou." The officer in question was named Li Sui. Zhuge Suizhi had overcome the enemy's magic and inflicted a severe defeat on them; Ma Sui had broken Wang Ze's lip and rendered him unable to recite his spells and practice his demonic magic; and now the commander had met this third Sui, which was why he was so happy. "What plan do you have for capturing him?" he asked.

"I have five hundred sappers under my command. Now that Fish Soup Li has revealed the true situation inside the city, we'll draw up a map showing all the wards and streets in their true proportions. Let me question him again as to the details, then use the map to calculate the relevant distances. I shall need only my five hundred sappers to dig a tunnel north of the walls. What's to prevent us from entering Beizhou, going to Wang Ze's headquarters, capturing the whole group of demons, and throwing open the gates to the army?"

Commander Wen was beside himself with joy. He rewarded both Fish Soup Li and Li Sui with a suit of clothes and appointed the former as a personal aide. He also ordered Fish Soup to give a detailed account of the situation of the yamen, the streets and the lanes, and told his mapmaker to draw a map to scale and give it to Li Sui. From the map Li Sui calculated distances and directions. "The tunneling has to be kept secret," he said, "and it can't be done in short order, either. I hope, sir, that you will see that all our forces are ready at all times so that they can come to our aid at a moment's notice. I should also like to have Fish Soup Li with me as a guide."

"You must take great care. If you manage to capture Wang Ze and retake Beizhou, I shall memorialize the court, and the honors you receive will be by no means insignificant." He summoned the five hundred sappers and issued gifts to them before sending them off to do their work.

Li Sui was just about to set off when Zhuge Suizhi stepped forward. "Commander, even though General Li is able to dig a tunnel into the city, I fear that he will not be able to capture Wang Ze."

"What makes you think that?"

"The people around Wang Ze in Beizhou are all demons. If General Li tunnels into the city, they're sure to know and will start employing their demonic arts. Not only will he be unable to capture Wang Ze, he himself will be killed."

"In that case, when will we *ever* be able to destroy these rebels?"

"There's no need to despair, Commander. I shall need to go with him. By using right to destroy wrong, I shall render them incapable of employing their demonic magic, and they will all be captured."

Commander Wen was overjoyed. "If you are willing to go, our great enterprise will succeed!" Zhuge Suizhi then prepared pig's and sheep's blood, horse's urine, and garlic, and accompanied Li Sui out of the tent.

Li Sui consulted the map with Fish Soup Li, calculated the distance from the city wall, and together with Zhuge Suizhi gave directions to the sappers as they drove a tunnel into Beizhou. When they had tunneled to a point that Li Sui estimated was just beside the prefectural yamen, he told the sappers to come to the surface. As they broke through, he asked Fish Soup, "Where are we now?" Fish Soup took a look and found they were just in front of Wang Ze's residence. It was the fourth watch, and with Fish Soup Li as their guide, they yelled their war cries and rushed into Wang Ze's bedroom.

Wang Ze was accustomed to thinking like this: Since I have Zuo Chu, Pellet Priest, Zhang Luan, Bu Ji, and others here to help me, how could Commander Wen, even with his hundred thousand men outside the walls, ever get in here and do me any harm? As a result he had banished all worries from his mind and was making love to Eterna in a relaxed mood when suddenly he heard war cries in the building and was frightened out of his wits.

Because a host of men rushed into his room to seize him, certain consequences followed—all the things he had done in the past came back to haunt him. In truth

> You may flee as far as the farthest heaven,
> But riding on clouds they will track you down.

Did Wang Ze and Eterna Hu survive? Turn to the next chapter to find out.

20

THE DEMONS SUFFER DEATH BY DISMEMBERMENT IN BEIZHOU;

AFTER QUELLING THE DEMONS, WEN RETURNS TO THE CAPITAL.

POEM:

The seizure of power has always been wrong;
How can a rebel usurp the throne in peace?
Let Wang Ze's capture by the Duke of Lu
Serve as a warning that demons should cease.

That night Li Sui and Fish Soup Li led a squad of soldiers as they fought their way to Wang Ze's bedroom door. Wang Ze heard them coming and exclaimed to Eterna, "My dear! What misery you have brought me!" He was desperate to use his spells, but the split lip that Ma Sui had given him, together with the loss of two front teeth, prevented him from reciting them. Eterna, in an equal state of panic, failed to apply her invisibility magic in time, and this pair of lovers, stark naked as they were, could do nothing more than pull on their underclothes. Li Sui and his men took two hemp ropes and bound both of them to the bed. Zhuge Suizhi had already worked his countermagic, and the spells of the other demons could not be recited. The soldiers also took the pig's and sheep's blood, horse's urine, and garlic and splashed them all over Wang Ze and Eterna. Li Sui then ordered a number of swordsmen to surround the pair while half the army entered the city through the tunnel. The officers themselves went and killed the men guarding the gates, then threw the gates open and let down the drawbridge. Commander Wen promptly entered the city and took his seat in the yamen. Li Sui brought Wang Ze and Eterna before him, and the commander had them locked up securely in prison to await sentencing. At the same time he sent out search parties, with Fish Soup Li as guide, to arrest the demons. Fish Soup knew their whereabouts, and in no time at all they were arrested and bound. Since all of them were demons capable of magic, why were they unable to exercise their magic and avoid capture? The reason was that Zhuge Suizhi, with right triumphing over wrong . . . they had been splashed with pig's and sheep's blood, horse urine, and garlic . . . and couldn't move an inch.[1]

The only one missing was Zuo Chu. They were about to start a citywide search for him when an officer raced in and reported to Wang Xin, "General, our men have chased Zuo Chu into a grain mill." Taking some soldiers with him, Wang Xin rushed to the mill. He had his men surround the front and back entrances while he went in to make a search. "What is it about my mill that's causing all this fuss and bother?" asked the startled miller.

"A demon called Zuo Chu has fled into your mill. If you have any sense, you'll deliver him to us and keep yourself out of trouble."

"But General, *nobody* has hidden in my mill!"

Wang Xin's men had just conducted a fruitless search when Zhuge Suizhi arrived. "Let me go in and take a look," he said. "Then we'll know if he's really here or not." He went in and looked all around. "No wonder you weren't able to find him! He's turned into a piece of equipment!"

"Incredible!" said Wang Xin.

"Does this pestle belong to you?" Zhuge Suizhi asked the miller.

"No, that idle pestle is not one of ours."

"Zuo Chu may be good at transforming himself, but he can't escape me!" said Zhuge Suizhi. He told his men to fetch a rope and take the pestle to the yamen.

"Why are you taking it there?" asked Wang Xin with a smile.

"This pestle *is* Zuo Chu. He may know thousands of transformations, but he can't deceive me!" Zhuge Suizhi told his men to splash the pestle with pig's and sheep's blood, horse's urine, and garlic. Before they did so, it was no more than a pestle, but as soon as the liquid splashed down upon it . . . [gap of one page]

[Deputy Commander Cao argues against Commander Wen's recommendation of harsh measures against the local populace] ". . . incited by [the demons], they fell into a trap. This really has nothing to do with the common people. Were you to annihilate them, you would not only be condemning innocent persons, you would also be offending against the concern of heaven and earth for the sparing of life. At your convenience, sir, you should draw up another memorial seeking to spare the ignorant populace of the region." Commander Wen accepted his deputy commander's advice and wrote a second memorial to the court asserting that the people were innocent and had been incited by the demons. At the same time he issued large notices that were hung at the gates of the major thoroughfares informing the people that the criminal responsibility was restricted to Wang Ze and his band of well-known demons; for their lesser confederates as well as for the people of the entire city he was appealing for a pardon; meanwhile the civil and military populations should go peacefully about their business and not be alarmed. The common people saw the notices and relaxed, burning incense morning and evening and praying to heaven as they waited for official word of the pardon. Before many days had passed, the court sent down an imperial rescript to Commander Wen stating, "We accept your recommendation."

Commander Wen, having obtained the imperial decree, brought out the band of demons and had tablets made listing their crimes. He forced them onto wooden donkeys[2] and condemned them to death by dismemberment, then had the donkeys pushed out of the yamen. Wang Ze, Eterna Hu, and the whole demon band, their eyes filled with tears, gazed apprehensively at one other, unable to utter a sound. The people of Beizhou crowded around to watch the scene:

Two taps on a broken drum,
A single beat on a cracked gong.
Black silk flags unfurl like clouds,
Willow-leaf spears crisscross like snow.
The lists of their crimes are affixed high above;
People say that, once gone, they will not return.
White paper flowers flutter in pairs;[3]
Everyone says they cannot be reborn.
How hard it was to swallow that final meal
Or to sip the parting cup of wine!
On his great horse the spell-breaking abbot resembles Yama,
  king of Hell;
Among the massed swords the executioners seem like avenging
  ghosts.
Look at those to be dismembered this day—
All are rebels who practiced the black art.[4]

NOTES

INTRODUCTION

1. Patrick Hanan, "The Composition of the *P'ing Yao Chuan*," *Harvard Journal of Asiatic Studies* 31 (1971): 201. See also page 202 of this source for a discussion of where extant early printings can be found.

CHAPTER 1

1. A Daoist deity, usually known as the God of the Dark Heaven (Xuantian Shangdi).
2. Zhenwu (true and warlike) is another name for Xuantian Shangdi.
3. To indicate his devoutness.
4. Polaris.
5. The progression calls for a "six" here. "Green" (*lü*) is a near homonym of "six" (*liu* or *lu*). There is a version of this same stock set piece in the early story "Yinzhi ji shan." For more on this story, see Patrick Hanan, *The Chinese Short Story: Studies in Dating, Authorship, and Composition*, Harvard-Yenching Institute Monograph Series, vol. 21 (Cambridge, Mass.: Harvard University Press, 1973), 8. Interestingly, instead of "green willows" it has "six lakes" (*liu hai*), which was possibly the original form.
6. I.e., the busy heart of the city.
7. This piece is found in different forms in other fiction, notably *Jing shi tongyan* 11. For more on *Jing shi tongyan* 11, see Hanan, *The Chinese Short*

Story, 13. It is also similar to a well-known riddle (the answer is the wind) that is probably its origin.

8. The text does not indicate that this remark is directed at the master. It is presumably meant to assure him that the woman will be found.
9. I.e., the moon.
10. The moon.
11. I.e., the land within the four seas, China.
12. I.e., the million worlds of Buddhist belief.
13. I.e., the moon.

CHAPTER 2

1. By the Song poet Zhang Qiu. It is contained in the popular Song anthology of verse and fiction *Qingsuo gaoyi*. For more on this anthology, see Patrick Hanan, *The Chinese Short Story: Studies in Dating, Authorship, and Composition*, Harvard-Yenching Institute Monograph Series, vol. 21 (Cambridge, Mass.: Harvard University Press, 1973), 218. The father of the poem is seeking patronage.
2. Baosi was the favorite of the last emperor of the western Zhou. To draw a smile from her, he had the signal fires lit in a false alarm that had the feudal lords rushing to his aid.
3. Zhou Yu was a youthful general of Wu in Three Kingdoms time. He set fire to Cao Cao's fleet at Red Cliff.

CHAPTER 3

1. Jiutian Xuannü, a Daoist deity who has been described as the goddess of sorcery.

CHAPTER 4

1. Wulei Zhengfa. The ritual of an exorcising movement that emerged in the twelfth century and became influential. See Edward L. Davis, *Society and the Supernatural in Song China* (Honolulu: University of Hawai`i Press, 2001), 21–32. In Chinese fiction, the Thunder God Rites are a force for good, devoted to exorcising demons.
2. I.e., the text says "gold sand," which was refined by alchemists into a cinnabar drug to promote immortality.

CHAPTER 5

1. Traditionally the prospective bridegroom himself delivered a goose to his in-laws, but not in this case, for obvious reasons.
2. This note appears in smaller print in the Chinese text.
3. A demon king depicted with three faces and eight arms.
4. See Wu Cheng'en, *Xiyouji* (Journey to the west) (Beijing: Zuojia chubanshe, 1954), chapter 23.
5. A concubine of the Yellow Emperor's. A classic reference for an ugly woman.
6. Wife of the Duke of Qi in Warring States times. Another classic reference for an ugly woman.
7. The details are being kept from the reader.

CHAPTER 7

1. See Shi Naian, Luo Guanzhong, *Shuihu quanzhuan* (The complete *Water Margin*) (Beijing: Renmin wenxue chubanshe, 1959), chapter 42.
2. I.e., the Dark Goddess (Jiutian Xuannü).
3. The goddess who provides the peaches of immortality.
4. Almost identical with a set piece in *Shuihu zhuan*, chapter 2.
5. Rather confusingly, the reference is not to the prefect but to Bu Ji.

CHAPTER 8

1. A popular sect of the Northern Song. See Edward L. Davis, *Society and the Supernatural in Song China* (Honolulu: University of Hawai`i Press, 2001), 121–22. In Chinese fiction, Diamond Chan (Jingang Chan) is always a subversive force, employing demonic magic.
2. A reference to Nezha. Originally a Buddhist guardian god, he is a fabled warrior in much fantastic fiction.
3. A disciple of Confucius's who, on the strength of *Analects* VII.11, is said to have killed a tiger with his bare hands.
4. A famous assassin of the Spring and Autumn period. He was said to look like a hungry tiger.
5. A popular saying derived originally from the poem "Bei shan" in the *Poetry Classic*. See Sheng Guangzhi, annotator, *Shijing sanbai shou yixi* (The *Classic of Poetry*, translation and analysis) (Changchun: Jilin wenshi chubanshe, 2005).

6. Hebei province in the Song dynasty was much larger than the modern Hebei, incorporating parts of modern Henan and Shandong.

CHAPTER 9

1. 999–1062. In fiction he is regarded as the ideal judge.
2. I.e., the runners were held strictly accountable. The mirror is a symbol of perfect justice.
3. Presumably a somewhat mangy lion.
4. The *si* period, which is from 9 to 11 a.m.

CHAPTER 10

1. Chunyu Fen is the hero of the famous Tang-dynasty tale "Nanke taishou zhuan" by Li Gongzuo. See Lu Xun, ed., *Tang Song chuanqi ji* (Collected tales of the marvelous from Tang and Song) (Hangzhou: Zhejiang wenyi chubanshe, 2013).
2. The famous story of Zhuang Zi and the butterfly is found in the *Zhuang Zi*; see Yang Shu'an, annotator, *Zhuang Zi* (Beijing: Zhongguo wenxue chubanshe, 1997).
3. Bian Zhuang, a hero of Warring States time, is famous for killing two tigers. (The tigers, it has to be said, had already exhausted themselves fighting each other.)
4. The reference, perhaps comic, is to a phrase in the *Classic of Changes* (*Yi jing*), under hexagram 63. See Xu Qinting, *Yijing jieyi* (The *Book of Changes* explicated and translated) (Xinbei shi: Shenghuan tushu, 2012).
5. The significance of Baitieban is not clear.
6. Erhuizi, a secret sect in the Song that is portrayed in fiction as specializing in demonic magic; cf. Diamond Chan (Jingang Chan) and the Heretical Way (Zuo Dao). "Double Adepts" is the way the title is explained in chapter 17. See, in this volume, chapter 17, n. 3.

CHAPTER 11

1. The Buddha, the doctrine, and the priesthood.
2. If he were to leave. A standard reference for a beloved local official.
3. The famous Tang-dynasty poets Li Bai and Du Fu.

4. The model Han officials Gong Sui and Huang Ba.
5. This obscure sentence may refer to the transmission of the teaching.

CHAPTER 12

1. A sticky pole was a device for catching birds and, evidently, bats.
2. Stock praise for a perceptive, incorruptible official.
3. The three images in the main hall of monasteries, Sakyamuni flanked by Avalokesvara on the left and Bhaisajya on the right.
4. A pavilion outside the city for welcoming newly arrived officials.
5. *Lijia.*

CHAPTER 13

1. This word for what seems to be a kind of morgue is found only here, it seems.
2. In the Song dynasty, in addition to the imperial army there were armies attached to the individual prefectures. The prefectural armies were made up, broadly speaking, of paid professional career men and local militias, of which the former carried the greater prestige. See Lau Nap-Yin and Huang K'uan-chung, "Founding and Consolidation of the Song Dynasty under T'ai-tsu (960–976), T'ai-tsung (976–997), and Chen-tsung (997–1022)," in *The Cambridge History of China, Volume 5, Part 1: The Sung Dynasty and Its Precursors, 907–1279*, ed. Denis Twitchett and Paul Jakov Smith, 206–78 (Cambridge: Cambridge University Press, 2009).
3. Chang'e, the goddess of the moon.
4. Weaving Maid, a figure from folklore who once a year at the time of the Autumn Festival meets her lover, the herd boy. That's when a flock of magpies makes a bridge across the Milky Way so that they can traverse it.
5. Both headdress and robe signify a Daoist priest or priestess.

CHAPTER 14

1. The text specifies the Zuo Dao, the Heretical Way, which is portrayed in fiction as subversive, employing demonic magic.

CHAPTER 16

1. Characters illegible.

CHAPTER 17

1. A kind of ceremonial parasol.
2. The handle of a whip was rapped on the floor three times to call for silence.
3. Diamond Chan (Jingang Chan) was the name of a sect popular in eleventh-century China. The Heretical Way (Zuo Dao) and Erhuizi, which this text interprets as meaning "double adepts," were similar popular sects. All three are described in fiction as subversive, devoted to demonic magic, whereas the religion and magic of the Five Thunder Gods (Wu Lei Zhengfa), sometimes called the Five Thunder Gods Celestial Heart (Wulei Tianxin Zhengfa), are devoted to exorcising demonic influences. See Edward L. Davis, *Society and the Supernatural in Song China* (Honolulu: University of Hawai`i Press, 2001), 45–66, 121–22.

CHAPTER 18

1. The typical guise of the exorcist. See Edward L. Davis, *Society and the Supernatural in Song China* (Honolulu: University of Hawai`i Press, 2001), 59.
2. A Daoist ritual, originally known as the Dance of Yu, which included pacing out the stars of the Big Dipper. The object was to invoke the magic of the spirits.

CHAPTER 19

1. Du Yu, the king of Shu in the Warring States period. He abdicated and, according to legend, changed into a cuckoo. Cuckoos cry, mourning the passing of spring, until they cry blood.
2. The poet Song Yu, supposedly a follower of Qu Yuan's, wrote poems lamenting the passing of spring.
3. A Three Kingdoms figure. He had a dagger that a fortune-teller had said only a prime minister should have. He gave the dagger away—and the recipient fulfilled the prophecy.

4. An expert on astronomy, Lei Huan knew from the stars that a famous sword could be found in Fengcheng. He dug up two such swords and gave one of them away. It was later lost.

CHAPTER 20

1. The ellipses represent groups of indecipherable characters in the text.
2. A wooden donkey was a wheeled contraption to which the person condemned to death was bound.
3. On the heads of the condemned.
4. The text is elided at this point. These last two lines are taken from the forty-chapter version. It is found under the title *Bei Song San Sui Pingyao zhuan* in the Naikaku Bunko edition of 1620. A second edition bears the subtitle *Xin Pingyao zhuan* and is also in the Naikaku Bunko. Both were edited by Feng Menglong.

TRANSLATIONS FROM THE ASIAN CLASSICS

Major Plays of Chikamatsu, tr. Donald Keene 1961

Four Major Plays of Chikamatsu, tr. Donald Keene. Paperback ed. only. 1961; rev. ed. 1997

Records of the Grand Historian of China, translated from the Shih chi of Ssu-ma Ch'ien, tr. Burton Watson, 2 vols. 1961

Instructions for Practical Living and Other Neo-Confucian Writings by Wang Yang-ming, tr. Wing-tsit Chan 1963

Hsün Tzu: Basic Writings, tr. Burton Watson, paperback ed. only. 1963; rev. ed. 1996

Chuang Tzu: Basic Writings, tr. Burton Watson, paperback ed. only. 1964; rev. ed. 1996

The Mahābhārata, tr. Chakravarthi V. Narasimhan. Also in paperback ed. 1965; rev. ed. 1997

The Manyōshū, Nippon Gakujutsu Shinkōkai edition 1965

Su Tung-p'o: Selections from a Sung Dynasty Poet, tr. Burton Watson. Also in paperback ed. 1965

Bhartrihari: Poems, tr. Barbara Stoler Miller. Also in paperback ed. 1967

Basic Writings of Mo Tzu, Hsün Tzu, and Han Fei Tzu, tr. Burton Watson. Also in separate paperback eds. 1967

The Awakening of Faith, Attributed to Aśvaghosha, tr. Yoshito S. Hakeda. Also in paperback ed. 1967

Reflections on Things at Hand: The Neo-Confucian Anthology, comp. Chu Hsi and Lü Tsu-ch'ien, tr. Wing-tsit Chan 1967

The Platform Sutra of the Sixth Patriarch, tr. Philip B. Yampolsky. Also in paperback ed. 1967

Essays in Idleness: The Tsurezuregusa of Kenkō, tr. Donald Keene. Also in paperback ed. 1967

The Pillow Book of Sei Shōnagon, tr. Ivan Morris, 2 vols. 1967

Two Plays of Ancient India: The Little Clay Cart and the Minister's Seal, tr. J. A. B. van Buitenen 1968

The Complete Works of Chuang Tzu, tr. Burton Watson 1968

The Romance of the Western Chamber (*Hsi Hsiang Chi*), tr. S. I. Hsiung. Also in paperback ed. 1968

The Manyōshū, Nippon Gakujutsu Shinkōkai edition. Paperback ed. only. 1969

Records of the Historian: Chapters from the Shih chi of Ssu-ma Ch'ien, tr. Burton Watson. Paperback ed. only. 1969

Cold Mountain: 100 Poems by the T'ang Poet Han-shan, tr. Burton Watson. Also in paperback ed. 1970

Twenty Plays of the Nō Theatre, ed. Donald Keene. Also in paperback ed. 1970

Chūshingura: The Treasury of Loyal Retainers, tr. Donald Keene. Also in paperback ed. 1971; rev. ed. 1997

The Zen Master Hakuin: Selected Writings, tr. Philip B. Yampolsky 1971

Chinese Rhyme-Prose: Poems in the Fu Form from the Han and Six Dynasties Periods, tr. Burton Watson. Also in paperback ed. 1971

Kūkai: Major Works, tr. Yoshito S. Hakeda. Also in paperback ed. 1972

The Old Man Who Does as He Pleases: Selections from the Poetry and Prose of Lu Yu, tr. Burton Watson 1973

The Lion's Roar of Queen Śrīmālā, tr. Alex and Hideko Wayman 1974

Courtier and Commoner in Ancient China: Selections from the History of the Former Han by Pan Ku, tr. Burton Watson. Also in paperback ed. 1974

Japanese Literature in Chinese, vol. 1: *Poetry and Prose in Chinese by Japanese Writers of the Early Period*, tr. Burton Watson 1975

Japanese Literature in Chinese, vol. 2: *Poetry and Prose in Chinese by Japanese Writers of the Later Period*, tr. Burton Watson 1976

Love Song of the Dark Lord: Jayadeva's Gītagovinda, tr. Barbara Stoler Miller. Also in paperback ed. Cloth ed. includes critical text of the Sanskrit. 1977; rev. ed. 1997

Ryōkan: Zen Monk-Poet of Japan, tr. Burton Watson 1977

Calming the Mind and Discerning the Real: From the Lam rim chen mo of Tsoṇ-kha-pa, tr. Alex Wayman 1978

The Hermit and the Love-Thief: Sanskrit Poems of Bhartrihari and Bilhaṇa, tr. Barbara Stoler Miller 1978

The Lute: Kao Ming's P'i-p'a chi, tr. Jean Mulligan. Also in paperback ed. 1980

A Chronicle of Gods and Sovereigns: Jinnō Shōtōki of Kitabatake Chikafusa, tr. H. Paul Varley 1980

Among the Flowers: The Hua-chien chi, tr. Lois Fusek 1982

Grass Hill: Poems and Prose by the Japanese Monk Gensei, tr. Burton Watson 1983

Doctors, Diviners, and Magicians of Ancient China: Biographies of Fang-shih, tr. Kenneth J. DeWoskin. Also in paperback ed. 1983

Theater of Memory: The Plays of Kālidāsa, ed. Barbara Stoler Miller. Also in paperback ed. 1984

The Columbia Book of Chinese Poetry: From Early Times to the Thirteenth Century, ed. and tr. Burton Watson. Also in paperback ed. 1984

Poems of Love and War: From the Eight Anthologies and the Ten Long Poems of Classical Tamil, tr. A. K. Ramanujan. Also in paperback ed. 1985

The Bhagavad Gita: Krishna's Counsel in Time of War, tr. Barbara Stoler Miller 1986

The Columbia Book of Later Chinese Poetry, ed. and tr. Jonathan Chaves. Also in paperback ed. 1986

The Tso Chuan: Selections from China's Oldest Narrative History, tr. Burton Watson 1989

Waiting for the Wind: Thirty-Six Poets of Japan's Late Medieval Age, tr. Steven Carter 1989

Selected Writings of Nichiren, ed. Philip B. Yampolsky 1990

Saigyō, Poems of a Mountain Home, tr. Burton Watson 1990

The Book of Lieh Tzu: A Classic of the Tao, tr. A. C. Graham. Morningside ed. 1990

The Tale of an Anklet: An Epic of South India—The Cilappatikāram of Iḷaṅkō Aṭikaḷ, tr. R. Parthasarathy 1993

Waiting for the Dawn: A Plan for the Prince, tr. with introduction by Wm. Theodore de Bary 1993

Yoshitsune and the Thousand Cherry Trees: A Masterpiece of the Eighteenth-Century Japanese Puppet Theater, tr., annotated, and with introduction by Stanleigh H. Jones Jr. 1993

The Lotus Sutra, tr. Burton Watson. Also in paperback ed. 1993

The Classic of Changes: A New Translation of the I Ching as Interpreted by Wang Bi, tr. Richard John Lynn 1994

Beyond Spring: Tz'u Poems of the Sung Dynasty, tr. Julie Landau 1994

The Columbia Anthology of Traditional Chinese Literature, ed. Victor H. Mair 1994

Scenes for Mandarins: The Elite Theater of the Ming, tr. Cyril Birch 1995

Letters of Nichiren, ed. Philip B. Yampolsky; tr. Burton Watson et al. 1996

Unforgotten Dreams: Poems by the Zen Monk Shōtetsu, tr. Steven D. Carter 1997

The Vimalakirti Sutra, tr. Burton Watson 1997

Japanese and Chinese Poems to Sing: The Wakan rōei shū, tr. J. Thomas Rimer and Jonathan Chaves 1997

Breeze Through Bamboo: Kanshi of Ema Saikō, tr. Hiroaki Sato 1998

A Tower for the Summer Heat, by Li Yu, tr. Patrick Hanan 1998

Traditional Japanese Theater: An Anthology of Plays, by Karen Brazell 1998

The Original Analects: Sayings of Confucius and His Successors (0479–0249), by E. Bruce Brooks and A. Taeko Brooks 1998

The Classic of the Way and Virtue: A New Translation of the Tao-te ching of Laozi as Interpreted by Wang Bi, tr. Richard John Lynn 1999

The Four Hundred Songs of War and Wisdom: An Anthology of Poems from Classical Tamil, The Puṟanāṉūṟu, ed. and tr. George L. Hart and Hank Heifetz 1999

Original Tao: Inward Training (Nei-yeh) *and the Foundations of Taoist Mysticism*, by Harold D. Roth 1999

Po Chü-i: Selected Poems, tr. Burton Watson 2000

Lao Tzu's Tao Te Ching: *A Translation of the Startling New Documents Found at Guodian*, by Robert G. Henricks 2000

The Shorter Columbia Anthology of Traditional Chinese Literature, ed. Victor H. Mair 2000

Mistress and Maid (Jiaohongji), by Meng Chengshun, tr. Cyril Birch 2001

Chikamatsu: Five Late Plays, tr. and ed. C. Andrew Gerstle 2001

The Essential Lotus: Selections from the Lotus Sutra, tr. Burton Watson 2002

Early Modern Japanese Literature: An Anthology, 1600–1900, ed. Haruo Shirane 2002; abridged 2008

The Columbia Anthology of Traditional Korean Poetry, ed. Peter H. Lee 2002

The Sound of the Kiss, or The Story That Must Never Be Told: Pingali Suranna's Kalapurnodayamu, tr. Vecheru Narayana Rao and David Shulman 2003

The Selected Poems of Du Fu, tr. Burton Watson 2003

Far Beyond the Field: Haiku by Japanese Women, tr. Makoto Ueda 2003

Just Living: Poems and Prose by the Japanese Monk Tonna, ed. and tr. Steven D. Carter 2003

Han Feizi: Basic Writings, tr. Burton Watson 2003

Mozi: Basic Writings, tr. Burton Watson 2003

Xunzi: Basic Writings, tr. Burton Watson 2003

Zhuangzi: Basic Writings, tr. Burton Watson 2003

The Awakening of Faith, Attributed to Aśvaghosha, tr. Yoshito S. Hakeda, introduction by Ryūichi Abé 2005

The Tales of the Heike, tr. Burton Watson, ed. Haruo Shirane 2006

Tales of Moonlight and Rain, by Ueda Akinari, tr. with introduction by Anthony H. Chambers 2007

Traditional Japanese Literature: An Anthology, Beginnings to 1600, ed. Haruo Shirane 2007

The Philosophy of Qi, by Kaibara Ekken, tr. Mary Evelyn Tucker 2007

The Analects of Confucius, tr. Burton Watson 2007

The Art of War: Sun Zi's Military Methods, tr. Victor Mair 2007

One Hundred Poets, One Poem Each: A Translation of the Ogura Hyakunin Isshu, tr. Peter McMillan 2008

Zeami: Performance Notes, tr. Tom Hare 2008

Zongmi on Chan, tr. Jeffrey Lyle Broughton 2009

Scripture of the Lotus Blossom of the Fine Dharma, rev. ed., tr. Leon Hurvitz, preface and introduction by Stephen R. Teiser 2009

Mencius, tr. Irene Bloom, ed. with an introduction by Philip J. Ivanhoe 2009

Clouds Thick, Whereabouts Unknown: Poems by Zen Monks of China, Charles Egan 2010

The Mozi: A Complete Translation, tr. Ian Johnston 2010

The Huainanzi: A Guide to the Theory and Practice of Government in Early Han China, by Liu An, tr. and ed. John S. Major, Sarah A. Queen, Andrew Seth Meyer, and Harold D. Roth, with Michael Puett and Judson Murray 2010

The Demon at Agi Bridge and Other Japanese Tales, tr. Burton Watson, ed. with introduction by Haruo Shirane 2011

Haiku Before Haiku: From the Renga Masters to Bashō, tr. with introduction by Steven D. Carter 2011

The Columbia Anthology of Chinese Folk and Popular Literature, ed. Victor H. Mair and Mark Bender 2011

Tamil Love Poetry: The Five Hundred Short Poems of the Aiṅkuṟunūṟu, tr. and ed. Martha Ann Selby 2011

The Teachings of Master Wuzhu: Zen and Religion of No-Religion, by Wendi L. Adamek 2011

The Essential Huainanzi, by Liu An, tr. and ed. John S. Major, Sarah A. Queen, Andrew Seth Meyer, and Harold D. Roth 2012

The Dao of the Military: Liu An's Art of War, tr. Andrew Seth Meyer 2012

Unearthing the Changes: Recently Discovered Manuscripts of the Yi Jing (I Ching) *and Related Texts*, Edward L. Shaughnessy 2013

Record of Miraculous Events in Japan: The Nihon ryōiki, tr. Burton Watson 2013

The Complete Works of Zhuangzi, tr. Burton Watson 2013

Lust, Commerce, and Corruption: An Account of What I Have Seen and Heard, *by an Edo Samurai*, tr. and ed. Mark Teeuwen and Kate Wildman Nakai with Miyazaki Fumiko, Anne Walthall, and John Breen 2014; abridged 2017

Exemplary Women of Early China: The Lienü zhuan *of Liu Xiang*, tr. Anne Behnke Kinney 2014

The Columbia Anthology of Yuan Drama, ed. C. T. Hsia, Wai-yee Li, and George Kao 2014

The Resurrected Skeleton: From Zhuangzi to Lu Xun, by Wilt L. Idema 2014

The Sarashina Diary: *A Woman's Life in Eleventh-Century Japan*, by Sugawara no Takasue no Musume, tr. with introduction by Sonja Arntzen and Itō Moriyuki 2014

The Kojiki*: An Account of Ancient Matters*, by Ō no Yasumaro, tr. Gustav Heldt 2014

The Orphan of Zhao *and Other Yuan Plays: The Earliest Known Versions*, tr. and introduced by Stephen H. West and Wilt L. Idema 2014

Luxuriant Gems of the Spring and Autumn, attributed to Dong Zhongshu, ed. and tr. Sarah A. Queen and John S. Major 2016

A Book to Burn and a Book to Keep (Hidden): Selected Writings, by Li Zhi, ed. and tr. Rivi Handler-Spitz, Pauline Lee, and Haun Saussy 2016

The Shenzi Fragments*: A Philosophical Analysis and Translation*, Eirik Lang Harris 2016

Record of Daily Knowledge *and* Poems and Essays*: Selections*, by Gu Yanwu, tr. and ed. Ian Johnston 2017

The Book of Lord Shang: Apologetics of State Power in Early China, by Shang Yang, ed. and tr. Yuri Pines 2017

The Songs of Chu: An Ancient Anthology of Works by Qu Yuan and Others, ed. and trans. Gopal Sukhu 2017

Ghalib: Selected Poems and Letters, by Mirza Asadullah Khan Ghalib, tr. Frances W. Pritchett and Owen T. A. Cornwall 2017